I0535384

PULLED OVER
WITH MY
PANTS OFF

....

H. C. MANN

Strike Press

Newport Beach, California

H.C. Mann
h.c.mann.author@gmail.com
Newport Beach, CA 92660
www.hcmann.com

Publisher's Note: This is a work of fiction. Names, characters, places, and incidents are a product of the author's imagination. Locales and public names are sometimes used for atmospheric purposes. Any resemblance to actual people, living or dead, or to businesses, companies, events, institutions, or locales is completely coincidental.

Book Layout ©2013 BookDesignTemplates.com

Pulled Over with My Pants Off/ H.C. Mann. – 2nd edition.

Dedicated to all the brave souls who courageously reclaim their lives as theirs and theirs alone.

Care about what other people think and you will always be their prisoner.

– LAO TZU

ONE

....

GG

His fingers tightened on my nipple, he breathed permission into my mouth, "Yes, you may cum now." He flexed his cock, pulled it out and slammed back into me. My back arched, my muscles clenched and I cried out my surrender, my climax. Heat flooded my body.

His eyes held my eyes, refusing to allow me to look away from him, making my climax all the more intense. I knew, in that moment, I had found more than sex, more than good fucking, more than I had ever imagined was possible. For once, my mind went still and I was content to be, just be, and to float there in a moment more intimate than anything I had ever experienced.

The phone rang and my fantasy crashed down around me in pieces. I groaned as I answered the phone, "Hi Stacy."

"Hi, GG! I am so excited. You'll never believe what we're going to do. Wait, what were you doing?"

"You know, this and that."

"Again? Girl, you so need to get laid. You are too old to be making yourself come all by yourself and too young to hang up your pussy for good. You need cock in that thing."

"Stacy, I love you, but this conversation won't get us anywhere. I'm still married to Theo, and he isn't going to suddenly want sex again, after all these years."

"That's why I've been making plans. We're going to a concert in Ohio in four weeks. You need a girls' weekend, GG, and I won't take no for an answer."

"If you say so, but I don't see how that's going to fix my problem."

"You leave that to me. I'll figure it out."

We talked further about inconsequential things. When I hung up, I stared out the window. I knew on the outside I looked happy, *the perfect wife.* But on the inside, I was a steaming mess of sexual need. I longed to have a cock inside me. I longed to hear the words "not yet" when I asked him, "Sir, may I cum?" I longed to feel hands on my ass, teeth on my shoulder; to feel fingers on my face, my nipples, my clit.

Everything had changed a year and a half ago with my Theo's sudden illness. He had a massive heart attack and almost died. I won't bore you with the details but this was quite a wakeup call, for me anyway. Up until this event I had grown complacent, lulled to sleep by the drone of the television and the powerful hum of the Mercedes. There was enough money I didn't have to worry ever again. We owned a huge house and property in one of the more affluent neighborhoods in the state. I could go to concerts and plays in Las Vegas or New York City, fly to visit friends and family in the mid-west, and take a few days at a spa in the desert without ever considering the cost. I stayed at the finest hotels, ate at the best restaurants, and could even invite a girlfriend to accompany me; all on my tab.

I'm sure you are wondering what I could possibly have to be unhappy about. How about no companionship, no passion, and the biggie, no sex? In the beginning, we were wildly in love, at least I was. As Theo grew his business and became more successful, the sex went from once a week to once a month to never. We lived in the same house, more as roommates than lovers. I was never sure why but all my attempts at seduction were deflected. Not only had I not had intercourse in ten years, my husband hadn't touched me so long I couldn't remember the last time.

Stacy, my best friend from high school, was incensed. Our conversations over the last couple of years had been consumed by my increasing frustration over this issue. We always circled back around to the same unanswerable question.

"What's wrong with your man?" she would ask. "I've known you for thirty-five years, GG, and you love sex as much as I do. No way is this healthy for you."

It was true. She knew me so well. We would read the same trashy novels and report back to each other the exact pages and paragraphs, where the dirty action would make us wet – or even cum – and count who had more orgasms per page.

"There is no way I'm letting this continue," she said. "I am making it my mission in life to get you good and royally fucked before this year is over."

"I won't take no for an answer, honey," Stacy said, when she phoned me with the details.

"I'm not going to tell you no, Stacy," I always replied. But I never thought she would pull off her scheme.

TWO

....

ST. LOUIS SEXTING

Every year, Stacy and I celebrated our many years of friendship, by attending a concert in our home state. Our annual event was fast approaching. She was gregarious and leveraged Facebook to accomplish her plan to get me laid. In anticipation of our jaunt, she talked me into considering the possibility of messaging an old friend of hers, who would also be attending the concert. "M," as she knew him, had attended our high school. I didn't remember him but Stacy was impressed with him and over-the-moon excited about the three of us getting together. I guess he had been a few years ahead of us. Stacy and I were freshman at the time he was a senior. Older men never stopped Stacy from flirting, but had always, and still does, stop me cold in my tracks.

Stacy and M had begun sexting.

"Um, Stacy?" I asked, "What's sexting?" She looked at me with exaggerated disbelief and she shared their erotic texts with me. I was titillated by what I read. It was raw and, I'll admit, turned me on more than a little. I tried to join in, but many years of disuse had left my dirty talk dead in the water. Stacy encouraged me to send some naked pictures.

"What?" I exclaimed, outraged. "Not going to happen."

Still, Stacy remained undaunted by these challenges. She continued her provocative chatting with M.

About three weeks before the big trip, Stacy called and begged me to come visit her in St. Louis. She was caught in the middle of "daughter drama," and she needed my support, to sort it out. Her youngest daughter was having a baby shower. Stacy thought her oldest daughter wasn't coming, since the two girls didn't get along. Megan, Stacy's oldest daughter, was like a niece to me, anyway. Since I had been Stacy's best friend forever and also grateful for any excuse to escape the hovering hubby, I immediately agreed.

To appease Theo, I attended a formal dinner at his annual convention where he received some industry award. Afterwards, I caught the redeye into St. Louis.

When I arrived early the next morning, I was beat. The scene was in full drama mode, and Stacy was sure Megan wasn't going to show up for the party. As we ran around picking up last minute items, I called Megan to confirm I would be seeing her and her husband at the party. "Of course, Aunt GG. I would never miss a chance to see you. I'm bringing Cory with me. It should be fun."

I got off the phone, "Ok Stacy, you can relax. Both Megan and Cory will be there. Now take me to the hotel. I'm beat and I stink."

"Oh GG, what would I do without you?" Stacy squealed.

"I don't know but let's not find out."

After a nap and a much-needed shower, we were on to the festivities. Things went well, and her daughters got along fine. Cory – a tall, solid man –, gave me the greatest bear hug ever. "You know, Cory, Megan is lucky to have you. You give great hug." He laughed and we chatted for a while. When one of Stacy's friends tried to pick me up, Cory whispered in my ear,

"No way, he's a slut, been to bed with most of the women Stacy knows."

After the party wound down, Stacy and I went back to the hotel and headed for the hot tub. Before I knew it, M and Stacy began sexting again. They were both swapping naked pictures and were determined to get me to join them. I was 50 years old and had never allowed anyone to take a naked picture of me.

"For heaven's sake, Stacy, leave it alone," I moaned. "I'm trying to relax."

"No, I won't leave it alone," Stacy huffed. "You are so repressed. Live a little, GG."

I looked around the abandoned pool area, bent over, pulled down my bikini bottom, and stuck my bare ass in Stacy's face. "Fine," I said, "take my picture."

So she did.

One photo changed everything. M christened my butt the "Ass of Destiny." I loosened up and joined their sexting. When I saw the photo, I thought, "Wow, nice ass." It was dimpled and round as a peach with a long sensuous crease down the middle. The kind of ass you just want to bite or spank.

The conversation between M and I took off from there. All three of us were looking forward to our weekend tryst; our grand sexual adventure.

I flew home the next morning, and Theo picked me up at the John Wayne Airport. I loaded my bags into the trunk of the Mercedes and let myself into the car. We made our usual small talk but I guess I couldn't hide my excitement.

"What's gotten into you, GG?" he asked.

"Nothing, hon. I'm just happy to be home." I hated to lie to him, but what could I say, *Theo darling, Stacy has arranged for me to have my pussy fucked, if that's ok with you?*

I leaned over to him, as he pulled on the 405 freeway and said, "Stacy said to tell you hello and to give you a kiss from her," and kissed him on his cheek.

We drove the next fifteen minutes home without talking; sports radio droning over the sounds of the highway, motorcycles, and sirens. He pulled the car into the garage, fetched my suitcase out of the trunk, and we made our way into the house.

I rolled my suitcase into the bedroom and walked back through the house. The view out our living room windows was breathtaking. It overlooked the hills and out onto the ocean. But Theo had the blinds pulled to cut the glare on his big screen TV. He had planted himself in his recliner to watch the big game.

I walked through the room unnoticed and into the kitchen. I seated myself at the breakfast table and sighed to myself. *None of this matters now,* I thought.

I stared out the kitchen window and up at the clear, California skies. I was going to do it; have sex again after ten years of going without. Smiling to myself, I called out to the other room, "I going to make myself some lunch. Can I get you anything, hon?"

THREE

....

THE GETAWAY DAY

The getaway day arrived, and I was up at 5 a.m. packing and making sure everything was in order for my journey. Theo loaded the suitcases in the trunk and we were on our way to the airport. The traffic was decent so we made the trek in fifteen minutes.

"Now, you behave yourself, young lady," Theo said, half joking, as he dropped me at departing flights. The porter retrieved my bags from the trunk and rolled them over to check-in.

I shot Theo a look, "I always behave myself, Theo. See you in four days." I added a chaste kiss on his cheek and off I went, walking away from the car and through the sliding doors, to my destiny; with a bounce in my step, a swivel in my hips and a smile on my face.

I landed at the Akron airport with butterflies filling my stomach. Stacy had flown in from St. Louis and I from Orange County, or OC as some call it. Our latest rock and roll adventure was underway. With Stacy's boisterous influence, I had been convinced, we were facing the most erotic adventure of our lives.

I made my way off the plane, walking and navigating between my fellow travelers. I had just stepped off the escalator and was heading for the baggage claim carousel when I heard a scream.

"GG!"

Stacy was running toward me with a bag over her shoulder and her suitcase dragging behind her. She dropped everything and ran into me, arms spread wide, almost toppling us over.

"I love this woman," she exclaimed, hugging me and spinning us around.

"I love you, too, Stacy," I said. She was my BFF, no question about it. We had been through hell and heaven together, and I loved her.

Stacy looked great; sexy and stylish with her shoulder length, dark-red hair, cut with bangs, hanging down all the way to her shiny green eyes. She wore a fur-collared, leather jacket, and short leather skirt. She looked like she had just stepped out of a British fashion magazine from London in the swinging sixties, a real English "bird."

"I'm so excited!" Stacy said, bouncing up and down. "I finally get to be with him. He is so hot. I've had a crush on him since high school."

"Well, don't tell him," I laughed. I was as excited and nervous about meeting M, as Stacy was, and I found him just as hot as she did.

My heart was racing as we waited for the car rental agent to finish writing up the contract. It took him forever. We loaded our bags into the trunk and hit the road.

Since we were both starved I left the airport and drove straight to our favorite diner. We had time to sit and talk, without Theo eavesdropping, about our expectations for the weekend and how we were going to choreograph our liaison with M.

It was clear both Stacy and I would be sleeping with M, but it was Stacy who had first suggested I be included in the threesome. M, of course, was enthusiastic about the possibility. "Stacy, you should be the first one to sleep with him," I said, "you started texting him, and you've had the crush on him since forever."

"GG, you are going to sleep with him first," Stacy said. "And I won't take no for an answer." I tried to dissuade her, but she wouldn't hear of it. "Ten years is just too long for anyone to go without sex," she insisted, "and you are not to go another day without getting some."

I swallowed a mouth full of burger and said, "I have to say, I'm pretty nervous about making love to him. After you told me he is an accomplished lover who is able to have intercourse for hours at a time, I nearly changed my mind."

"I'm so out of practice," I quipped, "there's no way I could go for so long. I'll need to tag out." We both broke into giggles; Stacy stood up, leaning over the burgers and fries, and hugged me.

"And besides," I said, "you are the one who contacted him. And you're single. You could have a relationship with him, if things work out." I knew Stacy was hoping for something a little more serious with him.

"GG, you're just nervous. You go first and that's that. It's like getting back on a horse after you've been thrown. You'll be fine."

We talked some more, working out the details. I didn't have any problem with the three of us making love together, but it was clear, the idea of having sexual intimacy with me present, made Stacy uncomfortable. Neither of us wanted to jeopardize our friendship, so it was decided we would share him, but not in the same bed at the same time.

I got on my cellphone to the hotel and changed the reservation so we had adjoining rooms.

We arrived at the hotel, gave the valet the keys to the car, and checked in. We followed the porter off the elevator and down the hallway. Stacy keyed us into the hotel room, flirting nonstop with the young porter. His cheeks were flushed red as he carried our bags into the room.

"GG, you are first class all the way, honey," Stacy said, looking around the suite. She walked off through the living room and disappeared into the bedroom.

"And you are such a tease. That poor boy might never recover," I said, as I walked through the living room, checking the wall of mirrors across from the couch, and admiring the incredible skyline with the lake beyond it.

I stepped into the bedroom. Stacy stuck her head out of the bathroom and waved to me.

"Whoa," she exclaimed, "come in here, girl. You've got to see this."

I turned the corner into the bathroom and was met by sparkling lights and glistening mirrors.

"Wow," I exclaimed. The large walk-in shower dominated the room. I saw the Jacuzzi tub, big enough for the three of us. "Perfect place to soak and sooth all those aching muscles after a workout between the sheets," Stacy exclaimed, with a smile on her face.

FOUR

....

WE THREE – ONE

We got settled in, taking turns using the master bath to shower, shave our private parts, fix our hair, dress and put on makeup.

There was nothing left to do but wait. Stacy went down to the first floor vending machines, to get us bottled water and soft drinks. I was vibrating with anticipation and more than a little turned on at the thought of Stacy and me, sharing M. I could even understand her wanting privacy with M, she had been crushing on him for decades.

I was pacing the length of our room when I heard giggling out in the hallway. I stopped and looked at the door as Stacy let herself in, followed by a tall, handsome man with a neatly trimmed beard. He wore a denim shirt, low cut denim jeans, and hiking boots. My breath caught for a moment. M, in the flesh, at last.

"Look who I found in the elevator," Stacy said, sliding herself under M's welcoming arm. He leaned down and planted a long, sensuous kiss on her eager mouth. He turned to me, extending his hand.

"GG," he said. His eyes crinkled with his irresistible, lopsided smile, "We meet, in the flesh, at last." Hmm, he just echoed my thoughts.

M released Stacy, took my hand, and held it for a moment. He pulled me into his arms, placing his soft, warm lips to mine and giving me a deep, moist kiss.

My cooch burst into life. The heat from his kiss filled my pussy with sultry sex juice. My bottom ached to be entered.

When M released me, I was reluctant to let go.

"Ladies," he said, "if you'll excuse me for a minute, it's been a long trip and I have to relieve myself."

As he disappeared into the bathroom, Stacy looked at me and we both pretended like we were screaming, but making no sound.

"Oh. My. God," she whispered. "There I was, stepping back into the elevator, when who should grab the door at the last moment, but M. We recognized each other immediately. The door closed, and he pulled me to him, caressed my hair with one hand and grabbed my ass with the other, and gave me the hottest kiss I've ever had. It was unbelievable, GG."

Stacy took me by both hands, led us over to the couch and sat us down in front of the mirrors. I could feel her hands trembling in mine. We sat there, side-by-side, vibrating in anticipation. I marveled at the two, sexy-looking, middle-aged women sitting across from us in the mirrors.

The bathroom door opened, and M walked out. I watched him in the mirror, crossing the room. Stacy and I slid to either side of the couch, making room for him to sit between us. M slid into the space, put his arms around us (Stacy to his left and me to his right) and pulled us to him. Stacy turned towards him, swung her leg over M's thigh and pushed her crotch against it. M pulled me to him, crushing my hard, braless nipples against his side. He turned his head to me and kissed me, slipping his tongue into my mouth. In the mirror, I watched him slide his hand down Stacy's back, past the hem of her shirt and over the bare skin below it. He began to slide the tips of his fingers into her jeans, but her pants were too tight.

He removed his arm from around my shoulder, reached over to Stacy, unbuckled and unbuttoned her pants, pulling down her zipper with one hand, making easy work for the other hand's searching fingers. M's hand disappeared deep into her pants and Stacy bit her lip, tilted her ass up and moaned. I could see the shape of his hand finding passage through the welcoming valley of her ass and lifting up the fabric as it passed into her crotch. Stacy's spread her legs wide across his thigh and shivered with her groaning orgasm. I turned away from them, leaned back into M's side, waiting for my turn, pushing my back up against his warm body. He returned his arm and wrapped it around me. He slid his hand into my shirt, over my erect nipples, cupping my breasts, one after the other, squeezing each nipple.

In the mirror, I watched M return his attention to Stacy. She looked up to him, hungry for his kisses and he delivered them. Her pants had been forced down over her tight little ass to mid-thigh by M's intruding hand. I could see her swollen pussy lips glisten beyond her smooth ass cheeks. His fingers danced on her sex. In and out of her hole he went; up and down the length of her slick slit. His fingers explored over and over. Stacy moaned and pushed her pussy against his hand, her head thrown back. Watching her cum pushed me to the edge. All this time, M had continued to caress my breast. He wrapped his fingers around my wanting nipple and pinched it, sending me right over the edge into a huge orgasm without even touching my pussy.

M lifted his arms from around us and brought his hands down to his own pants. He undid them, pulling down his zipper, reached in, and pulled out his cock. I gazed at his member, as my pussy rolled out the welcome mat. He possessed the archetypal phallus: long and thick, rock hard, with a big circumcised crown, purple and bulbous. I caught Stacy in the mirror eyeing it with a look somewhere between wonder and fear.

"Oh my," she said with a hush, stood up and excused herself to the bathroom.

I was still sitting with my back to M. He turned towards me, pushing his long, hot cock against my back. He reached up with both hands, pulled my hair back from my neck, and began kissing my ears, his warm breath sending shivers through my body. He unbuttoned my blouse and pulled it aside, at last freeing my aching tits. He slid his warm, supple hands over them, skimmed my yearning nipples, and continued down my belly, circling my navel several times with his palms. He kept outlining the shape of my pussy through my pants. I reached down, undoing my snap and zipper, and pushed the pants over my Venus mound and midway down past my knees. My clean-shaven pussy glowed naked, pink and moist, the shiny layers of lips unpeeled and awaiting his touch.

But M didn't touch it. Instead he chose to caress the exposed inches of flesh on the outsides of my thighs. He slid his hands around and back up my inner thighs. I began to cum as his agile fingers followed the inner crease of my slick cunt lips; beginning from just outside my soaked hole and following up to the exposed tip of my flaring clitoris.

Stacy emerged from the bathroom, clad in her yellow bikini.

"Well, I'm off to the pool," she said, averting her eyes from the lascivious scene on the couch. "You two text me when you get hungry," she finished, and disappeared out the door.

FIVE

....

AND THEN THERE WERE TWO

I turned to M and we looked at each other before our mouths met in a soul-searing kiss. Together, we stood, our mouths never separating as we helped each other strip out of our clothes, climbing into bed.

This was going to happen. After ten years of forced abstinence being the good wife, I was naked with this hot, gorgeous man.

M lay me down on my back, spread my legs as wide apart as they could go, then a little further. He crawled over me, up between my thighs, dragging the hot head of his prick along my sensitive inner thigh. From my prone position, I looked down between the rising and falling of my breasts. His impressive rod hung suspended above my aching gash. On the tip of M's cock was a shiny drip of pre-cum. He reached down with his free hand, lubed the crimson crown with his slippery juice, placed his member against my hungry fuck hole and pushed it into me.

Any doubt or hesitation I had about straying from my husband, vanished. This was what I had been dreaming of for years–to be taken by a hot man who knew his way around a pussy and knew how to use his cock. M was all that and more.

He ravaged me. Plundered my pussy over and over, from every direction and every imaginable position. Again and again, he drove me to explosive orgasms. When I thought I couldn't come again, he would mount a new and unique assault on my sex; me, face down on the bed and he, with his thighs on the outside of my thighs, his long shaft driving his cockhead down on my G-spot. He pinned me to the bed and assaulted my slit until I came with his balls slapping my clit. He pulled out, turned me over, reversed his direction and put his cock in my mouth and his mouth on my pussy. He sucked my clit into his mouth and inserted three fingers in my quivering gash. I came hard, and he just kept going.

An hour and half later he slid his cock out from my lathered cunt and climbed off of me, heading for the bathroom. A minute later he returned with a warm, wet washrag and a clean towel. He wiped down my perspiration soaked body, then laid the towel over me and kissed my forehead.

"Rest, my beautiful GG," he said, pulling his t-shirt over his head and putting on his jeans, sans underwear. "I'm going to see about our friend Stacy. I think she is in need of some special attention as well."

With a smile on my face, I closed my eyes and didn't open them again until the hotel room door opened, several hours later.

I awoke and lay motionless. I huddled under the covers for several minutes, not sure where I was and yet not caring. I squinted at the clock on the night table. I hadn't moved, hadn't stirred, not even to get up to pee, for four hours. Outside, daylight had long since faded. A red light blinked on the telephone announcing someone had called. Had I slept through the ringing? I felt a wonderful soreness between my legs and a delicious, raw sensitivity deep in my womb. My pussy throbbed ever so slightly with the memory of the thorough fucking I just experienced.

There was a noise at the door. It swung open and shut again, letting the light and sound of the hallway in to fill the room. I heard soft whispers, the sound of clothes coming off, then, a warm muscled body pushed up beside me.

"How is our GG?" came the deep tender voice of my new lover.

"We missed you, honey," the sweet, familiar voice of my best friend sounded from behind M.

"Stacy?" I asked, "You are in bed, with us? Are you sure about this?"

"Yes, honey," she cooed. "It's all good now. We decided there would be no harm in the three of us sleeping the night together." She reached over M and smoothed my hair.

"Oh good," I said in a swoon. "I love you guys."

I realized my bladder was about to burst. "Excuse me, I'm sorry, I have to go now." And I shot out of bed, making a beeline to the bathroom. I sat down with great relief and took a good, long pee.

I wiped my cooch, it was tender to the touch in a titillating way, and found my way back through the darkened room to my side of the bed and under the covers. I rolled on my left side and spooned up against M. I don't know how the man could do it, but he was erect again. To my delight, his hardness slipped between my thighs. Long and thick, it pressed up against the full length of my sex. The head protruded out past my clit. I reached down to caress it and I could feel his cock throb to his heartbeat.

I looked over my shoulder at M and saw Stacy was spooned up against his back. She reached over him and smoothed my hair. M lifted his arm off me and turned his torso half way back towards Stacy. Their lips met in a searing kiss. He pulled his cock from between my thighs, repositioning its tip at my heated hole. He pushed his hot helmet between my labia and up into me, just past its thick pronounced ridge, and held it there for a moment. I couldn't help myself, watching Stacy and M kiss. I turned back on to my side and pushed my ass back hard against M's cock. I needed his full length, his full girth in me, fucking me long, hard, and deep.

And fuck me, deep and hard, he did. While Stacy held my hand, M moved his hand down her belly to finger her pussy as he continued to slam into me. Stacy and I moaned in unison as we both came.

M just kept right on going. This continued throughout the night. When M was finished fucking one of us and fingering the other we would all lay back, exhausted, and sleep for a while.

I remember waking at one point to find Stacy on her back with her legs spread wide. M's arms were veined and rippled from the exertion of suspending himself above her. I lay there and watched him fuck her slow, deep, and steady. Stacy's legs wrapped around M's back and she was grinding her pelvis into his thrusts, cumming over and over again. She was doing her best not to make too much noise, so as not to wake me, but every so often a whimper would escape her clenched lips as M found an effective angle and rhythm. I was so excited watching those two fuck, when she put her head back, her face grimacing and her whole body clutching and shaking, I came, too, without even touching myself.

M noticed I was awake, climbed off Stacy and moved back over to me. He put his mouth on mine, our kiss full of wet passion. I reached out and took his cock in my hand, still wet from Stacy's pussy, and stroked it.

"GG," he whispered, "roll on to your belly and up on your hands and knees."

"Yes, M," I whispered, assuming the position.

Stacy watched him move around behind me, position his thick cock and find entry into my eager pussy. He held my ass in either hand, guiding me back on to it, each time pushing deeper.

"GG," he said, "you are almost there. Another deep thrust and you will take my cock, balls deep."

He was already pushing up against my cervix. I wasn't sure where else there was to go, but I was willing to find out. M grabbed my hips, tilted them back and drove his fucking stick, deeper in me. I'd never felt anything like it before, not even back in the day. It felt like his cock was all the way up in my throat. I came, hard and long, with his every deep thrust. Then, he slowed his pace and made his penetration shallow to let me rest for a moment before picking up his pace again and driving his cock deep into me, his balls slapping against my clit.

Stacy had risen to her knees beside him and was kissing him as he ravaged me. She had one hand on my back and the other on his ass. His cock-mass was growing now and with every plunge of his prick, he growled and grunted.

"M," Stacy cooed, "you've been fucking us since yesterday afternoon. You've earned it. Give my girl your cum, M, she's been waiting for this for ten years."

M increased his thrust and tempo, slamming in past my cervix and into the full dark mystery spot of my deepest, most hidden pleasure.

Stacy pushed my shoulders down to the bed so my ass was available, at M's command. He held my hot cheeks cleaved open so Stacy could watch his mammoth piece pound into my swollen cunt.

"Hold my balls, Stacy, and together we will give GG my hot load," he said.

Stacy reach behind him and grabbed his heavy ball sack. M bucked forward, bearing down on my pussy, his lungs heaving with the effort. His width doubled in my passion, stretching me to my limit. My moans were no match for M's deep grunts and guttural growls.

Then, M let loose the orgasm he had denied himself for twelve hours. His cum exploded into my pussy. My cunt contracted and clutched at his cock. The steaming founts of his ejaculate pumped me full as his thrusts forced his creamy seed out along the length of his engorged cock. His great size meant his full load of semen had nowhere to go. It backed up and out of my fuck hole, squirting out along my lathered labia, and dripped down my clitoris, on to the bed.

M emptied himself into me and collapsed on top of me, pressing me into the bed. His heavy breathing began to soften and slow in my ear. We lay still for a while, until M's supple cock slipped from my gash, allowing another stream of cum to leak from my spent pussy.

M rolled off me, pulling me to him under one arm and Stacy to him under the other, and the three of us fell asleep.

S I X

....

THE MORNING AFTER

The next morning we all woke and cuddled, kissed and caressed, then showered and dressed.

We grabbed our things and took the elevator down to the hotel lobby. M went to the reservation desk to check for messages. Stacy went out to bring around the car. I stood back and watched M at the counter, conferring with the attractive young woman attending to him. As M went back and forth between checking his phone and conversing with her, she never once took her eyes off him. When he looked back to his phone, she looked him up and down. I surprised myself with the burst of possessiveness that filled me.

What is this, GG? I thought, *jealousy? You've just met the man and the greened-eyed monster is showing its ugly little head already?*

M turned from the counter with a concerned look and walked back to me.

"Something has come up, GG. I won't be able to attend the concert with you this evening," M said, putting his arm around my waist, walking us towards the exit.

My heart sank to my toes. Was this how it was going to end? One passionate night together? Was I ever going to see him again? Of course, I kept those thoughts to myself. Instead I said, "I understand, M."

"I still have time for breakfast before I have to head out," he said.

He held me tight to his side as we walked. I fell into step with his long-legged gate. Although I was on the short side, I had learned to match stride and stay in sync, marching in Navy boot camp. Walking next to him felt so natural, so comfortable and yet, so hot.

No sooner had we walked out of the hotel than Stacy, wielding her cellphone camera like paparazzi, began photographing us. With a dramatic flair, M swept me up in his arms, lifting me off my feet, and planted a passionate kiss full on my mouth. When he released me, I giggled as I turned back toward Stacy. I was surprised by her expression.

"Well," she said, opening the door to the car, "don't you two make a fine looking couple?" She disappeared into the car and M gave me a funny look, raising his hands palms up and shrugging his shoulders. "What's got into her?" he mouthed as he opened the door for me to get in.

Ravenous, we made our way out of the hotel parking lot, looking for the nearest diner for a hearty breakfast.

The three of us enjoyed breakfast together. We were seated all in a row on one side of a booth with M in the middle. Our poor waitress didn't know what to make of us. M first whispering in Stacy's ear and kissing her on the neck, turning to me and doing the same. In our amorous self-involvement we were putting on quite a show for the after church crowd. An older couple, all dressed up in their Sunday morning finest, gave us looks of disapproval and left without finishing their meal.

I excused myself and went to the ladies room. When I returned to the table, Stacy's face was flushed with arousal. As I seated myself I noticed her skirt was riding a bit high on her thigh. She was sitting on M's hand, moving her hips. I knew she hadn't put on her panties; she was sitting bare ass, and bare pussy, on M's busy fingers. She let out a quiet moan and shivered, and M's hand reappeared on the table, his fingers wet from their excursion.

M's car had arrived, so he picked up the check and left the waitress a generous tip. He escorted us out to our car and we said our goodbyes. He gave us each a long passionate embrace and a deep, lingering kiss. Then the three of us hugged one last time, for a sweet, eternal moment. M disappeared into his limo and drove off.

Stacy and I sat in the rental car, staring out the front windshield. Neither one of us said as much as a word.

Then, Stacy broke the silence.

"You know, he has something special for you, don't you?" she asked.

I turned to her, "I'm not sure what you mean, Stacy."

She took her phone out of her pocket, brought up a photo, and passed it over to me. "A picture is worth a thousand words, and this photo says he's into you."

It was a picture Stacy had taken of M and I as we walked out of the hotel. He had his arm around my waist and I was snuggled up against him, with my head against his chest. In a private, unselfconscious moment, M was looking down at me. The expression on his face looked a lot like love.

"I don't know what you mean, Stacy. He's just being M. He's been loving with both of us," I said as the slightest of smiles curved up at the corners of my mouth.

SEVEN

....

BACK IN THE OC – JEE SUN'S SPA

Nothing would ever be the same for me and yet, the weeks following the fateful weekend, were much like the years preceding it.

Theo and I continued our predictable daily routine. Stacy and I texted every day. The *Ladies who Lunch* met every Wednesday at the club for drinks and gossip. I read trashy novels on my Kindle, shopped my favorite boutiques, and drove my baby: a red Mercedes - my ruby roadster - around town with the top down.

Oh, and I had my hair, lashes, and nails done at Jee Sun's Salon. I just love my appointments with Jee Sun. She is the one person who has unconditional love for me, as long as I tip her well and don't cancel on her at the last minute. Sure, my therapist knows me better than anyone else in the world, but Jee Sun understands me better.

"You have needs, GG. Good for you, honey, you're looking after yourself," Jee Sun said as she worked on my eyelashes. "But a word of advice, GG, don't get serious about this man. A man like him becomes a great lover because he gets a lot of practice with a lot of women."

"Get serious, Jee Sun?" I was leaned back and my eyes were closed. "I haven't heard from him since our weekend tryst. There's nothing to get serious about. Besides, it wasn't as if it was just the two of us. Stacy was right there in the bed with us."

Jee Sun stopped applying my lashes and put her hand on my shoulder. "All the better, hon. Keep your options open. You are a beautiful, sexy woman, GG. Perhaps your next relationship should be with a woman?"

"No, Jee Sun, it's not like that. Nothing happened between Stacy and me. We just shared him in the same bed. I mean, he made love to both of us at the same time, but we didn't touch each other."

"But eating a woman's 'boji' is something you would want?"

"I guess so," I said, wondering to myself. "You know me, I'll try anything twice." She switched over to my other eye and began applying lashes. "You never know, I guess. But honestly, the reason I was there was to have his huge cock in me. You know how I feel about a man's private parts."

She laughed, "Yes, there is no replacing big namgeun, is there?"

I think I must have blushed, but like I said, Jee Sun knows me well.

"I was hoping he would text or email me or something, but maybe I'm being unrealistic. He is a busy man. He travels the world. He can have any woman he pleases. So why would I think he would find me special?"

"GG, you still so old fashion." Jee Sun said. "This is the new millennium, girlfriend. We are liberated ladies now. Maybe this man, maybe he comes, seeks you out again, maybe he doesn't. But meanwhile, don't put all your fish into one net, girlfriend. You are finally breaking free. Your finger may still wear a wedding ring, but your passion does not. So don't cage yourself, again, GG. Take lovers. Make love. Take more lovers. Make more love. There are many, many hot men in the world, and they will make your *boji* happy and full, yes?"

It didn't take me but a moment to answer her, "Yes, Jee Sun. Yes, you are right, as always."

EIGHT

....

FIRST CLASS RED EYE

"You are never going to believe this!" Stacy squealed in my ear. "Stacy, are you sure?" I asked, my voice dripping with sarcasm.

"OK, you will believe it. But are you going to be so surprised! Tool Box is on tour and I got us tickets," Stacy purred, "in the front row."

"Sounds wonderful. When is it?" I asked.

"Is this weekend too soon?"

"It's a bit spur of the moment, Stacy, but I would love to come." It sounded like fun and a good excuse to get away from Theo for a couple days. Plus, it was a chance for us to see a favorite band from our youth. I broke the news to Theo and planned the trip. The redeye was the only option - a long flight and a long night, but I could rest all day when I got there.

The plane would lift off from John Wayne International Airport at 10 pm Pacific Time. With a connecting flight in San Francisco that wouldn't take off until after midnight, I had to steel myself for the ordeal with a trashy novel on my Kindle, a long warm dress to fend off the airplane air conditioning, and a neck pillow, for when I dosed off.

The flight from OC to San Francisco was pleasant enough. I treated myself to first class for the legroom and roomy seats. I entered the plane and rolled my carry-on luggage down to row four. There was a long-legged gentleman in the aisle seat, his head tilted forward, soft snores issuing from his mouth. I stowed my suitcase in the overhead compartment. In the hopes of not waking him, I hoisted up my dress and lifted my leg to step over his extended legs.

"Excuse me," I whispered under my breath, lifting one leg over him, trying to do the same with the other leg, to avoid waking him.

Surprised, his eyes popped open. "Oh," he exclaimed, bending his long legs up at the knees to get out of my way, "I'm so sorry."

His knee hooked my foot as I collapsed into the seat beside him. He got quite an eyeful before we could untangle our legs and rearrange my dress. For one embarrassing moment, I wished I had made the choice of modesty over comfort, foregoing flying "commando" for the evening.

I looked at him as I straightened my dress and put my handbag under the seat. He shined a sweet boyish smile on me, but his salt and pepper hair and the wrinkles around his eyes, gave him away as middle aged. After sitting back and buckling myself in, he leaned over to me, presenting his hand to shake mine and whispered, "I'm Gregory," he said as I presented my hand to him. "It's nice to meet you, um?"

"GG," I responded, "and it's nice to meet you Gregory." As I released his hand and sat back in my seat, he leaned over to me and said, "No worries, GG, your little secret is safe with me."

After blushing a hundred shades of red, the remainder of the hour flight was filled with his interesting, if non-stop, conversation. He was a charming fellow, remarried six months ago after a gruesome divorce a few years earlier. I found myself wondering what he and I might have been up to if he hadn't re-tied the knot. He seemed the adventurous type, and I had to admit, my hot little clit was pulsing like a homing beacon at the thought of a little illicit titillation.

"I swore I would never marry again, but Janice came along, and my resolve went right out the window."

He wasn't clear on his line of work, saying his travel took him away from Janice, too often. She was only able to join him when his travel was in the states and that wasn't the case the last few months. His demeanor was far too casual to be a corporate type, so I had him pegged as perhaps undercover, maybe even CIA. Fanciful thinking, I know, but fun to speculate.

We landed in San Francisco and said our goodbyes.

I made my way through the airport - bag over my shoulder, my carry-on rolling behind me - and boarded my connecting flight, heading back east. I walked down the aisle and to the last row in first-class, seating myself in the window seat. The stewardess passed out pillows and blankets, and I cuddled up, my legs folded up under me, my back to the empty seat beside me, staring out the window onto the night-darkened tarmac. I made myself comfortable.

The plane was ready to leave and the flight attendants were battening down the hatches, so it looked like I would have the row to myself, leaving even more room to stretch out.

Just as they were about to close the door, an out-of-breath fellow came bounding into the plane, apologizing all around about having ended up at the wrong gate. He made his way down the aisle and plopped himself down in the seat beside me.

It was Gregory.

"Well, hello there," he said. "We meet again."

We both laughed and he explained about getting all the way down to the wrong end of the terminal and then having to jog back so as not to miss the flight.

We chatted a bit longer. I said my good nights and rolled over with my head towards the window, legs curled under my dress and the blanket over my legs. I opened my Kindle to the new erotica I had downloaded the night before. Reading about other people's sexual exploits always seemed to send me off into dreamland in the most delicious way.

I was beginning to doze off when I felt Gregory get up and walk to the front of the plane to the bathrooms. I continued to read and the naughty sex was having its desired effect. My pussy was wet and my clit ached. I looked over my shoulder, and since Gregory hadn't returned, I made sure the blanket was well placed as I slid my skirt up and spread my thighs just wide enough to let my fingers into my hungry pussy. I shut off my Kindle and dipped into the delicious slutty heat between my swollen lips, wetting my fingers and bringing them up to work over my clit. Imagining myself as the main character in the book, I wove swift steady circles about my throbbing nub, picturing myself being taken by three well-hung studs. I didn't have much time until my seatmate returned, so I rubbed out an intense O, moaning into my pillow and clutching my thighs tight against my hand.

It took a moment to get my wits back about me. Where had Gregory gone to for so long, anyway? When I looked over my shoulder, there he stood in the darkened cabin, looking down at me. I couldn't be sure in the low light, but had I seen him reposition himself in his pants? I looked away from him and back out of the window into the night. He stood in the aisle for another minute before seating himself beside me.

Relaxed and fulfilled, I put my head back down and began drifting off into blissful sleep. But my aisle mate had become restless. Every time I would fall asleep, he would move around in his seat. If he had indeed watched my little cum fest, it was understandable he might have something on his mind, and in his hand, which he would need to tend to. There was a steady rhythm shaking his seat, so I thought it best to just pretend I was asleep so he might take care of his business.

I had to admit the thought of what Gregory was up to was turning me on. *But what should I do if he makes a move on me?* I wondered. *Well, what would Stacy do?* I thought, smiling to myself.

A moment later, I thought I felt a tugging at my blanket. Had I flung part of it onto Gregory's seat in my frenzy to rub one out? As I felt the blanket lifting off my hips I thought, *oh my, I didn't pull my dress back down after I came*

Just then, a hand reached under my blanket and caressed my ass, grabbing a handful and squeezing it. He followed the curve of my buttocks, continuing down the wet valley of my crack, and then planting a finger in my gooey gash. When I looked over my shoulder at him, Gregory was stroking his long slender cock with one hand and fingering my pussy with his other. I freed my hand from the blanket and reached back, circling his hot nob with my thumb and index finger. He caught my eye and held my gaze as the rim of his glans became too big for me to circle with my fingers. He thrust his hips toward me while he penetrated me with his finger. It took a moment for him to bring us both to orgasm. I pushed back hard on his hand to get his finger all the way up into my begging pussy. My cunt gripped it as I came and I moaned into the pillow. He grunted, shooting several long streams of cum over my ass cheeks and the back of my dress, where it dripped down over my thumb and index finger.

He withdrew his finger, wiping off my juices on his handkerchief, handing it to me to wipe off his man cream from my thighs and the back of my dress.

I stood up, taking my cellphone from my purse, and excused myself, walking to the first-class bathroom. I opened the door and bolted it closed behind me. I twisted around, taking a photo. The cum on my ass was dripping down my thigh, so I opened my legs, angled the camera just right, capturing my swollen labia and the blob of man cream now oozing down my inner thigh. I took two more shots as the cum made its way down my thigh. I snapped off a few shots of the cum stuck on my thumb and fingers. I twisted my dress around, back to front, and found the lion's share of his load. *Oh my*, I thought, *Gregory did need to unload, didn't he?*

There on the back of my dress was a big smear of white and juicy sperm. I sat down on the tiny toilet, opened my legs wide and lifted my feet up, placing one on the sink and the other, on the door. I placed my dress, sans cum rag, across my belly just above my clean-shaven pussy and lifted the camera up and over the mess to get a cum slut selfie for Stacy.

I composed a quick email, embedded the pics, and sent the hot stuff off to her.

"Just the way you like it, Stacy."

NINE

....

BILLY HANGING MEAT

Stacy arrived at the hotel just as I stepped out of my bath. She planned on helping me get ready for the concert, but it was just an excuse for us to chat. Stacy sat on the counter, bouncing up and down with excitement while I put on my makeup.

"Spill the beans, why are you so hyped?" I asked her.

"Well, GG, what do you remember from high school?" Stacy replied.

It was just like Stacy to ask an open-ended question. "What specific part of high school are you referring to? If you mean us going to concerts, I can recall your mad crush on Tommy Tool, the lead singer from Tool Box and you dragging me all over the state to catch his shows."

Stacy gave me an exasperated look, like how could I be so stupid as to not know what she was referring to.

"And...who else was there?" Stacy teased.

"I can't remember, Stacy, please, just spit it out," I was trying to put on my eyeliner and needed to focus.

"Does Billy Rowan ring a bell?" she said, looking proud of herself.

"Really, Stacy? Billy will be there, too? What a nice surprise," I said and leaned over and kissed her cheek. "Thanks, girl," I said, returning to the eyeliner, "I haven't thought about Billy in years."

Stacy and I knew Bill Rowen - Billy the Roadie - growing up in Ohio. He was a fixture of the local music scene when we were underage and sneaking into the 18 and older rock clubs. He began working with local bands, but it wasn't long before he landed a job as a roadie with a national act. He was smarter than most and reliable as well, so he soon advanced to a position of responsibility: road manager. Thirty years down the line he was still at it, now a respected tour manager. He had worked with some of the biggest names in the music business, and with so many classic rock bands reforming and touring again, he was in high demand. Stacy had reconnected with him through Facebook so when he hired on as tour manager for Tool Box, he invited Stacy to attend the band's concert in St. Louis. According to Stacy, he made a point of asking if I would be coming as well.

When I finished getting ready, we drove together to the auditorium. We went to will-call to retrieve our complimentary tickets, but when they handed over the envelope, with Stacy's name on it, the tickets were missing. In their place were two backstage passes.

"This is just too cool," Stacy said to me. "Billy came through big time. And won't he be excited to see you again."

We made our way through security and down several flights of stairs to the meet and greet area. We were both excited to be back stage at a real rock concert, even at our age. We were looking for something to drink, when we ran into Billy.

"GG," he called from across the room waving to us, "come over here." He was standing talking to a tall, lanky guy with hair extensions.

We navigated our way through the other guests and over to Billy. As we neared them, Stacy leaned over and whispered in my ear, "Oh my God. Do you know who is standing with Billy?" She grabbed on to my arm and squeezed it hard, "That's Tommy Tool."

Tommy was the lead singer of Tool Box. Stacy had had a thing for him for years, but then again, so had every other girl with a turntable or cassette player. Around the time vinyl records had passed the baton to CDs, Tommy and his band had crashed and burned in a blaze of drugs and squandered riches. Still, classic rock bands refuse to die. They're resurrected for reunions and package tours with other aging relics in recovery.

As we reached them, Billy turned and introduced the three of us. "Tommy, these two lovely ladies and I go all the way back to high school. This is my dear friend, GG and her best friend, Stacy. And this, ladies, is Tommy Tool." Stacy didn't miss a beat. I don't know how she does it, I'm way too shy to even try, but she was chatting Tommy up, gazing at him from under her straight, red bangs with her best doe-eyed, 'I'm available' look. Tommy seemed every bit as enamored with her, with her short leather skirt and tight, low cut blouse. My girl knows how to "flaunt it when she wants it."

Billy and I left those two flirting with each other and made our way to the bar. "Your friend hasn't changed a bit, has she?" he said, smiling over at me. "She always had a thing for lead singers. But tell me, GG, how have you been? It is great to see you."

We stood at the bar, chatted, and ordered drinks; a club soda for me and a diet cola for Billy. "It is so nice of you to get us the back stage passes, Billy, but it wasn't necessary," I said.

He reached up, his hand circling my forearm, and said, "Oh, it was no problem, GG, it's just great to see you again. Just like the old days, isn't it? You and me hanging out, talking by the stage door while your friend runs off with the front man." At this we both laughed. We made some more small talk as Billy looked at his watch.

"Well, time to punch the clock," he said. "This is why they pay me the big bucks. Being a tour managing is like being a cat herder." We both laughed, however, an unexpected, uncomfortable silence fell, once again.

"You're staying at the Sheraton downtown, aren't you?" I nodded yes to Billy. "We are, too. If you're not doing anything after the show, would you like to meet me in the hotel bar for a drink?"

"Sure, Billy," I said, "that would be nice."

"Great," he said. "I should be there by 1:30. Looking forward to it."

LIFE DOES HAVE A WAY OF FOLDING BACK ON ITSELF. Back in the day, Stacy and I would go out on the weekends and listen to all the local bands. We would get so excited, anticipating seeing the boys with their tight pants and shiny guitars. We would select our Friday night wardrobes by Wednesday afternoon. While I was a late bloomer, Stacy was a natural born groupie and by the time we were old enough to drive, she had dated every cute boy with a microphone in his hand and a potato in his pants.

I met Billy when she tried to fix me up with the drummer of a popular local hair band. It didn't work out since he preferred guys. I did have the hots for the lead guitar player, but he already had a girlfriend. So when Stacy and the lead singer were having at it in the back of the equipment truck, I could be found over by the stage door talking with Billy. He was a nice looking guy with big ears and red hair, all business until he cracked his big, charming smile. We became close friends after a time. He wasn't like the others, he didn't drink or get high. We would stand out back, smoke cigarettes, and talk about the business part of the music business; which is pretty weird for a couple of teenagers, I know, but he was more serious than most.

Stacy thought he was gay, because he never had a girlfriend, and he never hit on me. But I just thought he was the shy and serious type. When everyone else was getting stoned and getting drunk, he was the guy holding the whole thing together. It sure paid off for him, all the clean living and hard work. He had saved his money and saved his looks as well.

Stacy and I watched the show from just off stage, and let me tell you, it was so exciting. The band sounded great, and Tommy still had the moves, the somersaults, and the hot little twitch with his hips. It was still, more or less, the band we remembered. But, as was often the case, some original members were still with the group and the other players were stand-ins and look-a-likes.

After the encores, we braved the traffic and drove back to the hotel. On the way, Stacy got a text from Tommy. "He wants to meet me at Blue Magoo for a drink," she said. "Would you mind if I just dropped you off, GG? I won't go if you feel like I'm abandoning you."

"Honey, you know me better than that," I said and leaned over to give her a kiss on the cheek. She let me off at the hotel, and I took the elevator up to the room. I had an hour to kill before I met Billy so I ran myself a hot bath and relaxed.

I was just getting ready to head out the door when my cell phone rang. It was Billy.

"Hey," he said. "Looks like the hotel lounge closed up at 1:00. I have a suite on the thirtieth floor. It has a full bar, if you'd like to stop by here instead?"

"Sure," I said, "as long as it's well stocked with club soda."

"And diet soda," he laughed. "See you in a few."

Well, being tour manager for a resurrected eighties super group does have its perks. Billy's suite was first class. It looked out on the arch and had an incredible view of the city.

Billy took my jacket and purse and handed me a glass of Pellegrino. We sat side-by-side on a sofa facing a great expanse of windows, looking out over the city lights and chatting about our lives and loves. I told Billy about my twenty years in Newport Beach, and how I had put my life on the back burner, but I was changing now, hinting at my recent indiscretion.

Billy, on the other hand, had been around the world several times and had rubbed elbows with just about every famous rock star you could name. He was full of funny stories of the performers he had worked for: Bruce Springsteen, Paul McCartney, The Eagles, etc. He was charming, but never in a superficial way, and so self-effacing and modest about his success. I couldn't help but like the guy he had grown into. He was successful beyond his wildest dreams, but right beneath the surface, I could still see the red-headed kid with the big ears. He was still my good buddy, Billy.

I was surprised to hear Billy had a ten-year-old daughter from a brief marriage. He was proud of her and seemed sad about the divorce. "It must be difficult sustaining a relationship being gone all the time, making your living out on the road," I said. He agreed, and then added, "But it wasn't my absence which ended the marriage. It was, well, a personal matter."

Oh, I thought, so maybe Stacy was right after all.

"I understand, Billy," I said. "I'm so sorry. But at least attitudes towards alternative lifestyles have changed. People are much more accepting these days."

He looked at me funny for a moment and then laughed. "Oh," he said. "You think I'm gay, GG?"

I felt so embarrassed. "No!" I squeaked, "Well, I don't know. You never had a girlfriend and you never asked me out. Shit. Me and my big mouth. Please forgive me, Billy."

"Oh, it's okay, GG. Just so you understand, I always wanted to ask you out, but I was afraid to. You see, I have a deformity. It has made it impossible for me to be intimate with women. It's so extreme my wife refused to have intercourse with me after my daughter was conceived. I am in the one percentile."

I was nodding my head up and down, in an understanding way, but I had no idea what he was talking about. "Billy, I'm sorry but I'm still not quite sure what you mean?"

We were sitting side-by-side, looking out over the city. We had gotten cozy, he had his arm over my shoulder, and my hand was on his thigh, but it was feeling more like friends than anything else.

"Well, simply put, one percent of the male population is endowed to such a degree that intercourse is nearly impossible."

"Really?" I said. I was feeling embarrassed and excited by the conversation. I had never experienced a sizeable penis until M, but large penises had always intrigued me; I've been known to stuff my pussy as full as I possibly could, every opportunity I got. "How big are we talking about?"

"Well, too big for almost any woman to reasonably take inside of her vagina," he replied, matter-of-factly. "The one percentile is considered to be anything over twelve inches long and three inches thick."

I swallowed hard and blushed, inadvertently squeezing his thigh as I did so.

"In fact you have your hand on my penis right now and you just squeezed it."

"Oh my," I exclaimed, aware of his cock under my hand. "I hope I didn't hurt you." The leg of his loose dress jeans was indeed filled with a long, thick organ and my hand was resting on it. I could feel his heartbeat against my palm.

I went to lift my hand and he placed his hand on mine, pressing downward and moaning. He pulled me closer to him and whispered in my ear, "Would you mind if I make myself more comfortable?"

At first I wasn't sure what he meant, but then, he lifted my hand and stood up. He unbuckled his belt, unbuttoned his pants, unzipped them and let them drop to the floor.

Yes, it was colossal. I don't know if I would call it deformed, I thought it rather extraordinary. It hung nearly down to his knee and was as big around as my arm. Perfectly proportioned, super-sized. I couldn't help myself, I had to touch it. I reached out and ran my open hand down its full length, from beside his lemon size testicles, along its great veined, rippled shaft down to the monstrous swollen helmet head at its end. When my hand slid off the end it sprang upright, growing and stiffening before my eyes.

My mouth hung open, watering. My pussy was in a puddle. The lips and labia were engorged and throbbing. I wanted to try and get his gargantuan cock up inside of me and at once.

"Billy, it's beautiful," my voice was quaking. "I know it's too much for most women, but I promise you, it's just what I've been dreaming of all these years." I grabbed it with both hands, encircling it as best as I could with my fingers and began pumping it in long continuous strokes. His head fell back and his eyes closed, his hips thrusting in time to my motion. I was grinding my bottom into the couch in rhythm with his thrust.

"Until last month, I hadn't been with a well-endowed man in years, and never with anything like this." His club of a cock was as erect as a flagpole and I needed to run my pussy up it right now. "I hope you don't think I'm some kind of a slut, it's just, I prefer big, and I mean really, really big."

I leaned back and slid my ass forward so my skirt slid up over my hips, exposing my sopping wet panties.

"Please, Billy," I said, spreading my legs wide open while I pulled him towards me grasping his mighty cock, "please fuck my hot, empty pussy until you split me wide open."

Well, that was all he needed to hear. He went absolute animal on me, ripping my panties off, lifting me off the couch, placing my legs over his shoulders, his hands and arms under my slippery ass.

"Take me, Billy. I want you to shoot my pussy so full of cum, it squirts out across the room every time you slam your meat hammer into me." I couldn't believe the words falling out of my mouth. He had my ankles in either hand and spread them apart, holding my legs wide open in the shadow of his ridged monster.

"Fuck me now, Billy." And he did. He positioned the giant nob of that thing right up against my hot aching pussy lips; slowly, steadily, pushing that gargantuan beast, inch after inch, up into my slick pussy. I couldn't believe the pain, exquisite pain, which flooded my body. I kept begging him to give me more. And he did. He put the entire massive organ all the way up my cunt until his fat balls slammed against my asshole. I was stuffed so full of cock, I couldn't help myself. I came, bucking up against him. He rode me like a rodeo bull, both hands gripping my breasts and fingers wrapped around my nipples. Every time he slammed his huge man meat back into me, I came again, howling like a shameless slut and calling his name. When he started cumming, he got so big all I could do was wrap my legs around him and hold on for dear life. He stood up, lifting me along with him, impaling me on his hot fleshy post, holding me savagely down on it, grunting and pumping his hot gushing spunk, filling me up and spilling it out, over and over again, down my thighs and over my ass.

We collapsed together into a soaking pile of satiated flesh and salty, slick, sex fluid. When I could breathe, I looked up at him and grinned, "Do you think we could do that again?"

TEN

....

AFTER-CONCERT

Stacy let herself into my room. "Good morning, sleepy head," she said, heading straight to the windows to open the blinds. I squinted at the clock. I had arrived back to my room at 5:00 a.m. after a long night of fucking. It was 10:30. "I hope you brought coffee," I moaned, "I'm in need of a strong cup."

"As a matter of fact, I did," she said.

Stacy was all sunny and shiny, her red hair lit up and her green eyes sparkling. She came over and plopped down on the side of my bed, handing me coffee.

"Oh my God, GG, what a night. Tommy was just amazing. We had drinks and went back to his room, ordered room service and watched HBO. We talked and talked. He is such an amazing person. I think he likes me. He wants to see me when they come through Kansas City in six weeks," Stacy was gleeful.

"But you won't believe this," she said in her most conspiratorial tone. "His hair, you know all the beads and braids and dyed strands? It's a wig!" I didn't have the heart to tell her it was obvious. I mean, he had to be almost sixty; few men still had a full head of hair at his age. And if he did, why would he want to take care of it every day?

"He's completely bald!" she said. "I mean completely. And there's not a single hair on his entire body. Not even pubic hair," she said with amazement. "Is that normal, GG? Do you think he shaves his body? It seems like a lot of shaving to do every day," she said. A concerned looked crossed her pretty face, "Or maybe he's sick? I mean, do you think he has a disease that makes all his hair fall out?"

"I don't know, Stacy," I said. "Maybe he's a neat freak. You know, maybe he's compulsively clean, or something?"

Stacy thought for a minute. "Maybe. I was kind of surprised when he wanted all the lights off when we had sex. And then he wouldn't touch me. He only wanted a blow job."

"Well, was he, you know, like he looks in his pants? Big?" I said, remembering his swagger and how he would grind his hips and stomp his foot like a bull while he gripped the microphone. Then, he would paw the ground and snort like he was about to charge.

"Not really. He was kind of, "she seemed a little disappointed, "average."

"But he's a great guy," she said, excited again. "And we had so much in common. You know how much I love Jeeps, right? You won't believe this. He loves Jeeps, too! I think that makes us soul mates, don't you. He could have any car in the world and he has a Jeep, just like me."

My Stacy. The little things could make her so happy. She fell silent and gazed off into space, amazed at her good fortune.

"So, what did you end up doing, honey?" Stacy said, snapping back to reality.

"Billy and I arranged to meet in the bar after the show, but..."

"So how did it go, hon? Tell me all the juicy details," she said. Billy had seemed kind of sensitive about his, um, condition, so I thought discretion was the better part of valor and skipped the details.

"Well, you know. He's Billy. He's still a good guy. He's lonely, but loneliness comes with the job, I guess. I think we will always be friends." I threw off the covers and got out of bed.

"But…did you have sex?" she called to my back as I made for the bathroom.

"Yes, we had sex," I said.

"Was it hot, was he good in bed?" she asked.

"Yes and yes," I answered back, laughing.

"Did you get any more OC butt slut photos for me?" she asked sounding hopeful.

"No," I answered, feigning impatience, "did you get any for me?"

"No," she giggled. "It's kind of hard to take a picture when all the lights are out and you have your hands and mouth full."

We both paused for a moment, and then laughed at the idea of trying to take pictures in the dark.

"Tommy said the band will be on the road for the rest of the year," she called through the bathroom door. "The mid-west and east coast, and then South America. They will be all over Europe, hitting South Africa. Then, on to Asia and Australia. Finally, ending up on the West Coast."

"So Billy will be gone for a long time, then," I said. "He said he would call me the next time he's in L.A. We will see what happens then, I guess."

Stacy stuck her head in the bathroom as I turned the shower on. "You could always fly out and join me when they come to Kansas City next month."

The warm water caressed my skin. I lathered up and washed off the last of Billy from my body. My pussy felt stretched, aching, and tender to the touch. The physical memory of him filling me full made me shiver and cum anew as I soaped up my sore cooch.

ELEVEN

....

GG, OC, LA, AND M

Just another day in paradise. I was sitting in my office, thinking over the last few weeks. The trip I'd just gone on with Stacy, to see Tool Box, had been fun. The encounter on the plane had been hot, unexpected, and scandalous. Reconnecting with Billy had been a stunning surprise, the biggest cock I'd ever seen. He had stuffed my pussy full, and I had walked funny for days after.

Stacy had her own 80's throwback hookup with Tommy and shared every detail with me. I had shared the photos from the airplane bathroom with her but I hadn't shared Billy's secret with her. I didn't think it was my place. I was still unsure if I would see Billy again, if he came through town. Then, there was the unbelievable night we had spent with M. I felt a spark there and was so certain he did as well, but I had heard nothing from him since.

I'd been wild in ways I haven't been since college. Stacy always brought out my most outrageous behavior. Thank goodness Theo hadn't noticed. But then, he never did notice much about me anyway.

My workload of the day consisted of checking the payroll and sending it back to the bookkeeper so she could write the checks. I needed to plan the next day's lunch for the club ladies, and make some progress on my assigned tasks for the upcoming fundraiser, we were doing for the homeless shelter. Not unimportant, but not riveting, either.

I was staring off into space thinking of my one unforgettable night with M. Sex with Billy had been hot but it was M who stuck in my mind. I wasn't sure what it was about him, but I just couldn't seem to forget him.

My phone vibrated. *Oh no, what does Theo want now?* Every time I started daydreaming and rubbing my clit, I was interrupted with another request from the needy hubby. When I looked at the phone I was shocked speechless - it was M?

"GG, I will be in LA this evening. Would you consider joining me for dinner at WP24?"

Unbelievable! After four weeks, this is how he opened a conversation? I should have given him a piece of my mind, the inconsiderate jerk!

"Is that the restaurant on top of the Ritz at LA Live?" I responded.

"Yes, it is. I was thinking 8pm," M replied. "Should I send a car?"

"No, I can drive. Where have you been all this time? I was surprised - not even one text," I fumed. "I figured you'd had your threesome and moved on."

"I'm sorry GG, I thought Stacy told you, I was called out of the country. I didn't have your number, just your Facebook messenger account and I wasn't able to use to that program where I was."

Oh yeah, he's smooth, I thought to myself. But I'm not a doormat. I've got to stand up for myself.

As I tried to think of a caustic comment, my phone vibrated again.

"GG, I have thought of little else but your milky white thighs and beautiful ass since our night together. And the way your pussy takes all of my dick? Just so perfect."

"Oh M, I want to be mad at you but now, I can't. I've thought of nothing but you since our one night together. I'll be there for dinner at 8pm, WP24."

I ARRIVED AT THE HOTEL AT 7:45. As I dropped my cherry-red Mercedes at valet, I smoothed my dress. I asked the handsome young man the directions to WP24. He pointed me through the lobby and to the left, behind the lovely water wall. I'd been there once before, when Theo and I came up to see Bill Mayer, at the Nokia Theatre.

I turned into the elevator alcove and noticed a handsome dark-skinned man leaning on the wall across from the elevators. I turned my back to him and pushed the call button.

"GG, you are more beautiful in person than in my memory." I turned to see M's brown eyes glowing in his dark, tanned face. His arms went around my waist and I leaned into him, lips parted, eyes locked on his.

His lips descended, capturing mine. Soft, warm lips massaged my mouth, leaving me breathless. His tongue lapped at my lower lip. I heard the elevator ding, and M walked me backwards into it and pinned me to the wall. He pushed the button for the 24th floor without breaking our kiss. His hands burrowed into my hair, deepening our kiss, sending ribbons of desire curling through my insides. When the elevator door opened, we didn't move, didn't stop our audacious exploration of each other.

I heard someone clear his throat. M glanced over his shoulder. "This one's taken," he growled as the door closed. He nuzzled my ear, "Are you hungry, GG?"

"Only for your cock," I replied as my hand found his cock and began stroking him through his jeans.

"Ah, room service it is," M said as the door slid open. He took my hand and pulled me out of the elevator and down the hall. I was breathless from kissing and desperate to get naked with him. I had forgotten the astonishing energy I felt when our skin touched. How could this be? This man turned me into a needy teenager, wanting his cock inside me, hands all over me, lips locked on mine. Just thinking about him made my clit pulse with desire.

M opened the door to his room and pulled me inside. For a moment we just stared at each other. He opened his arms, and I launched myself into them, burying my face in his neck, struggling to regain my composure.

"GG," M said as he nuzzled my ear, "I need to see you naked, now."

"Likewise, M." I tilted my face up for a kiss as my fingers unfastened his shirt buttons. I pushed the shirt off his shoulders as my dress dropped to the floor. I stood there in nothing but my shoes.

"GG, I have missed your curves," M ran his hands down my waist and rested them on my hips. I hadn't been slender and lacking in curves, since my youth; to have a man look at me like I was the most beautiful woman on the planet had never happened to me. His lips dropped to mine as he walked me backward to the bed. When my knees hit the bed, I sat. M knelt in front of me and kissed my throat, down to my breasts. He sucked one nipple as his fingers stroked the other.

My breath caught in my throat as he continued kissing down to my belly. I slid my fingers through his hair, feeling the soft curls, tracing the line of his brow. I was so turned on I thought I would combust right then. He looked up at me and grinned.

"GG, lay back on the bed." His hands pushed my legs apart and his fingers found my wet gash. He began stroking me from top to bottom. His mouth closed over my clit as two fingers slid into my wet pussy. His tongue licked circles around my clit; his fingers plundered my pussy, looking for my G-spot. My hips bucked when he found the spot. He sucked my clit into his mouth, flicking the tip of my clit with his tongue, while his fingers tap-danced on my G-spot. I came hard, pressing my pussy into his face. Hot cum fire lanced from my clit throughout my body.

"M, please get undressed and let me return the favor," I crooned as he brought me to a second orgasm. "M, please. I want to feel your cock in my mouth. I need to suck your cock."

M lifted his head, chuckling, "Any woman who can talk while cumming should get what she wants." He stood up and shucked off his pants. I moved all the way onto the bed as M slid in beside me, claiming my lips in a kiss. I so loved kissing a man with my pussy juice all over his face. My hands explored his body, feeling his muscular arms and flat abs before moving on to my objective, his glorious cock. Long, with a distinctive head, thicker at the bottom - M's cock was gorgeous. I have never seen a man's cock look so good. I ran my tongue from the base to the head, reveling in the feel of his skin on my tongue. When I covered the head with my lips, I looked up at him and found him grinning like the Cheshire cat. "What?" I asked.

"You look so beautiful with your mouth on my dick and your ass sticking up in the air," M replied.

I smiled and set about attempting to deep throat his big, beautiful man meat. The taste of his pre-cum on my tongue made my toes curl. I tried and tried but M just got harder and larger, no chance I was going to deep throat him tonight. Our eyes met and I moved up to kiss him. He rolled me onto my back, guiding his cock into my pussy. Taking his time, he slid into me, all the way, until his balls rested against my ass. I felt like the missing puzzle piece of me had just been found. Our eyes locked together and he began to move, slow at first and then faster. Each thrust filled me, stretching my hole to fit him. My skin flushed as my orgasm started, muscles clenching around M's cock. My eyes closed and my back arched as I wrapped my legs around him. Oh, the glorious pleasure of having a man inside me, riding me. How had I lived without this for all those years? Then, when my orgasm would not be denied, all thought left my mind. M's cock rammed into me again and again, lengthening my orgasm as he came, shooting hot man juice into my juice hole.

We both drifted off to sleep, awakening later when the sun was down and the artificial brightness from the lights of LA filled the room. We kissed, the tender kiss of lovers. I felt the ground shift under me and knew this would be no simple sexual dalliance. This man made me feel complete; more so than I already did. M felt like coming home to fresh baked chocolate chip cookies. More than anything, he just felt like he belonged in my arms.

"Can you stay?" M asked me.

"Yes, I can stay," I answered although I was thinking I shouldn't. Theo would be irritated, followed by cranky. I brutally shoved the practical side of my brain into the corner. "Let me make a call, then I'm all yours."

TWELVE

....

NIKOLAI MIONCHINSKAIA

I lay there for a minute, lingering in that place between waking and sleeping. The room was ever so still. The only hint I had to my location came from the slow, steady sound of my lover's breathe. I rested on my side under the sheet, one leg extended, one bent, with my arm pulled up under my head. His hand lay heavy on my thigh, warm and welcome. How was this even possible?

I smiled to myself and rolled over to face him, careful so as not to wake him. The dim, dispersed moonlight flickered through a break in the hotel curtains and lighted his tanned face, just enough for me to make out his handsome features. Features more bold and raw than tamed and civilized. Dark brown hair turning to salt and pepper, fell around his face. His sleek ponytail had gone wild during our love making, with long, wavy strands of escaped locks, tucked behind the sculpted curves of his suntanned ears or falling over his smooth forehead. Dark eyebrows rose above his long, full eyelashes. Under those eyelids, piercing brown eyes slept. Some would call them bedroom eyes, with their seductive glint and slight, sad downturn at their corners. But those intense eyes were striking, with the power to see all of you, into you, and through you.

His strong nose stood out bold and straight, much as his other prominent organ he so masterfully wielded. His short, trimmed beard was almost a shadow, carving the contours of his cheeks and framing his slight, sensuous mouth. A mouth as adept at coaxing out results from his team as it was at passionate kissing. As adept at negotiating a hundred-million-dollar-deal as it was at eating out a quivering pussy. He ran the gambit from fond to formidable.

That evening, I caressed the fur on his chest as he hovered, suspended over me, the muscles of his arms taut with exertion, his hips pounding into me with steady, deliberate motion which brought him so much pleasure and brought me overwhelming orgasms.

His long, muscled legs and strong, rounded buttocks lay there, perfect. And there, lying across his thigh, his full, loose balls with his magnificent penis, still weighty and thick in its placid state. His gift, as it were, to womankind. I drank him in with my eyes, savoring the vision of this magnificent man. Though I fought it in my mind and thoughts, in my heart and feelings, I knew. I could fall in love with this man.

M stirred beside me as if he had heard the voice in my head and reached out for me again, opening his eyes and focusing on me. "I was dreaming about you, GG," he said to me, his smooth, deep voice just above a whisper. "I dreamt we were on a train riding across the snowy country side, traveling to visit my grandparents in Kiev in the Ukraine."

"You know, I never met my grandparents," he said. "My parents came to the US in the 1930's. My father was a carpenter and my mother a singer. My father became a developer in the 50s. He was responsible for the row of apartment buildings on Superior Avenue, up in the Heights. He named them after my brother, my sister, and me."

M had been in a talkative mood, last evening. After making love, our loose, comfortable conversation went from sports to philosophy, from business to family, from our memories to our dreams. It was a new experience for me to get to know someone after being lovers.

"How did you come to be called M?" I asked him.

"In high school, of course," he said, flashing his rascal smile. "With a long, foreign name like Nikolai Mionchinskaia, is it any wonder? The teachers called me Nikolai or Nick, but to my friends, I've always just been M."

M had graduated from high school with honors and had received his degree in architecture from Rhode Island School of Design, graduating at the top of his class. His talent and credentials led him to an international career, with clients around the globe.

"Sometimes I miss it," he confessed, "sitting down at the drafting table or the computer and digging in, being the designer, the architect, again. But my skills have taken me into other aspects of the business altogether. I enjoy the travel, the people, and the challenge."

He had just arrived from Toronto, the night before, and would be flying out to close a deal in Shanghai, the following evening. He was developing projects all around the globe, keeping him in continual motion.

"Maybe you would like to accompany me abroad sometime, GG? Some place like Africa or China, or maybe Dubai?" he said. "Traveling outside the United States is a real eye-opener. One's view of the world becomes myopic when never having seen outside the four borders of any one country or one culture."

I loved listening to him, the sound of his voice, but also his big ideas and big view of the world. I had to admit, it was a tempting offer, travel the world at M's side.

"Oh, I would love to, M. Unfortunately, there's no way I'll convince Theo ten days in China is just a weekend excursion with 'The Ladies Who Lunch'," I said and we both laughed.

"Well then, how about a weekend trip back east with me?" he asked, with a glint in his eye. "Nothing suspicious about that, is there?"

I thought about it for a moment and replied, "It sure would be hot fun, wouldn't it?" A smile crossed my lips as I imagined us traveling together. I shot a look in M's direction and caught him smiling as well.

"Ok, let's see if I can pull it off," I said. "But understand it's going to take some planning. I think I could get Stacy to cover for me. Let me work on it."

THIRTEEN

....

THE YEAR OF 100 HOTELS

And so began the year of 100 hotels. I was on an adventure beyond my imagination. No matter where I went, M was my destination. For now, our encounters were spontaneous and undercover, our little secret. Who knew? Maybe there might be so much more, so many places to visit, events to attend and hot encounters, expected and unexpected. Anything was possible, if I could arrange it.

Our hookups continued whenever M was in southern California. And when he was on the road, our texting was unbridled and oh so clandestine.

My usual life went on without any outward indication of the inner transformation that had begun. It was pretty easy to keep my affair hidden from Theo. He wasn't much interested in my life anyway. Sitting with *The Ladies Who Lunch*, hearing their complaints about unskilled lovers and husbands, I was so tempted to brag, but thought better of it. The affair was quite illicit, and women, even so called friends, can be so catty and backstabbing.

Believe me, I was aware of how fortunate I was. It felt like I had won the lottery. Not only had I found a lover with superior skills, but also a lover whose greatest satisfaction was to see me sexually fulfilled. He reawakened my deepest, darkest longings. In doing so, he was making me his slut-tress.

Slut-tress, I thought to myself, "I like the sound of it. Anyone can be a mistress, it takes a woman of exceptional daring and courage to free her inner slut." This made me laugh out loud with glee. This slut-tress was finished answering to others' expectations: I was dropping pretense and claiming who I was, at last.

Which brought me to my conundrum. This was not a secret I could keep forever. At some point, I would have to make a decision to come out into the open by telling Theo, and risk losing all the perks of my OC life style. Or lose M. I wouldn't be able to keep living a double life forever. But, for now, it worked. No one was the wiser and no one need know any different.

A week later, M stopped in Los Angeles on his way back from Singapore, in route to New York City.

"GG," he texted me, he was at LAX, "I know this is last minute, but I managed to change my plane reservation to route me with a layover in L.A. I'll be flying out to NYC in the morning but I'm hoping you can join me this evening?"

"Ok," I texted back. I would have to make excuses with Theo, but it was doable. "Where shall I meet you and what time?"

"Great!" he texted, "I got us a nice suite at the Westin by the airport, room 1520. Meet me at there at 7:30."

It was all so new and so incredibly exciting.

As I walked into the hotel room, M greeted me with open arms. His handsome face was lit with an incredible smile. I walked into his arms and was instantly engulfed by his wonderful energy, making me feel like the only woman on earth. Our kiss transformed from light to deep, our tongues entwined, when M pulled away in mid-tongue.

"I want to read you something I know you'll enjoy," he said. We walked across the room hand in hand. He sat at the desk and I lay across the bed looking into his handsome face.

He picked up an erotic novel and began reading. The chapter described the initiation of a young woman into a prestigious sorority. There was a hazing ritual where she must be submissive to a dominant alpha male from the brother fraternity. It combined exhibitionism with bondage, spanking, nipple clamps, and anal intercourse. As M read to me, I was transported into the book, both transfixed by the subject matter and turned on by the action. I imagined myself being ravaged just like the young pledge. I was surprised by my excited reaction to the anal sex. The sluttier she became, the more the fantasy aroused me.

"Oh M," I exclaimed, "I want to 'surrender to my needs' like the girl in the book. 'Let go and live out my darkest urges.' Sounds amazing." I was squirming in my seat. Before I could change my mind I said, "And I want you to train me to be your 'slutress.'"

"Slutress?" he said, surprised. "Well, well, Ms. GG. What's come over you?"

I couldn't believe what I was saying, but I reached over and began rubbing his cock through his jeans. I wanted him to treat me like the girl in the book. My mouth watered and my pussy steamed. While he continued to read I reached down, unzipped his jeans, and pulled out his heavy meat. I stroked it until it was hard in my hand. M read on as the chapter ended with the college girl taking a large cock in her ass and waking up the fraternity house with her loud moans.

"Slutress indeed," M looked at me and we both grinned, "I think I like the sound of that."

I was flushed with arousal. He put down the book and we stripped out of our clothes. He lay back on the bed and I crouched between his legs. Covering the head of his cock with my mouth, I resumed stroking him with my hand. Oh, he was so hard! I repositioned my hips so his hand could reach my pussy. As he caressed me, I came, forgetting about his cock in my mouth. I refocused my energy on his hardness and tried to swallow him like the young woman in the book had swallowed the large frat boy cocks, but he was just too big for my throat. The tempo of his fingers on my clit increased and I began cumming. Then he slid his finger into my hot pussy. All I could think of was having him inside me. I sat up, prepared to straddle him when he said, "Lie on your back, GG, and open your legs for me."

"Yes, sir," I said, changing places with him. He climbed up between my legs, his big cock in hand, and rubbed the head over my clit. He parted my labia with his hot nob and pressed the veiny beast into me, sliding his long, thick cock all the way up into my vagina. I shuddered, wrapping my arms and legs around him. He leaned down, kissing me while he slid in and out of my pussy; first slowly; then, faster in a smooth, steady motion, bringing on my cum. My entire body felt like it was on fire, my face so hot it felt sunburned. I opened my eyes and looked deep into his as I moaned, beads of sweat formed on his forehead. Those beautiful brown eyes looked back into mine as his powerful thrusts sent me into yet another climax, this one so deep and so long I lost track of everything but the feel of his cock pummeling me.

Then M pulled his cock out of me, sat up and flashed me his trademark smile. He tugged at my leg, turning me onto my stomach. He came up behind me, rubbing his cock against my swollen lady parts and between my ass cheeks. He slipped it back into my wet cunt. He drove deep into my vagina, slamming past my cervix to the absolute end of me. I came again and again, muscles contracting and heat increasing as I writhed beneath him, wanting the moment to last forever.

He held me from behind by the hips and continued pounding me with deep and fluid motion. After a particularly strong climax I felt a gentle finger slide into my ass. As my ass opened to him, he began a tantalizing rhythm of sliding his finger in, as he slid his cock out, then, sliding his cock in, as his finger slid out. My body took over, my mind stopped functioning and I experienced one long, spine tingling, mind-altering explosion.

His movements stopped and he withdrew his finger, causing yet another wave of bliss to flood my body. His cock pulled out of my pussy and he rested its head against my slightly opened ass. I moaned with desire.

"Are ready for your first lesson in slutdom, GG?" he asked.

"Oh yes, please, M," I said.

"Ok, then," he said, "How do you ask to have your ass fucked?"

I was speechless. I flushed with fear and excitement at our naughty game. "Please, sir, may I?" I asked, surprised at how much I craved him in my brown hole.

"Yes, but please, sir, what?" he replied.

"Please, sir, may I have my ass fucked?" I whispered. Still he didn't move. What was he waiting for? Was he going to make me ask again?

"Please, sir. I have waited for this moment for so long. Please, sir, fuck my ass," I tried again.

I tried to lean my ass back onto his cock, but he leaned back as well, keeping our relative positions the same and denying me his penetration. I looked back over my shoulder and pleaded, "Please, sir. I long for you to fuck my ass hard and deep."

He smiled his mischievous smile and, taking pity on me, he pressed forward. I so wanted to take him in, but the head of his cock was much bigger than his finger. I gasped as it stretched me open, the swollen head pushing up my ass past its bulbous ridge. My distressed anus clenched as he forced his way deeper in. I took a deep breath, trying to relax the gripping to give him entry, but he was so damn big I wasn't sure I would survive total penetration.

The feeling, so overwhelming and so different from having my pussy fucked, left me breathless and unable to focus on anything but his cock in my ass. He reached a hand under me and rubbed my clit to orgasm, opening my ass a little more. My ass was so full but I wanted him still deeper. I begged him to fuck me harder.

He took me, full and deep, and I couldn't control myself any longer. I met his steady, insistent thrust and drove my ass back onto his cock as hard as I could. It just hurt so good. He released my hips and put his hands on my back, forcing me off my knees and face down on the mattress, pinning me to the bed. I surrendered to him and he began fucking me with the full force and full length of his cock, driving me into a frenzy until the fire flared up and consumed me in my first ass-gasm.

After a timeless moment, M pulled out of me, rose from the bed and stepped away from me, leaving my legs spread wide and my ass gaping open. Satiated, I lay on the bed in bliss, face pressed into the mattress, legs and arms splayed every which way, panting.

M returned after a moment and covered my neck and shoulders with kisses, his hands caressed my throbbing ass. He rolled me over onto my back, draped my legs over his shoulders and slid his cock back into my ass. At first it hurt from this new angle, but soon, I relaxed and it was ecstasy. While he was sliding in and out of my ass, he worked a finger into my cunt. Waves of orgasm rolled from ass to pussy and back again, washing over my body in a river of heat. He fingered my dripping cunt, his huge cock ravaged my ass. My swollen pussy held his finger tight. He was suspended above me, one arm holding him up while with his free hand finger fucked me. In my compromised position, with legs up over his shoulders, he had complete command over my ass and pussy. He used the position to great effect, gaining deep entry into my hungry holes.

He leaned forward, sweat dripping down his forehead, and kissed me. His thrusting hips and dancing fingers took on a more urgent tempo. He drove into me hard and set off a three-way orgasm of my clit, my G-spot, and my ass. Stunning in its intensity, it started like coiled springs, centered in my ass around his cock and my pussy around his finger, unwinding to fill my body with molten lava.

As my orgasm finished, I opened my eyes. He began driving into my ass with a renewed determination. His swelling size and building momentum meant he was about to fill me with his love essence.

His gaze found mine, and I struggled to overcome the natural desire to close my eyes during the coming orgasm. I was about to have my ass filled with cum, a moment I had fantasized about for so many years, and I wanted to watch his expression when he finally let loose. He drove his massive cock of his into me again and again, the muscles in his neck standing out and the color rising in his face. He threw his head back and roared, plunging his full length deep into me, one final time. He held it there and stayed still, save for the convulsive jerking of his cock as it shot its great geyser of jizz.

My ass was stretched to the max around his jerking cock. As big as he had been, he increased in size as he came; his balls contracting again and again, shooting streams of man cream and filling my ass with his load.

He finally collapsed on top of me and then rolled to the side. We lay there spent, neither of us moving for a long time. M's breath calmed and took on the steady, even, rhythm of sleep. Soon, I dosed off as well.

I dreamt of flying and making love to angels.

FOURTEEN

....

GG'S TRAINING

A week later, out of the blue, M sent me a cryptic text message, "Are you ready to continue?" Unsure I texted back, "Yes, but am I ready to continue, what?"

Two words arrived, "Your training."

This excited me to no end. This was even better than I had ever imagined. It was like being a character in one of the erotic romance novels I read. But it also frightened me. What did he mean by training? What was I getting myself into? What I was feeling? Was it fear or was it arousal?

I responded with one word, "Yes."

"Expect a delivery in thirty minutes. It will be a personal package. What address would you like it sent to?" he asked.

"Hubby is out of town for a couple of days so you can send it to my home address," I said, spelling it out for him.

"There will be a set of instructions in the package," M said. "Follow them to the letter, GG."

"Yes, sir," I replied, and he clicked off.

The delivery arrived at noon by courier, a large box with a bow and a card. Bemused, I opened the envelope and slid the gold embossed notecard out of the envelope. "GG, you are to wear the outfit and accessories in the box for our date this evening. A car will pick you up at 6pm. You are to take a seat in the bar. I will text you where and when to come meet me." My heart skipped a beat as I gazed at the box. M was the most imaginative man I had ever slept with and I knew I would never be able to guess what he had in store for us that evening.

I tipped the courier and carried the box inside where I could open it behind closed doors. My heart beat hard in my chest and wetness gathered between my thighs. I opened the box, pushed aside the tissue paper and revealed a perfect little black dress, like one I had seen on one of the red carpets this season. Under the dress was a leather garter and silk stockings. Under them I found a note reading, "This will be your wardrobe for the evening. You will find no panties and no bra, but you will find two silver balls to slip in your pussy, a large butt plug to insert in your tight anus, two nipple clamps and a clit clip, joined by a delicate chain. These items are to be worn under your dress at all times."

I took a shaky breath. Concentration on work for the rest of the day was going to be difficult. I managed to work until midafternoon when I quit for the day. It was pointless to continue, I was too distracted to focus, anyway. I took a long hot bath, shaved my legs and underarms and triple shaved my pussy, making sure to reach even the most delicate spots, leaving them smooth and hairless.

I got out of the tub, toweled off and dried my hair, combing it out and clipping it up while I applied my makeup. I had the little black dress laid out on the bed with the leather garter and silk stockings besides it. On the dresser, still in the gift box, were my accessories for the evening.

Let's see, now, I thought as I took each item out of the box, *where should I begin?* This was all new to me. The nipple clamps looked self-explanatory, but the clit-clip was another matter altogether. How was I going to coax my little clitoris out far enough to clip this thing on? It was either going to hurt like hell or feel delicious. The balls for my pussy I had heard of before, *Ben Wa* balls I think they are called. I wasn't sure what their appeal was, but I was ready to give them a go. Last out of the box was the butt plug. It looked awfully big. It was shaped like the ace of spades in a deck of cards but 3-D. It was narrow enough at the tip, blossoming out into a big fat bulb - as big as a cue ball - before tapering off again to a narrow neck, attached to a large flat base, which I thought must be the handle. If I could get it up in my ass, or I should say, when I got it up there, it was not going to slip out any time soon.

I began with the butt plug. I made my way to the bathroom, grabbed a jar of Vaseline and put a large glob of it on the thing. "If this thing is going up my ass I'm going to need all the help I can get," I said under my breath. I stood backwards to the mirror and bent over. I contorted myself around and, holding one ass cheek open, positioned the plug near my brown hole, but the angle wasn't right and there was no way I was going to have the torque to force it, in this position.

"Hmm, what to do?" I squatted down with my knees open wide reached down with one hand, felt around to find the point of entry and moved the big thing up against my tender nether-hole. I tried to slide it in slowly, but it was just too painful as it began stretching my ass open. I was going to have to insert it quickly or not at all, and not at all was not an option. Still squatting, I put its flat base on the floor so it stood upright and positioned my rectum so it hovered over the thing.

"Ok, GG. On the count of three," I said aloud, "One, two," and I sat down on the thing with my full weight. I yelped as my ass stretched wide open, spreading around the horrid thing before it popped into me. As I sat on the floor catching my breath, I felt around down there and sure enough, only the base of the plug was still exposed.

I stood up and tested the fit. It wouldn't be going anywhere without some serious effort. Now that the painful part was over, I could see its appeal. Walking around with it in my ass made me aware of every step. My bottom had never felt so full before, and my vagina felt the effect, too, becoming quite wet and swollen.

Next, came the two chrome balls. The metal was cold and they were heavier than they appeared. About as big around as Ping-Pong balls, they were hollowed out with another solid ball inside, this struck the sides of the outer balls with a noticeable vibration as I shifted them around on my hand. They slid right into my damp pussy. I was surprised at how delightful they felt. I walked around the house, and the balls jiggled inside of me with each step. There was no question - the balls and butt plug were getting me aroused.

Now it was time for the nipple clamps. My nipples are large and supersensitive so I knew the clamps would be easy to attach but I didn't know how much it would hurt. "Ooh," I thought as I attached one and then the other, "now this, I like." The steady pinching pressure hardened my nipples and sent shivers of delight through me.

The delicate chain connected the two nipple clamps with the clit clip. The clip looked a little like a roach clip with a big bead at its center to tighten and loosen it. I took ahold of it, opening it up, and began feeling around for where to attach it. I was surprised to find coaxing out my clitoris wasn't going to be an issue after all, the little guy was already stiff and distended. Standing there, I leaned forward to try and look closer, but my boobs dangled forward as well and blocked my view. I couldn't see where to attach the thing, so I had to lay down on the floor on my back and position myself in front of the full length mirror in my bedroom closet. In this position, my boobs flattened out and I let my knees fall open to either side for a full-on view of my wide-open pussy.

It's not often we women get a close up look at our own cooch. I do love the sight of an aroused pussy, all velvety and shiny wet. Intrigued, I began to play with it, inspecting its folds, sliding the labia one way and the other, rolling my clitoris around and dipping my fingers in my honey bucket. I slid my fingers in far enough to touch the Ben Wa balls and experimented with pushing them further in and shifting them around. With my other hand I captured the nipple clamp chain and pulled until my nipples were stretched.

"I'm going to massage my clit for just a bit, to make sure it's big enough and firm enough to attach the clip," I said to myself, and began rubbing it. Watching the salacious woman in the mirror play with herself was like watching an oversexed other woman, masturbate. The woman in the mirror rubbed her pussy until her hips jerked up a couple of times. As the intensity peaked, her thighs quivered, her knees slammed together, clamped tightly and she moaned, shivering with her cum. She stayed that way for several moments; her thighs fell open wide again.

Blushing, I looked into the mirror and smiled at myself. I sat up on one elbow and placed the clit-clip wide on either side of my clitoris. I slid the large bead forward over the two pincers and it pinched my clit between.

"Wow," I thought, "and I'm supposed to walk around all hooked up like this?"

I stood up to try it out. The chain was just long enough to reach from my nipples to my clit and the clip pulled on my aroused clit. When I walked around the house the bouncing of my boobs tugged on my swollen sex parts. I began dressing. My sex was sensitive from all the movement, the constraint and the pinching, making me cum.

When I was dressed and ready, I stood back and took inventory. The plug stretched my ass, the balls filled my pussy and shifted in an erotic tinkle as I moved. The delicate chain of the clamps and clip had been the most deceiving. My nipples were pinched and my clit was engorged and pulsing with my heartbeat. I was more aroused than I had ever been in my life and so anxious to get to M and feel him inside me. I closed the front door behind me and walked out as the car pulled up. Every movement I made reminded me of how filled and stretched I was.

"Good evening, Madam," the driver greeted me as he held the door for me. "I must say, Madam is looking ravishing this evening."

THE CAR PULLED UP TO THE RITZ CARLTON AT L. A. LIVE; I CLIMBED OUT AND WALKED IN. Many a man's head turned as I sashayed across the lobby into the elevator. I seated myself at the bar, as per M's instructions, ordered a sparkling water and waited for his text. The apparatus under my clothes was pulling, pinching and stretching my sex in a most distracting way. I was in a high state of arousal, with my every orifice excited. Only my mouth was unfulfilled. I lifted the lemon off the edge of my Perrier, licked it and lipped it, biting into it as I crossed and uncrossed my legs. A nice looking young man, at the end of the bar, must have noticed. He smiled, stood and walked over, taking the stool beside me.

He extended his hand to me and turned up the charm, "Good evening, my name is Eric. May I buy you a drink?" I sat up straight, putting my shoulders back and extended my hand to shake Eric's, which tugged up hard on my aching clitoris. I gasped under my breath, slouching forward and Eric said, "Are you all right, Miss? You've turned bright red. Can I get you anything?"

I laughed it off, saying, "No, no, Eric, thank you, I'll be fine in a moment." I was doing my best to regain my composure but whichever way I turned, something pulled at some part of my hypersensitive sex flesh.

Thankfully, M's text arrived and I excused myself from Eric. I walked across the bar - as nonchalantly as a damsel in distress can walk - to the elevator and down to room 2350. As I rode the elevator, I took deep breaths, trying to gain some semblance of control over my overheated body. I exited the elevator. The door to the room across from the elevator opened in front of me. No one was visible but I entered the room anyway and looked around. M was standing behind the door and closed it. He took my hand and led me over to the window. He tipped my face up and kissed me, only our mouths touching. I didn't think it was possible to be more turned on than I already was but the liquid between my legs began seeping down my thighs.

M turned me to the window, placing my hands on it and spreading my legs apart. "Don't move, lover," he whispered. His hands roved over me, skimming across my bare back down to my ass. As his hands cupped my cheeks he whispered in my ear, "The ass of destiny."

He pulled up the dress and moved his hand between my cheeks, grabbing a hold of the butt plug and jiggling it. I squirmed and shoved my ass into his hand. He chuckled as his hand continued its path forward to the clip holding my clit out and engorged, ready for his questing fingers. He flicked his fingers across my swollen clit, which made me jerk upright, sending fire racing across my skin. He reached around to cup my breast and rubbed the end of my nipple with his fingers. He pulled the nipple clamps, stretching my swollen nipples outward for a long moment. He released the clamps sending a sudden rush of blood into my sensitized nipples; a wash of heat traveling down to my clit. The two sensations collided, sending orgasmic shudders over my body.

M wrapped his arms around me, preventing me from collapsing to the floor. "I'm not done with you yet," he whispered in my ear. He guided me to sit on the bed. "Lay back and put your arms over your head." I did as he asked, panting with anticipation. He lifted my dress exposing my shaved pussy, caressing my stomach and down my legs, to my knees. He knelt in front of me and bent my legs up, forearms resting on my thighs. He nuzzled my stomach, his fingers finding my nipples and pulling them again. With one hand, he released the clit clip as his mouth reached my throbbing nub. I felt his warm breath blowing across it and began to tremble. He licked my clit. Then from my clit to my hole and back. My toes tingled and my brown hole gripped the butt plug as my entire focus moved to my pussy. My legs pushed against his arms; his fingers held tight to my nipples. As my nipples stretched, the warmth shot down to my clit and I came, pressing myself into his mouth, begging without words for more of his mouth on my pussy. I was blazing hot, the fire of orgasm radiating off my body in waves. His mouth claimed my clit, sucking as he massaged it with his tongue, holding it with his teeth. The next orgasm flooded my body, racing outward like a wild fire.

M slid his fingers into my pussy, finding my G-spot and rubbing, keeping my orgasm going and going until I was out of breath. His fingers stilled and I shuddered one last time before I stilled as well.

M lifted his head and smiled at me. In that moment, I knew I was lost forever. This handsome man stole not only my heart but also my body. No one could ever equal his mastery, his creativity, his outright joy in making love. I prayed fervently I would never know life without him, for it would be no life at all.

"Did I make you cum?" he joked, knowing full well he had. He helped me sit up, pulled my dress down and smoothed my hair. "Come, lover, let's have dinner." He helped me up and led me into the other room.

The table was beautiful, set with a linen tablecloth, crystal glasses, and fine bone china. M pulled out my chair and I sat myself down - my ass still full with the butt plug, my pussy with the *Ben Wa* balls - he poured me a glass of sparkling water.

"To us," he said touching my glass with his glass and my lips with his lips. I was relaxed, enjoying the glow which follows multiple orgasms. As M took his seat, I smiled, "Thank you, love, for an already unforgettable evening." After the aggravating week I'd experienced, I was more than ready for some play and pampering.

M served our dinner from the warming box: an impressive yet, simple meal of salmon, asparagus, and mashed sweet potatoes. For dessert, we ate strawberry shortcake, my favorite. As we finished and sat drinking our coffee, M caressed my neck, nibbling on my ear. "Are you ready for the rest of your fantasy?" he purred. My belly tightened and my skin quivered. "Yes, Sir, I am ready," I whispered. He reached between my legs remarking, "So wet and so hot, you must be ready."

He pulled me to my feet and led me into the bedroom. Candles provided gentle light, rose petals covered the floor and the bed. M stopped me just short of the bed and pulled me into his arms, rocking back and forth in a slow dance-kind-of way. His lips captured mine and taught me more about kissing than I had ever imagined. It was as if his lips slow danced with mine, first gliding, then dipping and twirling my tongue in a loving caress. My pussy muscles tightened and the balls shifted a bit, sending spikes of lust along my nerves. I ground my pussy against M's hard cock, enjoying the slow dance but unable to hold back my passion.

"Ready already, GG?" M queried.

"Oh M, these balls in my pussy and plug in my ass have me all wound up," I replied. "I'm not sure I've ever been this aroused without having an orgasm. Please, I need to cum."

"I'm glad you are enjoying them. We'll leave them in little longer. I'd like you to lay on the bed. No, GG leave your clothes on, I'll take them off when I'm ready." M lay me out on the bed and pulled out his iPhone. "I hope you don't mind, I'd like to take some pictures."

"I don't mind, just hurry, please. I'm in desperate need of an orgasm, M." I was ready to cum but I knew M would want me to wait. As he pointed the camera at me, I couldn't help but give him a little pout. Only the certain knowledge my wait would be repaid, allowed me to retain some semblance of sanity.

"GG, could you lean back on your elbows, spread your legs, and bend your knees? Just like that." I flashed him the look but he was so concentrated on taking pictures, he didn't even notice. I pulled my knees together. "No, GG just a minute longer while I get a close-up." M clicked away. I let my head fall back and closed my eyes. For M, I would wait a minute.

I felt his fingers stroking my clit as he sat next to me. "GG, you have to see this, your clit is huge and slick with juices. Absolutely beautiful." He was right. Looking at my picture, I said, "Wow, that's me? I do look beautiful."

"My darling, GG, you are so much more than beautiful. Here, look at this picture and this one." M began flipping through the pics he had taken as I looked on in growing wonder. Not only was I beautiful, I was sexy. And the look I had thrown at him at the beginning looked sultry, not angry. "The world sees you differently than you see yourself," M said as he put the phone aside and began kissing me. His lips came down on mine, claiming me.

My mind continued to churn. How fortunate I was to have found this man. He already fulfilled all of my sexual needs; now, he was coming close to filling my emotional needs, as well. Not for the first time, I thought, *I'm in trouble with this man.* I gave myself over to his kiss, letting myself live this moment, to truly appreciate this experience.

"GG, let's get those balls out of you. I really need to fuck some pussy." M reached his fingers into my wet gash and coaxed out the balls with his fingers. He removed my shoes as I pulled the little black dress over my head. His hands moved up my stockings to my belly. He leaned over and licked my belly button then, sucked my nipple into his mouth. What sweet bliss. I felt his cock slide into me, filling all my aching parts. He began to thrust, not so much fucking me as making love. He bit my nipple and pummeled my pussy with his hard cock. My body responded with heat; the flash of an orgasm, gone as fast as it came. My body had never been so alive, so focused on the feel of his hair, his lips, his balls hitting my ass and his pubic bone rubbing my clit. His eyes captured mine, "Are you ready?"

"Yes, M, I'm ready," I replied. And together we came, looking into each other's souls as our bodies exploded in unison, bringing with it the greatest satisfaction I had ever known. We fell asleep in each other's arms, exhausted and content.

FIFTEEN

....

M'S DISTRACTION

I was spending a quiet evening at home, doing the good wife thing. Hubby and I were sitting on the couch watching James Bond, Goldfinger, for the ten thousandth time on the big screen TV. We had sent out for pizza. I had a plate with a slice of pepperoni and a salad, and he had the rest of the box for himself.

I was on my phone texting when Theo asked me what I was doing. "Stacy has been texting me for the last half an hour," I said. "She sends her love."

"Tell her hello," he said then, went back to watching the movie.

Bored, I checked in on Facebook and commented on a few posts. My phone buzzed me - a new text had arrived. I switched apps to see who it was.

My heart quickened. It was M.

"Hey," he typed.

"Hey," I typed back.

I wasn't worried about Theo looking over my shoulder and eavesdropping on the conversation. He had more important things to distract him.

"This meeting is so boring, I run the risk of waking myself up with my own snoring," he typed.

I chuckled out loud and shot a glance over at hubby to see if he noticed. Nothing short of a 6.0 earthquake was going to tear his eyes from the likes of Odd Job and his deadly derby.

M was in Hawaii on the big island, Honolulu, so with the three-hour time difference he was still in meetings. "How can I help out, my love?" I texted back.

Nothing came back from him for a couple of minutes, then, "I need a distraction."

"Maybe a dirty picture?" I texted. "I can take a trip to the bathroom and send you back a photo? Maybe some pussy squatting over the iPhone camera?"

Again, a long pause, and then, "A brilliant idea, but too conspicuous in the present company."

Hmm, I thought to myself, what can I do?

Then, another text, "Tell me a slutty GG story. Something you've never told to anyone before. A true confession, something you could never tell anyone, no matter what. But now you are going to tell me."

The idea of this made me squirm around on the couch. Theo shot a glance over at me and I made out like I was enjoying the movie, just trying to get comfortable.

M was discovering what a slut the fifty-year-old GG could be, but I had never shared my earlier indiscretions with him. Before my years of forced abstinence I had not been a "good" girl. I did have some steamy anecdotes to share. Just the kind of stories I thought M was hoping for.

I WAS MARRIED FOR THE FIRST TIME WHEN I WAS NINETEEN. I had been dating John for a year. We were both so young we didn't know any better. When I needed to escape from the chaos of my home life, marriage to John seemed like the perfect out.

John was a landscaper with the union. He worked days planting the bushes and shrubbery you see on the sides of the highways. I was a teller at a bank downtown in the small Midwest city we called home. We rented the upstairs of a duplex; we furnished it with second hand furniture. About what you'd expect from blue collar newlyweds.

We were young and didn't have much in common, but at our age, sexual compatibility was all you needed to have a relationship and that we had in aces. There wasn't a day that went by that we didn't have sex, and some days, we had it two or three times. It seemed natural to us. Our lovemaking had no finesse to it, it was all fast and furious, but it was all we knew, so we were fine with it.

One day, in the middle of the week, John and I were both home from work playing hooky. He had bought a small bag of pot from a friend at work. We had smoked a joint and were in bed watching television. John told me to take off all my clothes, so I stripped out of my t-shirt and panties thinking nothing of it. He told me to lie on the bed and he would take care of me. I liked the sound of that. The pot had made me lazy and the thought of letting him do all the work and get me off was fine with me. He squeezed my breasts and sucked my nipples. John wasn't one to take his time, which suited me fine. He began fingering me then he changed his position, which kind of surprised me because I couldn't reach his cock. He moved between my legs and began sliding fingers into my pussy. First, one finger then, another one. Getting fingered makes me cum pretty fast so I was squirming around, but he told me to stay still so I tried not to move. Then, he slid yet another finger inside my still squeaky tight pussy. He slid his three fingers in and out several times then, added his pinky almost as an afterthought. With his other hand he had begun to stroke my clit as well. He relentlessly fucked me with his four fingers all the while rubbing my clit, faster and faster, in circles. I came to a shuttering orgasm but he just kept on going. I had another big cum and then another.

He eased up on me, pulling out his fingers and resting his wrist. He cracked his knuckles and smiled and asked, "Do you want to go for five?"

Without waiting for an answer, he began pushing his hand into me. I was too speechless to protest. Oh God, it hurt so much I thought I might scream, but he kept right on working his whole hand in, pushing and turning, until abruptly his open hand slipped inside me, all the way up to his wrist.

At this point he stopped moving and stared into my eyes. I was highly aroused and also completely freaked out. After all, what went in was going to have to come out. Then, he began flexing one finger, then another. Every time his fingers moved I moaned, my entire body quaking from the intensity. I couldn't move. My entire focus centered on his hand filling my pussy.

Then, the phone rang.

We both looked at each other. I shook my head no, but he just smiled and leaned forward to pick up the phone with his free hand. His arm, now bent at the wrist, was resting against my clit. He began a long conversation with his boss as he continued to move his hand inside me, first flexing his fingers, then, in a moment of inspiration, he fisted them up. He began turning his hand back and forth, the tendons in his arm moving against my clit. I lay there, unable to move away with his hand in my pussy, trying not to make a sound, muffling my groans that followed every movement of his hand.

He continued his conversation while pushing his fist as far into me as it would go. Then, he pulled it out as far as he could, stretching my pussy without pulling his hand all the way out. Over and over again, he pushed it in, and pulled out, but only as far as the biggest part of his fist.

By this time, my hands were covering my mouth to muffle my moans. If you had told me I would enjoy being fisted, I would have said you were crazy. But there I was, coming hard, over and over again, my mind wiped clean of anything not orgasm related.

When he hung up the phone, he asked me if I'd had enough. I couldn't speak. He leaned over and kissed me, but then, began rapidly pulling his hand in and out of my pussy without removing it. The repeated stretching of my opening, with the penetration of his fist to my cervix, made me feel like I was losing my mind. He stopped, straightened out his fingers, and fisted them up again and penetrated deeper into me.

Finally, he put his free hand on my abdomen to extract his closed fist one final time. I screamed as the widest part of his hand stretched my opening wider than it ever had, pulling free from my pussy.

I convulsed a few of times, my whole body shaking with the orgasms. Still breathing hard, I lay perfectly still in a state of post-coital shock. He kissed my face over and over again, smoothed my hair and hugged me.

To this day, I still fantasize about that afternoon. It never fails to turn me on. I clicked "send" and my sexting was on its way to M.

About ten minutes later there was a reply. "GG. You have my attention. And you have me standing at attention," he wrote.

SIXTEEN

....

MR. FISTER

When we met next, we hadn't seen each other in weeks. M's travels had taken him from Hawaii to Shanghai, then on to Dubai, before his return to California.

I packed my little red Mercedes with my overnight bag, made my excuses to Theo, and set off north on the 405 freeway. It was 3:00 pm and I was hoping to beat the Friday rush hour traffic for our 5:00 pm rendezvous. I had the radio loud to LA's classic rock station when Frankie Mars and Her Majesty's "I'm Free as I Want to Be" came on.

Perfection, I thought, serenading Long Beach with my out of tune rendition. "Today, the gods are smiling on me. What better song is there? This is just for me."

M had reserved a room at our favorite spot in Los Angeles and left me a key at the desk, with instructions to come right up. When I let myself into the room, he was nowhere to be seen. I put my bag on the couch and walked through the suite before I met him coming out of the shower, with just a towel around his waist. He took me in his arms and kissed me, leading me straight to the bed. We sat on the edge of the bed and he leaned back. I pulled his cock out from under the towel and began by polishing his knob. He was especially hard and I was especially eager. I spread my legs and he reached up my skirt, taking my bare sex in hand and rubbing my clit with his thumb. I managed to remain calm for about a minute, but as soon as he slid a couple fingers into me and worked my pussy, I lost my composure. I was beyond turned on, my cooch soaking wet. So turned on, in fact, when M twiddled my G spot, I decided to deep throat him, which I had yet to do. Of course, as big as cock had grown, I still wasn't able to. I gagged on his long, thick manhood.

I slipped out of my clothes and we crawled into bed together. I could tell M needed to do some fucking. He lay on his side, and he lay me on my back, putting my legs over his legs. He put the hot, fat knob of his cock up against my pussy. He worked my clit, while he pushed his length up my pussy with long, forceful penetrations. He continued to fuck me with this toe tingling tempo, bringing on several colossal orgasms. He rolled me on my side, so my back was to him. He fucked my gash with his cock and put his finger in my ass. I was bent at the waist, on my side, and folded over; my ass was the only thing he was holding on to while he slammed into me.

I was so turned on, having my pussy so exposed to him, giving his big cock complete access. He started to work my ass, sliding a bundle of fingers in and out, while he fucked me. I wondered if he could feel his cock penetrating my pussy with his fingers in my bottom. In mid thought, I lost it, having what I call an ass cum; my ass muscles clenching down hard on his fingers while I rode them. When I slowed down, spent, M stopped for a moment, sliding his full length into me and hugging me close, wrapping both arms around me.

"You're really opening up this afternoon, GG," M said, catching his breath from all the exertion. "I've been thinking about your fisting story for weeks. It wasn't a story, was it?"

"No, M, not just a story," I confessed.

M smacked my ass hard and said, "Then I thinks it's time to open your bottom the rest of the way."

This excited me and frightened me at the same time. From M, this could only mean new extremes. He released me and rolled me onto my belly. He coaxed me up onto my knees and, sitting behind me, he massaged my ass, running his fingers down my pussy. He grabbed lubricant from the nightstand and greased up both hands, including his fingers. He began working his fingers into my pussy, then my ass, back to my pussy and back my ass, again. He added more fingers, until he had four fingers in my pussy. He proceeded to four-finger fuck me, deep and hard, until I let out a cum howl.

He slid them out of my pussy and, making sure I could see, he bunched his fingers together and sucked them, covering them with saliva. My slut nature overcame me and I arched my back, sticking my ass up in the air, to give him the fullest access to my pussy. Surprised, I felt him run his fingers over and around my nether hole. *Was he about to continue the training of my ass?* I couldn't help myself as I moaned and pushed my open ass back towards him. M began to slide his bunched fingers into my ass. He had done three fingers before but never four. M was teasing my clit with his other hand, making me squirm with delight, as he pushed all four fingers up my brown hole. I could hardly believe it, but his slow, steady entry caused me to cum. My ass gripped his fingers in orgasmic spasms. He rubbed my clit and I shook, losing control, coming hard and loud, and pushing my ass back on his fingers until I was filled with fingers to the knuckles.

I must have blacked out for a moment. My head was down on the mattress. My hair had fallen over my cum-blushed face. My breasts were pressed flat against the bed, with both arms extended out over my head, my hands gripping the sheets. My finger-filled ass was sticking straight up in the air and my thighs were spread wide apart.

M pushed me even further. He slid two fingers from his other hand up in my pussy. I was so tight and full, but he still found room to work my G-spot. He began with a steady rhythm and built up speed. My violent cum flooded my senses as my G-spot contracted with overwhelming force. My ass was clenching and unclenching around his fingers. He pulled his fingers out of my pussy, and squeezed my clit between his finger and thumb while he inched his hand out of my ass. I groaned and collapsed, shaking and moaning.

By this point, his cock was rock hard and jerking up and down with each heartbeat. His large member was massive when close to cumming and judging by his size, he was so close. He rolled me onto my back and slathered up his cock. My bottom was wide open by this point and that's when he put the purple cock-head deep in my ass, pushing it in all the way to his balls. My eyes opened wide with surprise. M looked back at me and gave my tight, swollen ass a good, hard fucking. He watched my face as he fingered my clit, my pussy and back to my clit again. With my legs up on his shoulders and my ass up off the bed, meeting his cock thrusts, he had complete access to my pussy as well. At this point, he had been working my ass and pussy for well over an hour. He was always careful and loving, progressing while staying well lubed, when he was opening me. While I watched M giving my ass a good, hard fucking, he had me lick his fingers until they dripped, slathering saliva over his knuckles and thumb. He noticed my puzzled expression.

"What do you say, GG? Ready to be fisted?"

M gave me no time to respond. He pulled his cock out of my ass and straightened his fingers with his thumb across his palm. He worked his compressed hand into my pussy, up past his knuckles and over his thumb. He put his cock back in my ass. He slid his open hand in and out, a counter rhythm to the thrusts of his prick. I was being double penetrated, both my holes fucked full at once. I was delirious with joy at the sensation. M was getting too big to stop cumming for much longer. He pulled his cock out, stepped back for the perfect angle and, with his hand still inside me, he closed his fingers and thumb into a full fist. His fist was motionless for a moment; he clenched it, expanding it and stretching my aching pussy even wider. I squirmed my ass around and pushed down hard on his fist. He withdrew his fist from my engorged pussy and I exploded in a monstrous orgasm. I lay back, writhing with ecstasy, gasping and shivering, my body jerking and pulsing with a super cum.

I lay there on my back for a moment until I felt M hoist my hips up high, placing my calves on his shoulders, giving him total access to my ass again. He pushed my legs up over my head and mounted my ass, pounding my nether hole, fucking it hard and fast. His forehead creased with concentration and I could feel him fighting the urge to abandon all control and shoot his load.

His cock was huge and still he pounded my sensitized ass. I gathered my scattered wits, reached up and squeezed his nipples hard, pushing him over the edge. His scrotum pulled up tight to his body, the cum rising out of his balls and pushing up through his great vein, into his cock. He assaulted my ass, pushing my legs high over my head and fucking me with savage abandon, his cock slamming balls-deep into me. I reached up and pinched his nipples again. He threw his head back in a roar, slamming his relentless shaft into me, shooting a huge load, pumping it into my ass, pumping it full, again and again. He came so hard, and for so long, I wondered if he was ever going to stop. He released my legs, collapsing on top of me, drained.

We lay there for a while wrapped up in each other, a hot and tangled mess. The afternoon had gotten away from us, and I knew I had better get up and get home before my long absence became too suspicious. I got up and dressed to leave. I walked back over to the side of the bed, eyeing M's long sleek physique. I leaned down, hugged him, kissed his serene face, turned and stepped to the door.

I looked back at him one last time, relaxed in the bed. I left closing the door behind me.

A minute later I was back at the door, letting myself in and making a beeline to the bathroom. M's huge deposit had begun dripping from my ass.

I finished up, tiptoed to the door and began to leave again, when M cleared his throat. GG?"

"Yes, M?" I whispered.

"I think I'm in love with you."

SEVENTEEN

....

THE SPANK OF LOVE

At last, M had returned to Southern California from another endless business trip. I drove to LA to hook up with him. Our last encounter left me craving him, even more than before. He was full of surprises, just the kind of surprises I had always dreamt of. I was filled with excitement and wondering what new experience he had in mind for us during his visit.

I parked in the garage beneath the airport hotel, popped the trunk, and grabbed my overnight bag. I clicked the automatic trunk closer and turned to walk to the lobby, when who should I find standing right behind me, eyeing me up and down, than my hot lover, himself.

"You do look good in a short skirt and heels, GG," he said, grabbing me around the waist with one hand, pulling me close to him and kissing me on the forehead. "FYI, lover, when you lean down to lift your bag out of the trunk you, your pink thong is clearly visible, tightly wedged in your lovely ass."

"And who's to say it's not my intention to share the "Ass of Destiny" with any appreciative onlookers who might be about?" I answered, feeling feisty, bumping my hip against his thigh.

M smacked my ass hard and the sound echoed through the parking garage. Ohhh, what fun! Our foreplay had begun with a bang, or should I say smack?

"Watch it, sir," I joked, "there are security cameras everywhere, and they will be witness to this assault."

"All the better," M said, and goosed me under my skirt.

I jumped and squealed with delight.

"Already getting damp, are we, GG?" M remarked as we rolled our bags into the elevator up to the lobby.

M let us into the room. Before the door had swung closed, we had dropped our bags and kissed. M reached around and unzipped my skirt and slid it down along with my panties. With his lips caressing my lips, his fingers began stroking my clit. Our public sexual activity had left my clit supercharged. M fingered me and I began to climax, my back arched, my head fell back and I moaned. His hand came up behind my head, grasped my hair, and pulled my mouth back to his. As his tongue dove deep into my mouth, his fingers slid up into my soaked pussy. I surrendered to him and came, muscles clenching around his fingers.

How can I be ready so fast? I thought as I caught my breath. A few simple strokes, a probing finger, and I'm all-afire.

My mind whirled around my body's complete immersion in the climax. M finished, pulled his fingers out of me and pushed me down onto my knees. He freed his stiff cock from his pants and rubbed it all around my face. He knew just how to free my inner slut. I opened my mouth wide, and he pushed in the fat, purple head. He held the back of my head and began fucking my mouth. He controlled me, pushing his cock against the back of my throat until I almost choked, pulling it out and rubbing it around my face again. My pussy juice dripped down my thighs.

He stood me up and led me to the bed, bent me over and began rubbing my cheeks with those skillful hands of his. He leaned over and covered me with his body, kissing my neck and whispering dirty nothings in my ear. He straightened my arms, moving my hands up over my head, and stood up, trailing his fingers down my back. He lifted my blouse up and over my head, but didn't take it off. Instead he used it as an impromptu restraint wrapped around my wrists.

He continued massaging my ass with both hands. With one hand, he reached between my thighs and stroked my still quivering quim; first, the outside then, inside of my labia. With his other strong, agile hand he began kneading my back muscles, eliciting a sigh of pure joy from me. The hand on my pussy found my clit and began stroking it, my breath coming in short gasps. Without warning, the hand massaging my back came down on my ass with a loud smack! I gasped with surprise, lifting up from the bed. M pushed me back down. "Stay where you are, GG."

I shivered in anticipation. His fingers increased their tempo on my pussy and my intensity began to build, screaming to be claimed. I forgot about everything when out of the blue, another smack; again and again, sharper and, this time, unexpected. The pain intensified and my orgasm exploded, red-hot heat flashing up from clit and ass, joining together to create a maelstrom of ecstatic sensation. Such a long, long climax.

"GG?" he said, and then again louder, startling me "GG?"

"Yes, sir," I answered.

"Have you earned your punishment?" M asked.

"Yes, sir, I think I have."

"And why is that, my slutty love?"

"I have been a very dirty girl, sir. I have looked at porn videos and dirty, dirty pictures," I confessed.

"Yes, you have been very bad, GG," M smacked me hard and I yelped. My ass stung and throbbed. "Anything else you need to admit to, young lady?"

"Yes, I've touched myself. I've touched myself many times, sir, until I made my pussy very wet. Then, I brought myself to many orgasms, sir."

Again, his hand came down, this time on the other cheek, with a loud, electric smack. My slutty ass tingled and pulsed in a most delectable way.

"And I've cum while I imagined I was eating pussy, sir. In my mind a slender stripper girl danced around for me. She lay down and held her pussy open for me. I licked it and sucked it and stuck my fingers in her. I fisted her pussy, sir, the way you fisted me. I absolutely enjoyed it, sir. I really liked fisting her."

Thwack, Thwack, two more times. This time I cried out from the sharp pleasure/pain of it and squirmed around.

"And what else, GG? You might as well admit to everything you desire, you depraved whore."

"I've cum fantasizing I was being fucked by two men at once, sir. And I'm ashamed to admit they were fucking me in my pussy and in my ass at the same time."

Smack, smack, smack, smack, in quick succession, back and forth from cheek to cheek.

"And I've cum fantasizing about sucking off a complete stranger in his car in a busy parking lot. And when another man saw what I was doing, then I sucked him off, too, sir."

He gave me no time to recover. One moment, his fingers sliding in and out of my pussy, the next, accosting my clit with fervor. He took me right to the edge of cumming, then, *whack,*

whack, whack. First one cheek; then, the other. My ass rising up in the air to meet his hand, begging for more. My orgasmic explosion was stinging fire, and it went on and on.

He gave me no recovery this time. He pulled his fingers out of my pussy and rubbed my clit, slid them back in, hooking into my G-spot, and alternating the rub with a spank! My entire body flushed and twitched, my orgasm multicolored ribbons of light and sensation coursing through my body.

This time, my orgasm lasted long, so long, it felt never ending. When M pulled his fingers out of my dripping pussy, he laid his palm against me and rubbed my throbbing ass with the other. I lay panting as if I'd just run a marathon.

My awareness returned when I felt him stand and unzip his pants. I felt so wet and so swollen, I wanted his cock inside me. My attention drifted until I felt a gentle slap against my butt cheek. *Wait,* I thought, *what's that?* It came again, a gentle slap of his belt. Oh no! I tensed against the bed. SMACK! Again and again, across my ass, my thighs, oh the pain, the pleasure, the unexpected sensations in my clit. I was cumming from being spanked with a belt. I pushed my legs apart and my ass up when *smack*, right on my pussy. Ohhhhhh, sweet god, I fell over the edge into the chasm. I sobbed my surrender and my cum into the bed. He owned me. M owned this OC butt slut.

I was in a haze of some new emotion - gratitude maybe? - as he finished spanking my ass with his belt. I was desperate to feel him inside me. He covered my body with his, sliding his enormous cock into my pussy, filling me up. I pushed back onto him, whimpering my need, repeating his name over and over. His hands slid under me and held me tight as he pounded me with his incredible cock. I know I must have climaxed; I cannot remember anything but the sensation of his body pressing me into the bed and his cock nailing me. My mind collapsed into the orgasm and thought was no more.

When he pulled out and stepped away, I slid onto the floor in a panting, boneless heap. He helped me onto the bed, caressing my face over and over.

"GG, I love you, I love you," he whispered.

EIGHTEEN

....

POOL-SOME

I couldn't sleep. Sometimes, after we experienced intense lovemaking, and always when I have to get up and go home, sleep eludes me for hours. Oh, for just once to be able to stay with M and not have to go running off, back to my 'day job.' Well, perhaps someday.

I got out of bed, careful not to wake Theo. I had been up reading for an hour when the green light on my phone started blinking. It was M. He couldn't sleep either. We chatted a bit and he began sending me pictures, steamy hot porn, graphic porn.

A couple of pictures later, he sent one labeled one "Gang Bang." I replied a gangbang was on my bucket list. I know, I'm a total smart ass. He told me about a gangbang he had witnessed at a casino in Monte Carlo, and I got so horny. M described how a high roller had lost big at poker, and the man's girlfriend agreed to have sex with all the men at the table to pay off his debt. M described the scene in intricate detail. I was so aroused by his story. I was always surprised at how much I wanted sex, even after having had the most mind-blowing orgasms of my life. M just made a comment or smiled at me, and boom, I was wet and ready to go, again.

In the middle of our sexting, he asked me how old I had been when I had my threesome. "Twenty-six," I replied, musing at how random the question seemed.

At some point, I had mentioned in passing, when I was in my twenties, I had a spontaneous threesome with two male friends at a swimming pool party. "Would you like to hear about it?" I texted, thinking it would be hot to describe it to him. "Of course, GG," came his instant reply, "You know I love to hear about your misspent youth."

BY THE TIME I ARRIVED, THE PARTY WAS IN FULL SWING. My sister had invited me to her house warming party. She had taken over the lease on my old house when I had been forced to move out due to a break up with a guy.

"Hi, GG, thanks for coming," Bev greeted me at the door, hugged me; she grabbed a glass of wine and put it into my hand. "Bird's hot friend is hanging out over there by the pool. You should go say hi." Bird was Bev's boyfriend.

"Ok Sis, I'm going," I replied. I had gone on one date with George to a concert. We had fun but I wasn't ready for a relationship. I looked around the room and didn't see anyone I knew, so I wandered out to the pool.

"GG! Over here," George called when he saw me.

"Hi, George." I kissed him on the cheek and sat down. "How's your day going?" I asked.

"Been a long one, glad it's Friday. Have you met my friend Paul?"

"Nice to meet you, Paul."

Our conversation turned to sports and current events. A couple of drinks later, I was relaxed and beginning to enjoy myself. When the sun went down, all the other guests went inside. The three of us stayed outside, drinking and talking. The moon came up, reflecting on the pool. It was quite late by this time. I was sitting between the guys and they each had an arm around me.

"Hey, want to go swimming?" George asked.

"Sounds good, but I don't have a suit here," I replied.

"GG, we don't need suits. There's no one else out here. Besides, it's night, no one can see."

I didn't take long to make up my mind. I loved to swim at night. In fact, I would swim every night before I went to bed, and I missed it now, since I was living elsewhere. We slipped out of our clothes and into the pool. We swam a little. Then, ended up floating together in the deep end. George nuzzled my neck, and Paul wrapped his arm around my waist. It was cozy and kind of hot. I could feel their dicks nudging my thighs. "GG, have you ever thought about two guys and you, having sex in this pool?"

My insides shivered and I pulled back enough to look into George's face. "I hadn't considered it until now, but why not? Let's." Paul began kissing the back of my neck while he reached around me and cradled my breasts in his hands. I found his dick with my right hand and George's with my left. George reached his arms around me and Paul, anchoring us together with me sandwiched between the two men. George kissed me, his tongue plundered my mouth. I guided his hard cock to my pussy while Paul supported us. As George fucked me, Paul's hard cock pressed between my butt cheeks, and his busy fingers caressed my breasts and pinched my nipples. I felt the heat growing; first, in my pussy, then, across my body. My back arched as I tried to match George's thrusts. Paul held me still, whispering in my ear "just lay back against me, GG. I got you."

He bit my ear and pinched my nipples as my cum took over my senses, flooding my body with heat and ecstasy. I moaned loudly and Paul put his hand over my mouth. As soon as my orgasm was over, George pulled out and turned me around to face Paul. He kissed me, his lips soft and full over mine. I felt George nestle his cock between my cheeks as he cradled my breasts, kneading them in his large, strong hands. The tip of Paul's cock found my opening and paused. I looked into Paul's eyes and smiled, trying to push myself onto his cock. As he pushed into me, his tongue invaded my mouth in time with his thrusting cock. One of George's hands had drifted down to rub my clit as Paul plundered my pussy. This time, I came fast and hard, crying out into Paul's mouth.

My head fell back onto George's shoulder as I lay between them, panting. They guided us to the side of the pool. I felt my feet touch the bottom. "GG, wrap your legs around me," Paul urged. I did and he thrust deep into me, as I was braced against George. I hung at the edge of cumming, holding myself there, waiting for Paul. I felt his rhythm change and let myself go, my muscles clamping down hard on his cock. He slammed into me once, twice, more; then, growled as his cum shot into me. We hung there in the water for a timeless moment while Paul sucked my nipples.

When he turned me around in their arms, George's lips found mine. "My turn, GG," he whispered. His cock was already hard again. Paul supported me as I spread my legs wide for George. He stepped between my legs, wrapped a hand under each leg and pushed his cock into my pussy. This time, he fucked me hard, slamming his man meat into my pussy.

Cushioned by Paul, I just hung on for the ride. I was getting a little sore from all the action in the swimming pool water so when I felt George's rhythm change, I tightened my pussy muscles around his cock, bringing him to ejaculation. Afterwards, we floated, looking up at the moon, my pussy juicy with their cum.

The next day, George got engaged to someone else.

NINTEEN

....

TIED UP AND TOYED

After additional hot sexting, M and I signed off for the night. I went to lay down in the spare bedroom, with my clit pounding in time to my heart. I was so tired and yet, so keyed up, in need of a good cum. I lay there on my stomach, arms stretched out to the sides, legs spread apart, like I was waiting to be penetrated. I ground my belly into the mattress and could feel the pressure all the way to my G-spot. I remembered fucking M from the weekend before. I visualized it in Technicolor detail, grinding my cunt as I came, and came again, before drifting off into sleep, mid-fantasy.

At 8:30 a.m., I woke up exhausted and craving coffee. No luck, we were out. You know you've been a negligent wife when you run out of coffee. With only four hours of sleep, I was feeling a bit rough around the edges. Theo was already at the work so I texted M "Hey love, want to get breakfast together?"

"Come on over, GG, I'll order room service with plenty of coffee. It should be here by the time you arrive."

When I got there, he was sitting at the table reading while eating toast and eggs. I sat down next to him and poured myself a big cup of java. We were chatting about inconsequential morning things when I mentioned I had fallen asleep after my threesome story, fantasizing of him tying me up. He put down his eggs and coffee and went to his suitcase, unzipped a hidden compartment and pulled out a set of straps and a harness.

As I watched him install the restraints on the bed, I felt a tightening in my clit. I loved to fantasize being tied up but had never experienced it. I can't explain it but wow, so hot. I got naked and went to the bathroom to try to pee, but no chance there. My muscles were too clenched for that.

When I walked out of the bathroom, he instructed me to lie down, with my head at the foot of the bed. "Yes, sir," I replied, and did as he asked.

His hand glided down my leg to my ankle; he pulled it out to the edge of the bed by the headboard. Wrapping the leather cuff around my ankle, he buckled it. He grabbed my other ankle, pulling my legs open wide, and did the same. My body began involuntary twitching, like I was ready to run a race, but was waiting for the starter's gun. The twitching got worse as he secured my hands. When he asked if I was all right, I choked out an answer, past the nervous quiver in my belly and tightness in my throat. He tightened the restraints, pulling me out in a spread-eagle position, and wetness began to trickle out of my pussy and slide down my crack to the bed.

When he finished, M stood at the end of the bed. His hard cock and hanging balls hung over my face. I tried to capture the head in my mouth but settled for licking the underside of his cock, down to his balls instead. As I concentrated on licking his balls, his fingers found the wetness of my pussy. He fingered my clit as I moaned into his balls. He pulled back to allow his cock into my mouth. He began sliding in and out, in a measured thrust. Oh how I love having my mouth filled with cock while fingers play my clit. I came fast and hard, the heat spreading over my naked body, rebuilding as the next orgasm shook me anew. He fucked my mouth with authority as he slid his fingers into my wet cunt. M gave me a good, hard finger-fucking, slamming his fingers into me in time with his cock hitting the back of my throat. I tried to hold back the orgasm so I could focus on sucking, but it was pointless. My back arched, and he pushed his cock as far down my throat as it would go. I gagged and waves of pleasure washed over me. M pulled out to let me breathe. His timing was perfect. I knew he would keep me safe even in our wildest sex-capades.

M reached into our bag of toys and pulled out a new vibrator. I watched him move around to the side of the bed. I was still panting and glowing from my last orgasm. He got between my legs and poured cold lube onto my pussy, rubbing it around and down into my ass. To my surprise, he forced the butt plug in my ass. My muscles clenched around it; first, in protest, then, in surrender. It felt so good to have my ass filled. M began stroking my clit and the sides of my labia with the vibrator. I moaned and tried to tilt my hips to follow the tip of the toy with my clit, but I was tied too well.

I was so turned on. I wanted him to slide his cock inside me right then, but he had other ideas. He continued stroking me, turned the vibrator to high and pressed it directly on my clit. I came instantly, uncontrollably. My vagina tightened and squeezed. My ass gripped the plug. My orgasm expanded and intensified. I began sliding from one orgasm to the next, with little space in between them. Each wave of pleasure crashed into the next, splashing the colors of an abstract cum painting through me.

He crawled across the bed and kissed me. As he looked down at me, I could see his mind working. "Let's try this," he said. He changed the straps around, pulling my hands down by my sides and lifting my legs up in the air, spread as wide apart as I could handle.

I think you'd better take yoga lessons again, my inner dirty girl whispered in my ear. In this position, I was exposed, ass lifted off the bed and pussy wide open, ready for the taking. M straddled me so that I could suck his cock. I gobbled him down, hardly noticing what he was doing with the vibrator until he inserted it into me. He slid it in my pussy and angled it onto my G-spot. Talk about an earth shattering orgasm. My G-spot got the ride of a lifetime.

With his cock stuffing my mouth, I was getting fucked in both ends. I was one heartbeat from another cum, but M kept me right on the edge of climax, not letting me go. I stayed there until he picked up his pace and slid his cock as far back into my throat as it would go. My body convulsed, and I came, superheated, so in the now. There was no room for extraneous thought or motion. I seized up with rapture.

Damn it, a muscle cramp in my thigh.

"Are you alright, GG," M saw my pained expression.

"Muscle crap in my thigh," I managed to squeak.

M quickly unstrapped my leg and rubbed out the spasm. He loosened the rest of the straps and pulled the covers over me. Warm and secure I began to drift off to sleep.

"I'm off to meetings, GG." M kissed me on the forehead. "Text me later, lover."

After a short nap, I got up, pulled out the butt plug, causing another orgasm, showered and left to join the hubby for lunch.

TWENTY

....

BURGER, MEDIUM-RARE

I thought *I'm addicted*. He was all I could think about. In my mind, I lay underneath him, filled beyond full. His cock buried to the balls in my pussy, his hand on my breast, my eyes captured by his intense gaze. Waiting on the precipice, waiting for his permission to cum, waiting for the twitch of his magnificent cock which would start my orgasmic avalanche.

"GG, are you alright?" It was Theo sitting across the table from me. "What the hell is going on with you?" We were at the club and a waitress stood tableside looking impatient. "You are certainly not yourself these days. Now, what would you like for lunch?"

Unfortunately, my body was not with my brain. My body was sitting at lunch with Theo, my mind was lying in bed next to M. I was watching ESPN on the big screen, not watching my lover make love to me.

"Hamburger, medium-rare, Linda," I said, "with sweet potato fries, please."

I had lunch with Theo. Then, return home to my so-called life, which felt more like a waiting room for "death by reruns:" Law and Order, all twenty seasons.

Text me M, I thought to myself, *please text me. Soon.*

TWENTY ONE

....

BALL WASHING – A+

When I walked into his hotel room and saw the look on his face, I knew I had chosen my outfit well. I wore a short skirt and a white sleeveless top, framing my cleavage. M grabbed me around the waist and kissed me, his light stubble grazed my face.

"You're looking especially hot this morning, GG," he said. His hands roamed over my body and under my skirt. All I could think about was getting into bed with him.

"Do you mind if I take a shower before we make love?" he asked.

"No, love, go right ahead," I replied, as I bent over to give him the view he loves the most, the "Ass of Destiny." My posing had the desired effect. He walked back to me and rubbed my butt cheeks with his hands. In a flash, my panties were around my ankles. He began fingering my pussy in his magical way. My man knew his way around a pussy. I craved having his hard cock inside me right now.

Sometimes, I thought he read my mind, but more likely, we were just in sync. He unzipped his pants and pulled out his cock. My fingers wrapped around him and gripped his thick erection, guiding it into me.

"Get on the bed," he commanded, "on your hands and knees." I started unbuttoning my blouse and he said, "No, leave your top on." My body shivered in anticipation as I climbed onto the bed. He teased my clit with his hot knob, rubbing back and forth across it. His hands smoothed the fabric of my top over my back; he gripped my hips and shoved his cock deep into my gash, filling and stretching me. He continued thrusting into me as his fingers found my clit. He was rubbing the one spot he's discovered, which always brought on my orgasm. I felt the pressure building, little shards of pleasure shooting from my clit to my G-spot and back. Just when I was sure I couldn't wait one more second, my lover hit the perfect rhythm and my climax exploded, sending a wave of heat across my back and up to my face.

When I started breathing again, he stopped moving and grabbed the lube. He dripped it on my ass and inserted a finger, spreading plenty of lube inside the opening of my hole. He lubed his cock and pushed the head into my ass. M smacked my ass cheek hard and said, "I think your ass training is going extremely well, GG. You now easily and eagerly accept deep insertion. I'm pleased."

"Thank you, M. I'm surprised by how much I like it."

He continued his penetration. My muscles clenched against his incursion then, loosened, allowing him access. It's so difficult to describe the pleasure of the moment he first inserted the head of his cock into me. It was almost as if every bit of my body and mind, halted what it was doing, to feel the unusual stretch of muscles, the instantaneous spread of heat across my skin, the localized ass-orgasm, focused around the invader, the ruler of my ass. When he moved so slow, the localized orgasm shot up my spine to my brain and all thought stopped. His long cock pushed in and out, going deeper every time. My back arched and I pushed back onto him hard as my muscles contracted and I came again. This time, it felt like fireworks painting my system with colors. In the moment when my ass was completely full of cock, all time stood still.

M continued his thrusts, sending ripples of pleasure through my body. He breathed hard with exertion, droplets of perspiration falling on my backside. I was panting as the pressure built again, slowly this time; as if some of the urgent need had been met and now, my body could slow down to enjoy the next climax. The moment extended into eternity. It was like I'd never been anywhere or done anything other than this. A rogue orgasmic wave hit me, and I rode his cock hard, shoving back on it frantically until my deep hunger was satisfied. As my muscles relaxed, he pushed me down on the bed.

He pulled out of me and rolled on his back. It was his turn. "GG, you will wash my balls with your tongue now."

"Yes, sir," I responded, eager to please him the way he always pleased me. I grabbed a washcloth from the bathroom and washed off his cock, and got down between his legs. I licked his hard cock up and down, then moved down to his balls. I used my tongue to cover every inch of him with saliva. When I had him good and wet, I went to work. I began by massaging his balls with my tongue. I pulled his right ball into my mouth and rolled it around. All the while I was stroking his staff, rubbing its great length with my hand while I washed his ball sack.

He was so close to cumming, but my wrist gave out. I so wanted to get him off, but I guess he could tell I needed an assist, because he took over for me, jerking his rigid man meat.

He lifted his hips, thrusting his pelvis into the air, and my tongue found its way into his bung hole, licking it with my stabbing tongue. His balls pulled up tight and he groaned. A great spout of jizm erupted out of his swollen cock-head. It shot straight up on the air, followed by another and another. His hot spunk covered his belly, landed on my face and in my hair.

He dropped back onto the bed, breathing deep and steady. He threw his head back and laughed. "What an amazing cum, GG. I guess you could tell I needed it."

"Yes, you did and that was my goal." I lay beside him, snuggling in under his arm and he kissed me on the forehead.

"By the way, your ball washing gets an A+ today, lover."

We snuggled together for twenty minutes or so. Then, we both showered and dressed. He continued on with his day and I returned to mine. On the outside, I looked to the entire world like nothing had happened, but on the inside, my thoughts and feelings were shifting.

TWENTY TWO

....

A MISMATCH MADE IN HEAVEN

So, with what you know about me now, you might ask, "How on earth did GG end up marrying a man who didn't like sex?" I was tricked into it then, lulled to sleep. I don't mean to say I had no responsibility because I know I am also at fault.

In the beginning, there was sex, enough to rope me in, I guess. Once we got married, it tapered off to once a week, then once a month, then once a year. And then zero, zilch, nada.

By then, I guess, he felt secure enough. I wasn't going anywhere, even if I was complaining about the drought in the bedroom. In his mind, he didn't marry me to have sex. He married me as a trophy to show off to his friends. We belonged to the club, we had our wonderful house with the view, we drove nice cars, and we had a comfortable life together. I had parties and volunteer work to keep me busy and to keep me out of his hair.

After I began my tryst with M, I moved into my own room. Long before M, it felt like we were roommates, not husband and wife. Most of my friends also have marriages of diminished expectation. We all came into them bright-eyed, thinking we were in love. Instead, we ended up cynical and alone in a room of two, trapped by the many things we possessed and the expectations of those we no longer love. Lulled into unconsciousness. Waiting in the anteroom of the afterlife.

Ok, a bit melodramatic, but it does feel more like waiting for death than truly living.

Twenty years in a passionless marriage was enough to turn this hot-blooded woman into a nervous wreck. I had pills for everything, a bunch of different pills to get me through the endless days. Everyone thought I was happy, but believe me, it was a chemical illusion. My happy life was prescribed by my happy doctors.

I had a ready smile and a good sense of humor. I looked good on the outside. I never had a bad word to say about my husband or my life. I floated through life on a cloud of pharmaceutical "everything is gonna be alright".

But, inside? Inside, I was screaming. *Oh my god*, I thought, *I'm only fifty. Will I have to live like this for forty more years?*

Well, as you've seen, my answer was, "Hell, no!"

TWENTY THREE

....

BI-CURIOUSER AND CURIOUSER

As the year went on, M's visits to California became more and more frequent. Theo had grown accustomed to my disappearing for several hours a day, and he stopped questioning me.

One such morning, M and I were finishing breakfast after a leisurely love making session, when he looked up from reading and mentioned Stacy had emailed him to say hello. "She brought up flying out to California to visit us," he said.

"Yes," I said, "she messaged me the same thing the other day. What do you think?"

M put down his Kindle and shut it off. "It's always a pleasure to see Stacy, and I do so enjoy being with you two in the same bed, but I know how frustrating it was for you, not being able to explore her sexually."

Stacy and I had shared M once before, when we three first met. And while it was delightful and fun for us, and even steamy hot, she and I could never be lovers. Our friendship, going all the way back to high school, was just that, a remarkable and loving friendship. When we got into bed together with M, it had been intimate but awkward. I had been open to the possibility of exploring each other sexually, even eager to do so, but Stacy had been less than enthusiastic. So while we held hands and slept in the same bed, and we both took great joy in pleasuring and being pleasured by M, our sexual interactions equaled zero. It was a disappointment for me. I so hungered to feel the soft curves and taste the sweet salty sauce of a woman, but I knew it was never going to happen with Stacy.

"Do you remember Erica?" M asked.

"Yes, of course," I said. "She sounds like such a lovely person and she is so beautiful."

M dated Erica before we met and they had remained good friends ever since. He shared they had a torrid affair, with a predilection for clandestine car hookups, sometimes in profoundly public places. When I had shown an interest in their story, he had told me about their erotic exploits. I found those hookups to be deliciously hot.

"Like you, she often spoke of someday making love to woman." M reached into his jacket pocket, pulled out his cellphone, and continued, "She recently broke it off with her fiancé. I'm going to reach out to her and set up a date for the three of us to get together. I was thinking maybe it was time for you and me to take a trip back east together."

Well, one mention was all it took. Just hearing M say it sent a shiver through my body, accompanied by an audible moan. Anyone else would have probably missed it but M picked right up on it.

IT WAS THE MIDDLE OF THE WEEK WHEN I WAS WORKING AT THE OFFICE. Hubby was at meetings so I had the place all to myself. The way I like it; I get work done with no interruptions. I heard my iPhone vibrating in my purse. I reached for it and thought, "Well, it will only be one of two people: M, in which case I'm thrilled, or Theo, in which case I'm not here."

To my surprise, it was neither. "Hi, GG. This is Erica. M texted me and suggested I reach out to you."

How sweet, I thought. "Hi, Erica, so nice to make your acquaintance. M has told me so much about you."

"And me, about you," she texted back. "If you text me your photo, I'll text you mine," she wrote.

I held the phone out at arm's length, looked at myself on the screen, removed my glasses, and took a selfie. I sent it off.

Her text came right back with her photo. "You're so pretty," she typed. "As you can see I'm in the bathtub." Her blond hair was up and clipped on top of her head. She was flushed with the heat of her bath, and she had the sweetest smile.

"I hope I'm not being too forward," she typed, "but M thought it might be fun for us to get to know each other a little better." *Hmm*, I thought, *I wonder where this is heading.* "Is it ok if I text you a more personal photo?"

Why not, I thought, *this is getting fun.* "Yes, of course, Erica, I would love to see your photo."

A moment later a snap shot appeared. She was in a bubble bath and I could see her smooth pink knees above the bubbles and the soft curve at the top of her ample cleavage just above the bubbles. "That's very nice, Erica. You have a lovely body," I texted.

"Thank you, GG. I have to be so careful not to drop the phone into the bathtub when I'm texting, you know?" I replied, "I know! LOL."

"I just finished shaving," she typed, "Let me show you." I waited for a photo of her legs, all smooth and hairless. To my surprise, up popped a lovely clear shot of her hairless, pouty pussy; all pink, the luscious lips open and her clit swollen and long. I felt a good, funny feeling in the pit of my stomach. I gulped to myself and typed, "Wow, Erica, you have a beautiful pussy. It looks smooth and inviting," my hands were shaking slightly.

"Thank you, GG. Any time you would like to send me some photos, please do. I know we can trust each other to keep them confidential," Erica texted, finishing with an emoticon of kissing lips.

"Can I tell you what I'm doing now?" she sent.

"Yes, Erica, if you'd like to. I'd love to hear." I had unbuttoned my jeans and had my hand down my pants, touching myself in preparation for what was coming next.

Erica went on texting. "I'm imagining you on your back, and I'm pushing my pussy into your mouth. You are licking and sucking it." She paused for a moment and asked, "Should I continue, GG?"

"Yes, please, Erica. I'm sitting at my desk reading your texts with my hand down my pants, touching myself," I replied.

"That turns me on, GG. I'm touching myself too, under the water. My pussy is very soft and smooth from my bath. I'm imagining I turn around and see M between your legs, putting his cock in your pussy. While I'm watching M's big cock disappear up your pussy, I squat down on your face. My pussy is on your mouth and you are eating me out."

"M starts sucking my nipples while he's fucking you, and I grind my aching cunt into your tongue. I watch your thighs shaking, like you're cumming hard. You grab my thighs with both hands and pull me down hard, sucking my clit into your mouth, making me come."

I lost it. I came so hard I nearly dropped the phone. Erica must have cum, too, because the texting stopped for a couple of minutes. When the phone vibrated, I retrieved it.

"Then, M pulls out of you and walks around behind me. Looking up, you see his cock wagging just above your face. I bend forward and put my head between your legs and slurp your juicy pussy. I can smell M's man scent all over you. Then, M puts his rock hard cock in my dripping cunt, slides it in and out the way he does, driving me crazy; he pulls it out, drops down and pushes it in your mouth."

I came again, even harder than the first time. I had never sexted with a woman, and it was driving me crazy. Erica was so hot. I couldn't wait for the three of us to be together.

"M keeps fucking your mouth until he's huge. Then, he pulls out, puts the great purple head against my slit and slowly splits my tight little pussy wide open. You watch him ramming into me from beneath us. You tongue my swollen little clit while he pounds away. All this time I'm eating your pussy, licking all around; sucking softly on your hard little clit, lightly flicking my tongue against it."

I did drop my phone, this time. I came so hard, my legs were shaking. I could hardly stop touching myself, cumming again and again.

After a couple of minutes I picked up the phone and replied to Erica, "OMG, Erica! That's the hottest thing I've ever read!"

A minute later, she texted me back, "I know! I don't know what got into me, GG. I had to put the phone down or I was going to drown it! I just came so hard I think I woke up the neighbors."

"LOL," I replied. "You are a real dynamo."

"No, I'm totally not. I'm generally reserved and modest, if you can believe it. I'm not quite sure what got into me," she finished typing, "but, I guess we will find out when the three of us get together someday."

TWENTY FOUR

....

HEAD BACK EAST

Believe me, it took some doing. My fancy footwork turned an idea into a plausible story, which Theo would buy and Stacy could back up. I made it happen. M and I were going away together. The day of our departure dawned so early, we barely had time for a kiss and a cup of coffee before we were out the hotel door and into the shuttle, for our 6:00 am flight out of Los Angeles' airport, LAX. We were finally on our get-away.

When we were seated, I leaned over to M for a kiss. What I got was so much more, a light flicking of his tongue across my lips and tongue. Still not completely awake, I sat back, mesmerized. The nerves in my sexual core lit up like Christmas morning, sending shudders up to my still-sleepy brain. I savored the moment. When I looked back at M, I saw his eyes twinkling with mischief. His smile could melt the mid-winter ice on the Great Lakes.

I slept most of the four-hour flight. Having the extra seat between us gave me enough room to get comfortable. I woke up when the stewardess walked by and told me I would have to straighten up my seat backs and fasten my seat belt for landing.

M and I walked leisurely through the airport and down to the baggage claim area. He grabbed our suitcases off the carousel. We wheeled them outside and climbed into our waiting limousine. On our way to the hotel, M leaned over and whispered to me "I can't wait to get you alone and strip you naked, GG." Just hearing him say it made me instantly wet.

We checked into the hotel and went up to our room. The bellhop brought our bags up for us. M tipped him and as the door closed behind him, we were out of our clothes, kissing and groping our way into bed. We were rolling around, half tickling, half wrestling. I was putting up a pretty good fight when M finally pinned my arms to the bed.

"GG," he said, "I do believe I will need to restrain you." M released me, got up and opened his suitcase. Out came his bag of tricks. He unzipped the canvas bag and pulled out a mass of leather straps. "This will only take a moment," he said with a wink, "I'm going to tie you to the bed."

My chaotic mind stood still and my body froze in place. I watched him install the restraints under the mattress, over the headboard, and up at the foot of the bed. My mind hyper-focused on his every movement, my body shivered in anticipation.

He captured my right hand first, attaching a strap around my wrist, doing the same with the left. He bound them together above my head and stretched my arms away from me. M moved to the foot of the bed, trailing his fingers along the length of my body as he went. He grasped both my ankles and lifted me up to center me on the bed. Being man handled made my pussy tighten in a delicious knot of anticipation.

Smiling at me, he spread my legs open wide. He secured both my ankles, tightening the restraints outwards, so I couldn't close my legs. He climbed onto the bed to check that my wrists were secure but not too tight. I looked up and there he was, all man, long, furry and lean, kneeling over me with his heavy manhood in hand. I eagerly raised my head and opened my mouth to wrap my lips around his perfect penis, but he had other ideas.

M gently pressed my head back to the bed, with his hand on my forehead. He waited until my eyes meet his, he placed the head of his cock against my lips. I opened my mouth wide to take it in and he slid his semi-erect penis between my lips. He was just getting hard, I could almost get him down my throat. He slid it into the back of my throat and stayed there, motionless for a moment. He slowly withdrew it, only to slide back in, again. He did this over and over, in an exquisite slow motion, which had my pussy dripping, without his hands even touching it. He had already gotten too big for me to choke down his thick knob.

M pulled out of my mouth and kneeled there with his magnificent man meat bobbing above me. He began spanking my face with his cock, rubbing the smooth, fleshy beast all over my face. What he was doing was so incredibly unexpected, so unbelievably hot, I came, arching up against the restraints. My juices dripped out of my pussy and down my ass, in an unexpected waterfall.

I was completely under his control. He could do anything he wanted to me and there was no way I could stop him. I was inside my most secret fantasy. M knew what I liked and he would take me to the greatest orgasmic heights I could have possibly dream of.

He turned around, straddling my face, his heavy balls hanging above me. He put his mouth down full on my pussy and sucked and licked my sex; he pushed his now-hard cock into my mouth and began fucking me with it. There's no other word to describe what he was doing to me. He was pushing into my throat, deeper and deeper. I could hardly breathe. I began gagging, saliva filling my mouth, coating his cock. Tears flowed from the corners of my eyes. His cock slid deeper into my throat than it had ever been before, and I strained against the ties, back arching, pussy muscles clenching and unclenching. He slathered my pussy lips with his tongue and lips and nibbled on my clit.

All motion stopped for an eternal instant, my body hung on the edge of an improbable climax; my mind went perfectly still and focused. His cock twitched and he began to shoot his load. My whole body tried to forcibly eject it from my throat, but he kept cumming, and I kept swallowing as fast as I could. Heat was racing from my cunt outward, burning away all thoughts. Ever watchful, he pulled his cock out of my mouth so I could breathe easy again. His cum dripped from the corners of my mouth. His softening rod fell across my face, forehead, cheeks, eyes, lips. I was panting, desperately pulling air into my lungs, my body quaking with powerful after-cum shudders.

Breathtaking, beyond words. M stood up and loosened my straps, freeing my arms and legs, helped me under the covers, and brought me a warm washcloth to wipe off our love juices. He kissed me on the forehead, pushing my hair off my face, and asked, "Was it too much, GG? If it's too much, you must always tell me."

I thought for a moment. Had it been too much? No, it hadn't. I had never, for a moment, felt in danger. Once again M had understood my limits and had taken me to their very edge.

"It was heaven, lover. Just heaven."

TWENTY FIVE

....

AN EPIC EVENING

M and I were back in our old stomping grounds for business and to see friends. After a power nap, and shopping with friends from high school, we met for dinner at our favorite diner.

"How was your day, GG?" M inquired.

"Relaxing, I saw Dory and Lisa for lunch. I tried to sleep but only managed a morning nap." M was fairly humming with excitement, unusual in such a contained man. "What's up M? You seem excited."

M smiled at me, "Remember the Tornado Shelter band from high school? They're having a reunion concert, tonight. Not only did I get us tickets, but Erica will be there, too." M knows I how much love rock concerts. And since Erica would be there, who knew what might happen. "Tonight is on its way to being epic." I bounced up and down and kissed M on the cheek, fondling his package under the table.

The concert was every bit as incredible as expected. We sat in the middle of a group of old friends he had invited, both his and mine. I never could figure out how he always knew the right people to invite, but my guess was, checking with Stacy.

Erica and I hit it off, right away. We spent the night chatting and enjoying the music, while M sat back, watching us.

The band played their obligatory two encores and the lights came back on. "I don't want it to be over," I moaned. M leaned over and kissed me. "I asked Erica if she would like to join us for a nightcap."

I looked at him, waiting, "She said a definite yes. She'll meet us back to the hotel." I was bubbling over with excitement. As we walked out through the parking lot to our rental car, I laced my arm through his arm and hugged into his side. "Wow, M, she's great. Why did you two break up?"

M gave me *the* look. "Circumstances, GG, it just worked out that way. She is extremely involved with her family, and I'm always on the move. But we've remained close friends."

"Well, I like her. She's so pretty and totally sexy, it's easy for me to see you with her."

"That's good, GG, since she's agreed to be our third tonight."

"M! You aren't just teasing me?"

"Not teasing, golden girl. She's always wanted to have a threesome and she is attracted to you as well. Just remember, GG, she's a little shy."

I had to laugh softly to myself after how she and I had been sexting.

"Oh, M! Thank you!"

ERICA HAD GONE IN THE BATHROOM FIRST, BRUSHING HER TEETH AND CHANGING INTO A LACY CAMISOLE. My usual state of dress in a hotel room is naked, but I decided to mirror Erica, leaving on my camisole and thong. When I came out of the bathroom, the lights were off, and they were sitting on the couch. "Come here, GG," M instructed. As I eased under his outstretched arm, I noticed he was naked. He had his other arm around Erica and was fondling her breast. As his fingers latched onto my nipple, his mouth crashed onto mine, stealing my breath and my thoughts. His tongue invaded my mouth as his hand caressed my breast. It excited me knowing he had Erica on his other side.

When he turned to Erica, and began kissing her, I snuggled closer and began stroking his cock, already so hard and large. My eyes had adjusted to the dim light, and the sight of M and Erica kissing, made heat race across my body. Erica's hand was in her lap. I began stroking it and pulled it over to M's cock. We began stroking his cock together, her hand on the head and mine on the shaft. M thrust into our hands as he switched his lips back to mine.

Our eyes met as his lips gently caressed mine, softly moving across them. I felt the tip of his tongue lick the underside of my lip, sending shivers into my core. My hand had cupped his balls as Erica took over stroking his cock. His arm held her closely while his hand disappeared into her panties. My attention was pulled back to M as his tongue curled around mine, making my insides quiver with anticipation. Our kiss lasted for a long moment. I was on the verge of an orgasm when M pulled away and went back to kissing Erica.

My excitement level would not allow for sitting still. I slid out from under M's arm, removing my remaining clothes as I went. My mouth found his cock before my knees hit the floor. I knew from our experience with Stacy that M found it hugely exciting to be kissing one woman while another sucks his cock. I was determined to give him his fantasy blowjob. My mouth eagerly cupped the head of his cock as my hand rubbed up and down the shaft. I took a deep breath and slid his cock into the back of my throat. I swallowed him down as far as I could, taking him down past my gag reflex. I felt the moisture flood my pussy as he bucked into my mouth. I held him as long as I could, then pulled up and caught my breath. Back down I went. Erica and M continued to kiss as I swallowed my man, getting that large cock as deep in my throat as I could. M moaned into Erica's mouth and put his hand on the back of my head, holding me there as he pumped in and out of my throat. The feeling was so intense I came right then, the spasm reaching up into my throat. I felt M's balls contract and thought oh no, you can't come yet!

M never comes until he is ready, so I wasn't too worried. I backed off of his cock anyway, giving him space to maintain control. I went after his cock again, mostly because I love sucking cock. It empowers me to bring a man so much pleasure, especially a man such as M who spoiled me rotten in every way. M was on fire now. As soon as I had my lips wrapped around him, with his hand on my head, he began fucking my mouth. I could feel Erica squirming against him and began running my hand up and down her thigh. M's hand was twiddling her twat and she gasped as she came. I felt M's body try to follow Erica, with a cum of its own, and kept sucking. His iron control allowed him to orgasm without ejaculation. I lay my head on his thigh completely out of breath, and so hot, I was certain I would surely combust. Erica had her head on M's shoulder and seemed out of breath. M's head rested on the couch.

My eyes met Erica's and we both laughed with delight. M looked at Erica then, down at me. "Ok, ladies, onto the bed." He helped us up and we walked to the bed arm-in-arm, smooching on the way. "How do you want us, M?" I inquired once we got there.

"On your backs ladies, side-by-side."

I could tell Erica was still a little nervous. How exactly would we be interacting? I was unsure as well, but I knew M would have a plan. As we took our positions, M knelt between the two of us, placing a hand on each pussy. His thumb landed on my clit, massaging it as he slid his fingers into my dripping gash. Swiftly the pleasure intensified, pooling in my core. Next to me, Erica gasped and began panting. My hand found hers as M brought us to simultaneous orgasms. Before I had time to think, those talented fingers brought me to the edge and kept me there, wanting release but waiting...waiting...*Oh please M!* His fingers continued stroking my pussy as I strained to move his fingers to my clit and find release. Just when I couldn't take it any longer, his thumb rubbed back and forth on my clit, bringing me to a raging orgasm. When I returned from orbit, I was on my side facing Erica. Her face looked like mine felt. We grinned at each other, enjoying M's incredible abilities.

"Erica, come here," M said as he rolled me onto my back and pushed my legs up. He took her hand and guided it to my clit, showing her how to touch me. He had her place her fingers inside my pussy, while he licked my clit. The tip of his tongue teased me. Then, he lapped me up and down, while Erica's fingers slid in and out. I balanced on the razor's edge when M quickly sucked my clit into his mouth. An avalanche of heat and sensation skittered across my body as he continued sucking. My mind fractured into a hundred little pieces as I floated on the feeling.

"Did you feel the way she clenches when she comes?" M asked Erica.

"So powerful, do I clench, too?" Erica inquired.

"You do. Now it's your turn to lick." M maneuvered Erica between my legs. She smiled at me and leaned down, hesitantly licking my clit. When I moaned, her hesitation evaporated and she began exploring. The first thing I noticed is how different the texture of her tongue felt - soft and smooth - compared to M's. Her long hair caressed the inside of my thighs, causing small spikes of pleasure up and down my legs. M continued to whisper encouragement into her ear and before I knew it, her mouth brought me to a blinding orgasm.

"Wow, you're a natural," I gasped. She laughed and M smiled. I saw his hand disappear behind her round bottom as she returned with new confidence to my pussy. The sight of her blonde head between my legs filled me with fierce joy. Her tongue thrust into my dripping gash sliding up to my clit. Erica's ass elevated high in the air as M brought her to orgasm. She moaned and ground her face into my pussy and my own moans filled the air. My hands found her head and stroked her hair; she looked up at me, clearly emboldened by her success.

M pulled her up and guided her onto her back. He motioned me to stay where I was and placed my hand on her breast. His face disappeared between Erica's thighs, and my parts quivered in anticipation. I began to massage her breast, so different from my own, soft and full. Her nipples were hard little points. I could tell M was getting Erica close. Her body began dancing and she knocked my hand away. Her bottom lifted straight off the mattress and her moans filled the room. I was impressed with the way M followed her every movement, keeping his mouth on her as she came again and again, bucking hard against his face. When he lifted his head, she lay shivering and quivering on the bed.

"Ok GG, on your hands and knees." As I moved into position, M kissed me and I tasted Erica's pussy on his lips. His cock was ginormous. I was more than ready to have it inside me. He gripped my ass and drove into my vagina fast and hard, his hands holding my hips as he controlled my movement. I came fast and hard, back arching as I howled my pleasure to the universe. Erica had joined us. She stood beside M and I felt her hand on my pussy and his cock. Her fingers reached under and found my clit. She knew just what to do, applying the perfect pressure and bringing me to an earth-shattering climax.

My arms were shaking so hard, I collapsed to the bed, face pressed into the mattress, as M pulled out. He turned to Erica and put her on her hands and knees. He entered her gently and began a slow, smooth rhythm. I moved so my hand mirrored the position Erica had just used so successfully on me. I could feel M's cock moving in and out of her vagina. My finger just found her clit when her orgasm took over, her body moving all over the place. I struggled to keep my hand in place but was unable to. I placed my hand around M's balls and let his body carry me with it. I felt M's balls tighten and knew he'd have to stop soon or risk exploding. When he pulled out, he kissed me and headed to the bathroom.

Erica and I lay there for a while, panting and sated, making small talk about the evening and our families. Without warning, we burst out laughing.

"This is amazing," she said.

"I agree. I've always been attracted to girls as well as men, but haven't had much chance to experience this."

When M returned he slid between the two of us. He wrapped his arms around us and pulled us close, our heads resting on his chest. He was looking back and forth between us when we got the giggles. "Ahhh, this has turned into a perfect night," M declared. I sighed with happiness as I snuggled closer.

"Beyond my wildest dreams," Erica replied. M kissed our foreheads. I floated in perfect connectedness, content to hear M's heartbeat and feel the breathing of my two companions. I was surprised to find the hotness of our encounter overshadowed by the togetherness that now connected us.

After a time, M hugged us tight and said, "We're not finished, ladies. GG needs to eat pussy, and you need your pussy eaten, Erica. Just one caution, you must remain as still as possible so you don't hurt GG. Her neck isn't as strong as a man's."

He held Erica as I knelt between her legs. Emboldened by her success, I got right down to it, tongue dipping into her wet gash, licking around her hole then sliding up her labia to her clit. Already swollen and sensitive from M's ministrations, her clit was irresistible. I licked around and around it. When I felt her close to an orgasm, I placed my mouth over her clit and sucked. Erica went wild, her pelvis grinding into my face, her moans sweet in my ears. I held her on the edge of cum as long as I could, then let her slide down the other side. What a feeling! My fingers found her gash and hooked into her G-spot as I sucked her swollen clit back into my mouth, rolling it over and over with my tongue. I felt her cum again, harder this time, as I came with her, hard and long. Her pelvis was moving all over but I held on, hands now on her thighs and mouth planted over her clit. I sucked and lapped and used the tip of my tongue to drive her beyond wild; our bodies so in tune, every cum of hers was mirrored by one of my own.

Her hands found my head and pushed at me, signaling an end to this phenomenal occurrence. Sitting up, I looked at her, hoping she was satisfied, hoping I hadn't gone too far in my enthusiasm. Her face seemed to glow, her eyes were unfocused. "You're a natural at this," she panted. M and I shared a smile. He held his arm open, and I slid beneath it as he kissed the pussy juice off my face.

The three of us lay in a heap, rehashing the night's events just like golfers do after 18 holes. "But M, isn't there something on your bucket list you might want to check off?" I asked out of curiosity. He thought for a moment, and then ordered us onto our backs right next to each other. He spread my legs as he rubbed his hard cock. He looked at us with a big grin on his face as he slammed into my wet hole. Fucked me hard and deep and long. I was panting and so was he when he pulled out and moved to Erica, pinning her with his big cock. He rode her hard, her body dancing all over the bed. I watched, enjoying the intensity on their faces. Back and forth he went, fucking us, making us come. His stamina dazzled me.

In the end, he was riding Erica again. I could see him getting close. I reached behind him, grabbed his balls and whispered to him, "Give her your cum, love. Give it to her." He came, so long and so loud, I was certain security would knock on the door.

Definitely an epic night.

TWENTY SIX

....

NAVY TIME

About five years into my first marriage I was done. This husband who had been a man when I was 18 now seemed more like an immature boy. Of course, the sex was still good, but I was growing annoyed at being the only adult in the house. He wanted toys and so he went out and got them. I never could get ahead on the bills since he was always spending money.

One of my friends - more of a mentor - suggested I consider joining the Navy. *Hmmm.* I looked into it and decided it sounded interesting. I took the *ASVAB* test and signed up on the spot to be a hospital corpsman. All this I did without telling the husband. I sprang it on him the week before Christmas, "Oh, by the way I joined the Navy and I'm leaving December 26th." To say he was surprised and upset would be an understatement.

Off I went to boot camp in sunny Florida. I thought I'd gone to heaven. No snow, temps in the eighties every day. All I had to do was get up and follow orders. I got into great physical shape and, the best thing of all, there were lots of men. Everywhere I looked, hot men. Of course, I couldn't touch them in boot camp, but when I went to hospital corps school, oh yeah! I left sunny Florida in early March and landed in the cold and windy city of Chicago.

I was having the childhood I never got to enjoy. My class began at 11am so I was able to sleep in every day. The coursework wasn't difficult so I had plenty of time for myself. I would go to the gym and lift weights with the guys after class. Late at night, I would run along the lake on the silent base. On weekends, we all planned trips together, to Chicago, camping at the state beach, and longer trips up into Minnesota, where many of my classmates were from. I had my choice of hot guys and got a little wild. (I know, you must be surprised!)

First, there was Jackson, a humorous guy from North Carolina with whom I studied. He was focused on his studies though and wandered away pretty quickly. Afterward, I took up with a handsome young man from South Africa who had a mesmerizing accent.

Chad was young and sweet, also oversexed, as I discovered to my delight. Our "courtship" lasted about three weeks of the twelve-week program. One Friday night, we walked outside the gate to the first motel we could find and rented a room.

As we entered the room, Chad reached for the buttons on my uniform and I reached for his pants. I had his zipper down and cock out in record time. I kissed him as I began massaging him. I slid down to my knees and beheld his cock for the first time. "Nice!" I said, taking in the large size and the slight bend to the left. As I took the head into my mouth, he placed his hands on my head and groaned. "GG, if you suck me much more, I'm going to cum." After some gentle sucking and some licking, I stood back up and took off my clothes. "We can't have you cumming now, when we have all night."

As he lost the rest of his clothes, we kissed our way onto the bed, his hands squeezing my breasts as I stroked his cock. He pushed me onto my back and mounted me, missionary style. He proved even teenagers could be good in bed. He fucked me hard and deep, bringing me to orgasm, shooting his load into my pussy. As he collapsed on me, I smiled, knowing we had all night.

We did not sleep as we explored each other's bodies, sucking and fucking like we were never going to get sex again. When I got on my hands and knees and looked over my shoulder at him, his cock got hard so fast I was amazed. He fucked my pussy long and hard, holding my waist and pounding into me. Later, I sucked his cock as he ate my pussy. Then, we did it all again. Such a wonderful night!

The next week we would steal kisses whenever possible but couldn't get away from base. In desperation, we went to the park by the lake. Although I had done some cock sucking the week before, I hadn't done a quality job. And I do love to suck cock. So, after kissing and walking, a little bit of groping, I found a large tree and had Chad lean against it. I pushed my breasts into his chest and ground my pussy on his leg. "Your job is to let me know if you see anyone coming toward us." He looked at me, perplexed. "What are you going to do?" I knelt on the ground and cupped his package in my hands. "Give you a proper blow job," I replied.

I nibbled my way from the head to the base of his cock and back up. He was quite hard and large by the time I returned to the head. I licked, slid my mouth onto him, taking his cock into my mouth and down my throat. "Ahhhh," I heard from him. I placed my hands on his hips and fucked his cock with my mouth. I gave him a top-flight blowjob, one he still talks about with awe in his voice.

The most memorable experience of our time in Great Lakes came in May. My friend Diane was coming to visit, and we were going to spend the weekend in Chicago, seeing the sites and enjoying the nightlife. Chad asked if he could come down to see us on Saturday with his friend. Victor was a handsome man with olive skin and black hair. We had flirted a bit before I got together with Chad. I told Diane about Victor and asked if she was up for a double date. "Of course I am, GG! I'm a fool for a hot guy in uniform!"

The weekend of her visit arrived. I picked Diane up at the airport and we spent a quiet Friday night. We ate at Berghoff's, and walked the streets, enjoying the big city feel. Di was a statuesque redhead with temper and a wicked sense of humor. She loved to date but refused to get serious, saying "we're much too young to get involved." The next morning we explored the Art Institute and then walked along the lakefront.

The guys joined us in the afternoon, changing out of their uniforms and into street clothes. We set off to find Rush Street and happy hour. Di and Victor hit it off right away. Chad and I were so horny we could barely keep our hands off each other. After a wild evening of dancing and bar hopping, we were ready to find a dark corner and get it on. I wanted the guys to stay the night but didn't want to pressure Di. On one of our restroom runs, I brought it up and she agreed. "Oh, GG, he's so hot. I want to rub my tits all over his naked body." I forgot to mention, she had great nipples. I've often wished she would rub them all over me.

In the cab, on the way back to the hotel, Victor and Di were kissing up a storm. Chad kissed me and whispered in my ear, "We should spend the night." As I arched into him, I replied, "as if I would let you leave." I unlocked the door to the room and we piled in, clothes flying every which way. Chad and I got right down to it, hardly noticing we were sharing a room with our friends. I pulled his cock until he was as big as ever.

He sucked one nipple then, the other, giving one a nip before his lips found mine, and his cock drove into my wet and waiting pussy. We fucked fast and hard, rolling over so I was on top riding him like I was in a rodeo. I came three times before he shot his load into me. I collapsed onto his chest, panting from the exertion.

When we caught our breath, we both looked over at Victor and Di. Victor was older than we were and much more experienced. Di was lost in the moment, Victor driving his cock into her while his fingers teased her clit. Her moans made me shiver with desire. Victor brought her to orgasm again and again as we watched. He looked over and winked at us. "Are you ready to go, my brother?" he asked. Chad's cock went from semi-hard to rock hard in an instant. "Fuck yeah, if it's ok with GG." I nodded, excited to see what would happen next.

Victor whispered to Di as he continued his ministrations, when she nodded yes, he withdrew and motioned Chad over. "Lay on your back, Di is going to ride you." As Victor directed my friend and my lover, one hand drifted to my gash while my other hand pinched my nipple. I settled in to watch and see what I could learn.

Di and Chad were kissing and Chad was thrusting his cock into her pussy. Victor took position behind her and put the head of his cock against her asshole. As he matched rhythm he pushed his cock into Di's ass. She froze for a moment before pushing back onto him. The sight of the two men, with their cocks inside her at the same time, made my skin flame. I thought I was sexually sophisticated, but I'd never even imagined this. The slow tempo continued until Chad and Victor had their rhythm matched; then, it sped up. Di was panting and moaning. I couldn't believe how turned on I was, rubbing myself to orgasm, again and again, yet still wanting more, wanting what was going on in front of me.

All three came at the same time, and they collapsed in a heap. I rolled onto my back and stared at the ceiling, mind reeling with newfound desires and possibilities. Two guys at once? That would be beyond incredible. With them filling both holes? A cock in my ass? So nasty, so dirty, so hot! But the thought of a cock in my pussy and a cock in my ass at the same time short-circuited my brain.

My mind was imagining how it would feel when I felt warm breath on my cheek. I opened my eyes to find Victor kneeling next to me, his lips inches from mine. "GG, you were so generous. Thank you, it's always been a fantasy of mine." I took a deep breath and said, "And now it's a fantasy of mine." He laughed, "Will you allow me to reward you for your generosity?"

I pretended to think about his request, knowing all along I would not deny him. "Ok Vic, since you asked." His lips brushed mine before he moved down my body, licking and sucking my nipples on the way. His tongue traced a lazy path down my belly, circling my belly button then down, down to my gash. My clit and lips were swollen from the furious attentions of earlier. Victor lapped my clit like it was a bowl of milk. My back arched, and I pushed my pussy toward his face. He put his hands on my pelvis, holding me still as he captured my nub between his teeth, flicking his tongue back and forth across my clit. My cum exploded across my body, heat and electric current mingling in the longest orgasm of my young life. When he let go of my clit, his fingers slid into my dripping pussy, filling me and reaching for the elusive G-spot I had read about in Cosmo. As his fingers continued to stroke me inside, his mouth ravaged the outside, sending me into a tsunami of cumming, each orgasm bigger than the last. I was floating on the ocean of post coital bliss when I felt Victor's fingers resting on my other hole. I stilled, feeling a little bit anxious. No man had ever touched me there. "Shhh, sweet GG," Victor crooned, "This will be a little invasion." He sucked my clit into his mouth and, as I relaxed, he slid his finger up into my ass. The feeling was indescribable, so different. My muscles clenched and released. He continued to work his finger in and out, then added another finger. My ass lit up like a Christmas tree as I bucked up into Victor's face, coming so hard I lost all track of time.

When I returned to my body, Victor helped me up and we joined Chad and Diane on the other bed. So comfortable to be snuggled together in a dog pile. We fell asleep and didn't wake up until morning.

TWENTY SEVEN

....

FREEWAY JAM

About a month after our epic evening with Erica, M and I again escaped for a glorious week together back east. He had meetings most evenings but we would sightsee during the days, waking up early and heading out for a cozy time together. Then, we split up as he headed out to work. I had the evenings to myself, and I enjoyed imagining what titillating trouble I could get into.

We did quite a bit of driving, so of course, there was a lot of car play. We were driving on the turnpike, heading out for a trip over to the islands, when he instructed me to remove my jeans.

"If you say so," I replied, "but I didn't wear panties today." He glanced out of the corner of his eye, feigning a stern look of displeasure at my hesitation. "Yes, sir, immediately, sir." I took off my seat belt. I unbuckled, unsnapped, unzipped, and worked my tight stretch jeans down over my ass and thighs, kicking them off one leg at a time. I was naked from the waist down, and clean-shaven, of course. The leather seats felt good on my bare ass and the air conditioning blew down between my legs onto my damp pussy, cooling my sizzling cooch. I opened my legs wider to let in the soothing breeze.

M noticed me positioning my pussy towards the cold air, and smiling said, "You are such a slut, GG. Now remove your t-shirt." M knows I never wear a bra. He often comments on how lovely it is to see my big stiff nipples pushing out through my shirt.

"But," I hesitated. Then, "Yes, sir." I twisted to lift the tight t-shirt over my head, leaving my breasts and big erect nipples uncovered, and slid down a little in the seat, feeling exposed.

The turnpike was bustling with traffic: cars, trucks, SUVs, and campers. We were in a low profile car, so anyone who cared to look down into our windows was going to get a hot eyeful.

"Feeling shy, GG? That's very unlike you," M knew me so well.

"Yes, M, a little," I replied softly.

"I see," he said, "thank you for being honest."

I felt a sense of relief, not wanting every trucker and horny husband in the Midwest to get a look at my goodies. But M did not tell me to get dressed, and I was determined to play our game. As we continued our drive, I sat in my seat trying to look nonchalant in my nakedness. We entered a crowded stretch of highway where the two major interstate routes intersected. The traffic slowed noticeably as the summer tourists and eighteen-wheelers entered the highway and merged lanes. I was feeling overexposed again, which was uncomfortable on the one hand and hot on the other. There was a delivery van riding parallel to our left and a motorhome keeping pace with us on the right. I could see the drivers, though neither was looking in my direction. I kept my legs crossed at the knees, thighs gripped together, and my arms crossed over my breast.

I've got this under control, I thought.

Then, M took his warm hand off the steering wheel and placed it on my cool, bare thigh. Like instinct, or maybe it was a physical reflex, my legs uncrossed and my thighs fell open. *Dammit*, I thought, *how does he get my body to respond so easily? One touch and my legs open wide, my pussy exposed and waiting for his masterful touch.* "Lean your seat back and put your feet on the dashboard so I can finger fuck you," he said.

I checked out the traffic. It was moving at a steady pace, with a semi beside us on the right, and a mini-van to our left. But it was no use trying to resist. If he had told me to get out of the car at a rest stop and suck off every trucker in the parking lot, I would have happily complied. "Yes, sir," I said, lifting the handle and tipping the seat back until I was almost horizontal. I put my heels up on the dashboard, my ankles crossed, trying to hide my nakedness.

M reached over, placing his hand on my thigh, just above my clenched knees, inserting his fingers just inside the narrow gap between them. He slid those magic fingers along my inner leg. My feet spread apart on the dashboard. The further up my thigh he went, the wider I spread my thighs. Within seconds, I had gone from completely closed, to wide open. My knees bent outward and my hips tilted upward, anticipating his touch reaching my pussy. I was already having little pre-orgasms, as he slid his fingers along the length of my hot, wet pussy, gathering my juicy slush and delivering it to my stiff, little nub.

The tip of my clit betrayed me, poking its hard little head from beneath its fleshy cowl and welcoming his adroit finger's advances. My arms swung open revealing my erect nipples, as I grabbed on to the armrest and the side of my seat. A minute of M's nimble touch and I was incoherent with cum. I had forgotten about any curious onlookers, cumming at once, as he rubbed my clit, cumming again as he fingered my pussy. Finally, a long, big orgasm, as he placed three fingers up my cunt, pounding against my G-spot, his fingers pounding in and out of me. I thrust my pelvis up to meet his every incursion, letting out an animal-like howl of pleasure with my orgasm.

As M pulled off the freeway, heading out on surface streets, I collapsed into a heap of hot titillation. I stared into the distance for several minutes, seeing nothing, as he made his way through traffic. I hardly noticed him making several turns, then stopping the car and shutting off the engine. "GG, hon, put your clothes on. The hotel is just across the way from here. I'm going in to order take out. I'll meet you inside."

TWENTY EIGHT

....

FOOD PORN

I looked around the parking lot and, sure enough, we were at our favorite Mexican fast food joint. M was out the door and heading inside. I collected myself and sat upright, my bottom sliding along the wet leather seat. I pulled my t-shirt over my head, down over my stiff nipples and pulled my skimpy jeans up over my swollen pussy. I stared down at my crotch noting the clear outline of my cunt. *A camel toe is what the young men call it,* I thought to myself. *I definitely have one. My swollen labia looks huge stuffed into these skimpy pants.* As I got out of the car I tried to pull the t-shirt down to cover my not so private parts, but it was useless.

I joined M at the front of the line, snuggling up next to him, still feeling half dazed from his exceptional attention. When it was my turn, I looked up to order. There waiting to fill my burrito bowl was the spitting image of my ex-husband's office intern. I had the hots for that man-boy for three years, but always kept my distance.

Early twenties, five-foot-ten, mixed race young man with green eyes, mischievous smile, and bulging biceps, spilling out from the sleeves of his company t-shirt. My camel toe gripped against the seam of my jeans as I eyed the muscular ripples beneath his shirt. He asked me what I'd like to order and under my breath I blurted out, "You! I'd like to order you." Our eyes met and a hot wind shot between us. Destiny snapped into place as we simultaneously blushed and averted our eyes.

Wow, I thought, *now that doesn't happen every day.* My clit shot to attention. It began sending Morse code to my brain. "SOS, SOS, SOS, 'So Over Sexed.'"

M saw all this too, checking out the situation. The young man and I both blushed again as I finished my order and thanked him. As I moved on down the line, he dared a glance at my nipples, pressing hard through my shirt.

M followed up behind me, ordering his food and carrying on a little playful banter with the young man, finding out his name. We moved down the line and paid up, collected our food and were heading out the door, when M said, "I've changed my mind, let's stay here and eat."

I looked at him kind of funny as we sat at a table across from the food service area and ate our dinner.

"I couldn't help but notice you were rather taken by young Michael over there. And he, by you," he said. "And you told me you weren't a cougar, GG."

Well I couldn't deny it. M would see right through me anyway, so I said, "Yes, M. I have a thing for young, athletic, dark skinned men," I said, "I just never have the nerve to approach them." I was feeling awkward about the situation but continued on anyway, "M," I said, "I would like your permission to ask Michael to meet me later, while you're working." I eyed him, feeling unsure of myself. He looked up from his food and took me in, seeing into me the way he did. "I will, of course, take photos when anything memorable happens," I continued.

"Yes," he said without hesitation, "judging by his reaction to you I think it's an excellent idea." He reached in his pocket, pulled out a piece of paper and a pen and wrote on it. He folded it in half and handed it over to me saying, "Take this note and hand it to him over the counter. When you hand it to him, simply say, 'I'll be waiting for you outside at closing time.'"

"M," I squeaked, "You are such an instigator." I went to open the note and M placed his hand on mine, stopping me. "'For his eyes only, GG."

I could feel the heat rising in my ears as I stood and walked to the front of the line. My adrenaline was pumping, making my hands shake. As M stood and watched from the back of the room, I caught Michael's attention. He looked puzzled but pleased to see me again. I delivered my spoken message to him, trying to keep the quiver out of my voice, and handed the note to him over the counter. He smiled back at me looking a bit shaky, the blood rising in his cheeks.

Saying "See you later, Michael," I turned to walk back to M. I could feel Michael's eyes burning into my denim-covered ass as I walked away.

M was waiting for me by the door. He had his phone out and my phone pinged as he put his phone back in his pocket. He winked at me and patted my ass as I walked by him and out the door. "Check your email, GG, food porn," he said.

Food porn? I thought.

We got back in the car and I checked my phone. Sure enough, he had snapped a photo of me standing at the front of the line. I was up on my tiptoes, leaning forward with my ass out, and my breasts pushed up, nipples protruding through the t-shirt. I was handing the message over to Michael who was looking back at me sheepishly.

"Look at me, I'm shameless," I remarked to M. "I am an OC butt slut, aren't I?"

M, with his left hand on the steering wheel, put his right hand, opened palm down, between my legs, grabbing ahold of my entire pussy and squeezing firmly. "Yes, you are, GG. Yes, you are."

M HAD JUST ENOUGH TIME TO CHECK US INTO THE HOTEL, BRING IN OUR LUGGAGE AND THEN HEAD OFF FOR HIS MEETINGS. I drew myself a hot bath, and soaked in the warm water. I have to admit I was feeling butterflies of anticipation in my belly, thinking about what might happen with Michael later. I was imagining everything from passionate love making to being stood up. But as I soaped my pussy, I found myself imagining kissing his rippled belly while I held his ball sack and listened to him moan, making me shiver all over. I coaxed an orgasm out of my eager pussy to take the edge off my heated imaginings.

I got out of the bath intending to dress and grab a latte in the hotel lobby to pass the time. But the hot water left me sleepy, so I wrapped a big bath towel around me and lay down for a quick nap. When I next rolled over it was already 9:30 pm. *Oh shit*, I thought and hurried to get dressed.

I walked around to the front of the restaurant and tried to stare in through the entrance window, but the lights were out and the sign had been shut off. Dejected, I turned back towards the hotel, continuing around the side of the building. There was a pickup truck parked there. Its lights were off but its motor was running. In the cab I could see Michael's handsome profile. His eyes were closed, but as I walked nearer, he turned his head to look, flashing his hot little grin.

Whew, I thought, smiling back at him, *it wasn't my imagination. This is some powerful stuff.*

He waved me around to the passenger side, pushing open the door for me to climb in. "Good evening, GG," he said, taking my hand and helping me into the truck, "I was wondering if you changed your mind."

"Good evening, Michael. After the moment we shared this afternoon? Not likely." He was still holding my hand. He kissed it as I sat down beside him, pulling me over to him.

We sat close for several minutes. It felt sweet and innocent and hot. He smelled sweaty but in a nice way. He smelled of masculine musk. We made small talk, savoring the anticipation. He was such a handsome young man with an earnestness about him, making him even more desirable. And those green eyes, oh my god, he must have driven the high school girls crazy.

He draped his arm over my shoulder and pulled me close to him. I fit under his arm, leaning up against his side. While M is long and sinewy, without an extra ounce of fat on his hard slender body, Michael's young muscular body was all hot sculpted curves, standing out from beneath his Affliction t-shirt. I couldn't help myself and soon found my hands sliding up his big arms, across his chest, and over the hard little nipples under his t-shirt. My fingers followed down to the contour of his rippled abdomen. His arm reached all the way around me and down to the hem of my skirt, his fingertips touching the soft skin of my thighs.

"Yes," he smiled, "it took all my concentration to keep the food orders straight after seeing you." Michael's fingers had worked the hem of my skirt up and they were exploring the soft thigh flesh under my dress. "Your husband is named M? He is a generous man, sharing you like this."

I gulped and my breath caught in my throat with excitement. What had M written in the note I had given Michael at the restaurant? My eyes wandered down the zipper of Michael's baggy jeans. I could see the shape of his erection through the fabric. My hand wandered down the front of his pants. I began tracing the outline of his cock and he moaned.

"M isn't actually my husband, Michael. He is my lover." He had reached over and he was cupping my breasts and squeezing them gently. His other hand made its way up my thigh and was rubbing against my damp panties. I turned my face up to Michael and he leaned down to meet me in a deep, wet kiss lasting for several minutes, our tongues made greedy with lust.

I unzipped his jeans, and his cock sprang out like a catapult being released. My skin flushed. He was rock hard and there was a dribble of juice on his broad tip just waiting for my tongue to lick off.

Michael was fumbling with the elastic of my panties, trying to get his fingers under to lift them aside. "Here, let me help you." I lifted my skirt up over my hips and pulled off my panties. My pussy was so swollen, the lips were fully parted, and my wet, rosy gash was spilling forth with juicy cream. To my relief, he sank his fingers into me to his knuckles. I bent down and took his cock down my throat, holding his balls as he pushed against the back of my throat. God, I wanted to climb on him and ride his young cock until I fucked it dry.

For the mouth fucking I was giving him, he was holding his seed well for a young man. When I was his age, the boys could barely take my lips around their rims and they would start shooting the bishop. Of course, they were also ready for another go before I could wipe the dribble off my chin.

He worked his fingers with a charming innocence. What he lacked in adeptness, he more than made up for in pure animal heat. I came wildly, pushing his entire cock down my throat as I gagged on his thick joint. "Oh my god, GG, you've got to stop," the sweet boy said, clamping his thighs together, "or I will cum in your mouth."

"And that's a problem?" I asked him, lifting my head to look at him.

"M's note, GG. His instructions for me when he shared you with me," Michael was close to cumming. His balls were pulled up tight and the head of his cock was as swollen as a red tulip.

"Tell me how M would have you do me, Michael. What was in his note? Tell me what you're going to do to me." I was dying to know what slut-play M had devised for me. Michael pushed his seat all the way back, and reclined it as well. "I'm going to need your camera phone, GG. M wants a picture of, well, you know."

What was this? Was Michael too shy and modest to say what he had been instructed to do? "Um Michael, I don't know what, 'you know' is. Please, tell me."

He seemed excited and not quite sure of himself as he continued. "M says I'm not to have sex with your vagina, it belongs to him tonight." Michael hesitated, searching for the right words. "He says I'm to have sex with your back door." As Michael said it my eyes closed and my bottom quaked. The ultimate taboo - too forbidden and too hot to imagine. M was going to have my hot young fantasy fuck my ass.

"The note instructed me to bring a jar of Vaseline. It said you would know what to do with it. He told me I was to make love to you and cum in you, but not in your pussy, because it's for him alone. I hope you won't be upset with me, but he told me I was to cum in your ass and take photos of it dripping out." Michael held up the jar to show me. I reached down, searched around in my purse and fished out my phone, turned it on and opened the camera app. I handed the phone to Michael and took the Vaseline from him in exchange.

With all the uncertainty, Michael had begun to go soft. But I knew what M had in mind, so I opened the jar and scoop a generous portion of Vaseline out. "Give me your hand," I said to him. Thankfully his nails were trimmed. I took the goop and rubbed it all over his fingers. Then I sat back, lifted my legs up against my breast and spread them open, showing him my entire bottom. He looked at me with a 'what now' expression and I pulled his index finger toward my ass-gina. He got the idea and slid it up my tight brown hole.

Well, that was all it took, one finger, and I was shaking and cumming. In another minute, I moaned, "Now two, Michael," and he added a second finger, sliding them both in and out in a slow, steady rhythm. I wrapped my hand around his now stiff cock and began massaging it, covering it with the thick goop. "Three, Michael, now three, please." The third finger went in smoothly, stretching my ass, the Vaseline easing the way. He had finally gotten the idea and with my ass relaxing he took it upon himself to insert his pinky as well. Four fingers bunched together in my ass and my pussy was dripping. His cock was hard again, so I lowered my legs, letting his hand slide out, sat up on my haunches, as I straddled him with my back to him. My puckering asshole was suspended over his beautiful full cock head, awaiting his instructions.

"Michael, do you want to fuck me now?" I asked him urgently. "If so you must tell me. You must tell me what it is you want to do to me."

He took my hips in his hands, his fat knob pressing up against my hinter-hole, and said, "GG, I'm going to fuck your ass now. I'm going to fuck it hard and deep." Then, he pulled my ass right down onto his cock.

I gripped the steering wheel with both hands and tilted my pelvis to better receive him. When he entered me, I began to cum. "Oh yes, Michael. Fill me up." He pulled my ass full down on his hard fat cock, filling my ass all the way to his balls. It was a punishing penetration. He split my tight, white ass wide open around his thick, black member. He was fucking my ass hard, and my pussy gushed as I felt his thrusts reaching a crescendo. His girth doubled in size right before his cum. He was grunting and slamming his hot shaft home, shooting over and over, emptying his balls up my ass. I moaned and howled, pushing my ass down on him, as hard as I could, to get every last inch of his cock up inside me, not wanting to lose a single drop of his sweet juicy man-boy cream.

The storm settled and we both stayed still for a long moment. I could feel him beginning to wane. "Michael, quick, the camera?" I asked. He reached over and picked up my phone and handed it to me. I switched it on and handed it back to him.

I was still crouched over him and leaning forward for him to get the right angle and a clear view. I heard the camera clicking away, so I lifted up off him, feeling his softening cock slipping out of me. "Here it comes Michael, get ready. Your cock is about to slip out." He switched settings and began the video just as he slid out. A large glob of cum seeped out of my ass and dripped onto his soft, shiny cock. I dripped for several minutes, amazed at how much cum juice my hot young man had deposited in me. I wasn't sure it was ever going to stop.

This was slut heaven, if ever there was one.

TWENTY NINE

....

PINNED

When I returned to the room, I was so tired. I got in bed next to the sleeping M, gave him a kiss and went right out myself.

I woke up the next morning to M kissing my cheek and rubbing my back. He whispered in my ear all the things he wanted to do me. "You were a very dirty girl last night, GG," M spoke in his sultry sex voice. "Did you make Michael cum in your ass?"

I blushed and lay still. "I did, sir," I replied, my voice shaking. "He filled my ass full of cum as you instructed him to, sir."

"I'm pleased, GG. Now I'm going to tie you to the bed, face down, and fuck your pussy." His words woke the beast in my belly and I began to squirm on the bed. "Or, better yet, I could pin you to the bed right now and fuck you in the ass too, my OC butt slut." I gasped at this and ground my pelvis into the bed, turning to face him and meet his eyes. He smiled at me and kissed me full on the lips. "Would you like that?" he whispered into my lips. I shook my head as I moaned a yes back into his lips.

My ass was still sensitive from Michael, but the idea of M fucking my ass, right after Michael, gave me butterflies in my belly and fireworks in my pussy. "Yes, sir," I whispered.

"Then you'll have to ask me," He said as I pulled my scattered wits together. He whispered into my ear, "Say, 'please, sir, will you fuck me in my ass?'"

"Please, sir," I managed to choke out around my growing excitement, "will you fuck me in my ass?"

Swiftly, he moved to cover me with his body, pinning me to the bed. He covered the head of his spectacular cock with saliva, placed it against my ass and slid it in balls deep. My ass stretched around him painfully yet perfectly. Unlike Michael's cock, M's was too big, and yet just right. M pulled out and then plunged back into me. His body covered mine, he kissed me; his tongue in my ear as his cock invaded my ass. This feeling, of being pinned to the bed unable to move, so turned me on. My euphoric nerve endings exploded and filled my entire being with white-hot heat. I moaned into his mouth as my ass muscles clenched around his cock. Still, he pumped in and out, and I could barely breathe. Right away I came again, this time my ass pushing up against him as best it could.

I managed to free one hand and gripped the top of the bed. M covered it with his own, interlacing our fingers, as his other hand slid under me and found my clit. With his gifted fingers strumming my clit and his cock slamming in and out of me, our heat became almost unbearable. I struggled to free myself from the overwhelming bliss. I opened my eyes and looked into his. M held firm and kept me on the edge of almost losing it without turning away. His cock plunged into my ass, again and again, driving me to new heights of erotic awareness. I lost the battle with him and the heat raced along my nerves and skin, burning away everything but the ecstasy.

My body filled by orgasm, my mind blasted clean.
I floated, pinned by his body to the bed.
I felt more at peace than I ever had before.

THIRTY

....

HOMEWORK ASSIGNMENT

We had driven the two hours to catch the ferry over to the island resort hosting M's conference. M had been quieter than usual, absorbed in thought. He is an observant man and when he did speak, he pointed out to me a little something which had eluded me.

M has always encouraged me, or more to the point, insisted of me, to be open and communicative about my sexuality. I mean, damn, it's not like I could hide when I'm turned on, anyway. When something or someone turns me on, I'm obligated to report back to him, sharing my "scandalous" arousals.

I can honestly say, no man has ever turned me on, or made love to me, the way M did. But after ten years of sitting on the sidelines, and watching the game of love from the bench, I was back on the field and I was ready to play and play hard.

OK, enough of the sports metaphors, what I'm trying to say is this, while on the one hand, I was forever proclaiming my complete obsession for all things M, he had also seen me turned on at the sight of complete strangers; like when we entered the restaurant, and I saw hot young Michael, with his boyish smile and flirty eyes. Or back at the hotel checking out, when the international business type in the tailored suit held the door for me and complemented me on my dress.

"GG, I do believe you have a wandering eye," M broke the afternoon silence. "You have been caged for years, lover. I'd say you need to spread your wings, or should I say, your legs, and fly where the hot summer winds may take you."

"But M," I protested, "no better lover than you could exist for me. You know how I feel, I want you."

"Ah, so you say, but your actions tell a different story." M's voice had the edge which both scared me and turned me on. Sometimes, I think he knew my libido better than I did. "As long as you are in denial of your inner tramp, and your most hidden and shameful desires go unfulfilled, you will be driven by them. Now that you've freed the beast, until you have fully experienced how lustful and slutty, deep down inside, you really are, you will be powerless over ever being faithful to one man again."

I'm not sure it was M's intention, but what he seemed to be suggesting was getting me dripping wet. Was he saying I should pursue my lusty fantasies to their salacious conclusions?

"The nun has left the classroom, GG. The gatekeeper has abandoned his post. There's no one and nothing to stop you now. You have stepped outside the realm of right and wrong, and into the heat of a raging fire, most women never dare face. You have been given permission by the gods to apprehend and achieve true sexual passion and fuck-stasy. I'm sorry, that's not quite accurate. The gods demand it of you."

This sent a little shiver through my belly and down deep in my pussy. I was curled up on the passenger seat, staring at the road ahead. The wipers were swiping back and forth, clearing a light rain off the windshield. "Are you hearing me, GG?"

"Yes, M, I think I'm hearing you." I hesitated. "But I'm not sure I'm understanding you. Seems like you are telling me to have sex with other guys." I paused, searching for an elusive thought. "Is there something you want me do this weekend, is that why you brought this up?" I awaited his reply with a titillating dread. Could I be aroused with anticipation and yet feeling a sense of impending doom?

"We will be at the island resort for three days, GG. I will be working for much of the time, but you will be free to explore and experience the local color. You have expressed to me on several occasions you feel you aren't as skillful at oral sex as you were as a young woman. You mentioned your desire to practice your oral technique, to rediscover the joys of sucking cock and pleasuring a man with your mouth, bringing him to orgasm," M paused for a moment.

Uh oh, I thought, *here it comes.*

"There will be an abundance of attractive men, both younger and older, vacationing on the island, this holiday weekend. No doubt several will peak your interest, as they so often do. Come Monday, when we have exited the ferry back to the mainland, you will have pleasured five men, bringing them to orgasm with your mouth."

I swallowed hard at the thought of it. Sucking dry five handsome strangers was kind of disgusting, but also, it was sizzling hot. I so love taking a cock deep in my throat. I've missed the moment when I've sucked a man so well, he loses control and shoots his cum, moaning and ejaculating with complete abandon. I found many opportunities to experience the thrill during my time in the Navy. There's nothing like having a man go over the top, losing it, filling your mouth so quickly, you don't have time to swallow it all; then, he falls back satiated, satisfied and used up.

"Yes, M," I said, "Thank you. Would you like me to take photos, sir?"

"That's our agreement, GG. When I share you, you will show me exactly how you've been a good, obedient, OC butt slut."

THE RESORT WAS LOVELY, LAID OUT LIKE AN ISLAND VILLAGE, CABINS SPREAD ACROSS THE GROUNDS. The lush vegetation reminded me of the tropics. Our quaint little cabin was at the end of a path, surrounded by tall bamboo, succulents and native grasses.

M left for his meetings, saying he would join me back at our cabin well after midnight. I had taken a seat at the end of the tiki bar, passing the time watching the guests arrive while flirting with the bartender. At 10:30 p.m. the action heated up. I had been sitting there for a couple of hours, sipping my Virgin Margarita, when two wedding parties arrived off the evening's last ferry. A bachelor party and a bachelorette party settled in on opposite ends of the pool. The tiki bar stood right in the middle, just beside the hot tub, and the celebrants descended on the bar for drinks, all the while checking each other out.

It was a lovely evening to watch the twenty-somethings, couples and singles, soaking and swimming. They moved from the bar to the hot tub, back to the bar. Then, to the swimming pool, laughing and talking, flirting and eyeing each other. I was enjoying their hard young bodies, the women and the men alike, and their amorous activities. The later the hour got, the freer the liquor flowed and the more open the groping became.

Two cute young men in particular, had taken an interest in me. Several times they had stopped by on their way back from the hot tub, trying to buy me drinks. They introduced themselves as Brian and Timothy, and explained about their best friend getting married the following week and how he was already passed out back in his room. They made a point of explaining the young women from the bachelorette party weren't their type. They were into mature women, like me. They were into MILFs.

"Into what?" I asked, laughing at their cute, half-drunk attempts at picking me up.

"You know," Brian said, looking hopeful, "a *MILF*, a 'Mom I'd Like to Fuck'." We all laughed.

Brian was tall with sandy colored hair. His long legged, baggy swim trunks were slung low on his hips, showing off his perfect abdomen. He was practically hairless, but for a single narrow line of dark pubic hair which began just below his navel and disappeared down into his trunks. Timothy was mostly hairless as well, but darker, with a soul patch at the center of his chest and a little rim of hair around his nipples.

"Hey, come on" Timothy said to me, "come in the hot tub with us."

I turned to Timothy, my breasts brushing against his arm. "You're so sweet," I said, "but I don't have my bathing suit on under my dress, see?" I pulled my meager skirt up over my legs, exposing my bare thighs and brief, see-through panties.

I could hear them both gulp at the sight of my smooth, white flesh. I swung my stool around, uncrossing my legs, standing up and slipping my arms through their arms. "Maybe you two would like to escort me back to my cabin where I left my swim suit?"

My awkward, half-drunk escorts, stumbled back to the cabin at my sides. I held their arms against me, pushing my hard nipples against their well-muscled arms. We climbed the steps and unlocked the cabin door. I turned to one and then the other. Standing on my tiptoes, I gave them each a hard kiss on the mouth, pushing up against their bulging swim trunks.

"Well, thank you Brian, thank you Timothy," I said, "for delivering me to my cabin door to retrieve my swimsuit. Perhaps I'll see you later in the pool."

They both looked so dejected. I had to chuckle to myself as I began to walk in through the door, then stopped, and turned back to them. "Oh, I'm sorry," I said, "how impolite of me. Please come in and make yourselves at home." I took both their hands, pulled them into the cabin and closed the door behind us.

"Can I offer you anything while I change?" I said, unbuttoning my blouse.

There they were, both awkward, standing in front of me. I felt like such a tease. I just couldn't help myself, I had to go down on them, just like in my fantasies. I was going to blow them, both at the same time.

I finished unbuttoning my shirt and walked over to them. Kissing one, then the other. I slid my hands down their naked chests, over their tight abdomens, and fell to my knees. I looked up at them, both looked back at me, not quite sure what to expect when I pulled their swim trunks down. Their hard, young man meat sprang up to meet me. I grabbed their cocks, rubbing them on my lips and around my face. I opened my mouth wide, taking them both in at the same time. I began kissing and tonguing their cocks. First, jerking them then, fondling and cupping their ball sacks.

Oh, it was just too hot. Their tan lines on their hairless bodies. Their silky, white cocks and full, red balls. Neither had even touched me and my pussy was already clutching and squeezing.

They stood there hip-to-hip, grunting and moaning. I reached behind them with both hands and grabbed a hold of their hard ass cheeks, pulling their hips towards me, gobbling their combined joy-joints, savoring the salty sap oozing from their hot swollen glands.

Still kneeling, I began going back and forth between them, jerking cock and sucking one hot purple knob then, the other, rubbing my hands on their taut young thighs and touching their hard, tanned bellies. I traced their rippled abdomens with my fingertips and fucked their cocks with my lips, mouth, and throat.

It was coming back to me. I had been great at giving head back in the day. My skills were practically legendary, and it seemed my muscle memory hadn't failed.

Again, I took both their rock hard cocks in my mouth and they put their hands on the back of my head. Together they both fucked my mouth, slapping their balls against my chin. I was gurgling, gagging, and drooling like a porn star.

I pushed Timothy back and gave him my cellphone to take a video of Brian cumming. He stood off to the side and pointed the camera at us and I doubled down on Brian, jerking the shaft and sucking him hard. It only took a minute until I sucked him into a huge, lathered orgasm, the foamy cum filled my mouth and dribbled down my chin.

Brian stumbled backwards and Timothy gave him the camera. He stepped right up to me, taking his friend's place, shoving his long thin, white cock deep in my throat. He held the back of my head and began mouth-fucking me. I gagged on his stiff prick and pissed my panties.

Just as he was about to shoot, Timothy pulled back, grabbed his cock and began jerking his cum into my eager mouth, shooting long thick streams of white jizz down my throat. I swallowed as fast as I could, but he had a huge load and, as fast as I swallowed, even more dribbled out of my mouth. Timothy jerked himself dry. I leaned forward as he finished up and licked up the last of his cum from his cock.

Brian turned off my phone and Timothy staggered backwards and collapsed onto the couch. I sat back on my haunches and looked at the two of them. "Wow, Timmy," Brian said, "What a huge load."

The three of us sat there for a moment, spent. We looked around at each other grinning from ear-to-ear. "This was fucking awesome," Timothy said. "Yeah, thank you," Brian said. "You are amazing." They pulled up their swim trunks and took turns in the bathroom.

When Timothy and Brian let themselves out, they called back good night. I leaned out the front door to see them off and there, sitting on the swing on the porch, was M. "Well hello," I said. "How long have you been out here?"

M smiled without looking up, "Long enough, GG. Am I correct to assume you only have three to go?"

"Yes, sir," I said, "Those boys were numbers one and two."

"Well, the night is still young, GG. I'm off for a nightcap with the resort owners. I will meet you back here at 2:30 am. I'm sure you will think of something to keep yourself busy until then," he said.

THIRTY ONE

....

THE TIKI BAR

I made my way back to the tiki bar, feeling disappointed and more than a little frustrated. After all that foreplay, Brian and Timothy were nowhere in sight, and now M wouldn't be back for who knew how long.

I seated myself at the end of the bar and ordered a virgin piña colada. I tugged at my skirt, trying to keep warm and crossed my legs. The pressure from my thighs squeezing together made my pussy drip like an orange in an orange juice squeezer. I shivered a little with the unexpected pleasure and, when I looked up, Tony, the cute bar tender I had been flirting with earlier, had noticed and was smiling at me. Embarrassed, I smiled back and looked away at the busy hot tub.

The night air had cooled so the party had moved to the steaming waters or, for the dance crowd, inside to the disco. From where I was sitting I had the perfect view of the unrestrained action. The occupants played some kind of game, a drunken, fraternity house version of spin the bottle. One drunken person removed her swimsuit, stepping to the center of the tub. She closed her eyes and, acting as the bottle, she was twirled by the others who groped her as she spun. When she became too dizzy to stand up any longer, she fell sideways and it was the next player's turn, this time a young man, to receive this titillating treatment.

I was surprised at how the young women boldly grabbed the young man's stiff penis as he spun around, taking turns stroking it, licking and kissing it. It only took a drunken moment until he toppled over and the group laughed and slapped his ass.

"Me next, me next," a cute little blonde with big breasts called out. "It's my turn now." She stood up, stripping out of her one-piece suit, revealing her extra-large nipples and clean-shaven pussy. The young men and women hooted at the sight of her naked body. She played it up for all it was worth, scrunching her boobs together with her arms, licking her lips and shaking all over.

She closed her eyes, placed her hands above her head so her heavy breasts and luscious body were available for groping, and began to turn around.

From every side, the hands descended upon her welcoming curves and beckoning folds. The man-boys and woman-girls slid their hands in and out of every inch of her, concentrating on her perfect round ass, stiff nipple breasts and swelling pussy. She inhaled as a thirty-something woman with an asymmetrical haircut boldly slid four fingers down from her navel over her pubic bone, rubbing right over her clitoris, separating her labia and pushing in and out of her vagina with several quick motions before withdrawing. Never opening her eyes, she quaked and doubled over for a moment, then straightened up, refusing to fall over.

"I would get so turned on having those horny young hands all over me," I said out loud to myself, then looked around to see if anyone had heard me mumble it. The thought made my thighs hot, wet, and sticky.

Blondie kept right on spinning, hands running over her breasts and up between her legs, hands squeezing her beautiful round ass cheeks and touching her pussy. She was licking her lips and trying her best not to lose it as she was caressed from every direction. Her big nipples rose to a point and the tip of her clitoris stuck out from between her puffy pussy lips. When three separate hands simultaneously pushed their fingers between her thighs, one from the front and two from the back, she lost it and could stand no longer. She collapsed, shivering and moaning, into the waiting arms of a beautiful young couple seated on the hot tub's steps.

"So what do you think?" came a voice from the stool behind me.

"I think I'm getting turned on," I replied as I turned towards the voice. Seated beside me was the handsome bartender, Tony with whom I had flirted with earlier.

"What are you doing on this side of the bar, mister?" I joked, leaning over, placing my hand on his thigh and giving him a kiss on the cheek. He looked even more handsome up close. Tony had to be Italian, with his close trimmed beard and fine black eyelashes. His shirt hung open to the center of his chest, showing off his dark fur and a tiny gold cross.

"Getting closer to the hottest woman on the island," he said, slipping his hand up my skirt and between my warm, slick thighs. "Well, well," he smiled, "someone is hot and bothered."

That was all the provocation I needed. I slid my hand up his thigh and onto his package and pushed my mouth against his. We kissed and right there, sitting at the bar, he pushed his hand against my wet gash, pulled my panties aside, and slipped his finger in my pussy. The whole thing was just too naughty. I was on the edge of orgasm from my earlier double suck;

Tony's fingering almost made me cum, but he abruptly withdrew his finger from my pussy and pointed towards the lurid scene over in the hot tub.

"What do you say we take a dip in the hot tub, babe?" he said, licking those fingers which had just been up inside me.

"Sounds great," I said, "but I don't have my suit on under my dress and as you can probably tell, I'm not wearing a bra." He reached up and pinched my erect nipple.

The spinning game had stopped, but the hot tub still had eight or ten young couples seated in and around the water, all kissing and caressing and in various stages of undress.

"GG," he said, "I'd say clothing is optional, wouldn't you?" He was right of course. "But if you're feeling self-conscious, maybe this will help." Tony reached back over the top bar and felt around for a minute. "Ah, there it is," he said, and flicked a switch turning off all the lights in the hot tub area.

He stood up, offering me his arm, and we made our way through the beach chairs and discarded clothing to the water. He pulled his t-shirt over his head and dropped his baggy shorts to the ground, stepping out of them and into the water. His uncircumcised cock, a first for me, bobbed proudly. I pulled my blouse over my cold, hard nipples and off over my head, dropping it to the ground. I unzipped my skirt, dropping it around my ankles. My panties were still pulled to one side. I adjusted them but they were soaked clear through and stuck to my pussy lips and clit, giving any gawker a clear view of my goodies. Thank goodness it was dark. Besides, the crowd around the tub was too busy to notice how exposed I was.

Tony offered me his hand and we stepped down into the steamy bubbling waters. He led me around to a narrow opening in the writhing swarm of bodies. He took me into his arms and sat us down, pulling me up against him. His rigid cock pushed against my thigh and our passionate, hungry mouths met in a deep kiss, our tongues interlocking. I wrapped my thighs around his hip, grinding my aching slit hard against him. I was drunk with the delicious lust which follows delayed gratification and I reached down and grabbed ahold of his hardness with both hands. "I need cock inside me," I whispered in his ear, "fuck my slutty hole and make me cum, please."

I jerked him with one hand and rubbed his knob with the other. He threw his head back with an ecstatic moan. I was about to mount him when two hands grabbed my ass from behind and tilted my hips up. Surprised, I glanced over my shoulder and saw Timothy, one of my cabin boys, smiling broadly. Not satisfied with cumming down my throat, he was back for more, his hard young penis ready to cum in my pussy this time. He had a wonderful cock, long and slender, a good 9 inches. I felt him pushing it between my slick pussy lips. Tony was watching all of this and pushed my head down under the water onto his cock. I gagged and my pussy clutched Timothy's hot prick tight. Timothy's hands wrapped around my waist, holding me while he pumped my aching hole. Hands from somewhere found my nipples and another hand found my clit.

We were creating quite the scene. Our lustful exhibition inspired an all-out orgy in the hot tub as it erupted in wild uninhibited groping. I wasn't sure what to do so I just held on, sucking harder or fucking harder, but the fingers flicking my clit sent me into a massive cum. Tony was holding my head, thrusting his hips up into my face and fucking my mouth. I felt Timothy's excitement as he grew bigger inside me with his ever-faster gash-shafting.

I cupped Tony's balls with one hand and gripped his rigid cock with the other. He began shooting wildly into my mouth. I tried my best to take his hard thrusts down my throat, but there was just too much man-cream and I gagged, my cunt convulsing around Timothy's cock. that was just what he needed to push him over the edge. He moaned and delivered me his second big load of the evening, this time it didn't drip down my chin. He continued slamming into me, emptying his balls. My vagina contracted in an orgy orgasm, squeezing the excess cum out of my filled fuck-hole, and dribbling down over my clit.

I looked up and saw a turned-on young woman rubbing herself frantically. She was using her cell phone to video our threesome. She saw she had been discovered and tried to hide the phone, looking ashamed. "Thank god," I said to her. She looked at me, uncertain. "No really. Can you email me your video?"

THIRTY TWO

....

MORNING AFTER DELIGHT

M woke me out of a deep, blissful sleep with his deep, blissful penetration. As always, being taken by M was a mind shattering experience: the combination of his unmatched skill as a lover, his intimate knowledge and acceptance of my unique and unusual fetishes, created a perfect synergy. During the long years of my passion drought, I had often fantasized, as I lay alone in my marriage bed, of being ravaged by a man such as M. Lovingly yet forcibly taken right as I awoke, entering me as I lay prone, pushing my feet up over my head and fucking me hard and fast, me cumming, again and again.

Many times, I lay alone in my bed, face down with both hands between my thighs, grinding my cunt into my fists, fantasizing about a great white-backed gorilla grabbing my ass and mounting me from behind. Fucking me like a wild, savage animal. Pounding me mercilessly into orgasm after orgasm. Stripping away any facade I had of being civilized.

Following our morning passion, I showered and dried my hair. When I came out into the living room, I saw M had ordered up a lovely breakfast of toast, eggs, and coffee. He took a last gulp of coffee and collected his things.

"I'm off for a morning meeting, GG," he said. "But before I go I have a surprise for you." My ears perked up. M's surprises were always exciting.

"I have scored us tickets to a limited engagement performance by Frankie Mars at the Westland Casino. He will perform in the small cabaret for one night only, and we have third row seats."

M knew I just adored Frankie Mars. He had gone solo, but during his many years as the lead singer of the band "Her Majesty", he had written some of the greatest rock anthems of all time.

"Oh M, thank you," I exclaimed, throwing my arms around his neck. He knew how much I loved Frankie, and those tickets were impossible to come by.

"I will be finished with my meetings this afternoon so be ready to check out early. We will be catching the four o'clock ferry back to the mainland. Have your bags packed and ready to go, GG," M smiled at me, blew me a kiss and winked. "And I expect you to have your homework assignment completed by then as well."

M departed, leaving me to stare at the closed door behind him. Where was I going to find two more willing recipients? It had been easy the night before when everyone was drunk, but now all those amorous young men would be hung over or laying by the pool with their girlfriends.

After I thought about it for a bit, the challenge excited me. I had six hours to go and, men being men, how hard could it be?

"Our sex play is such fun," I smiled as I walked down to the clubhouse. It was so liberating to have a partner who not only understood my needs but also encouraged my fantasies. *What was the worst M could do if I didn't give head twice more before four o'clock? Punish me?*

I felt a pang of fear in my stomach. I wasn't feeling so sure of myself after all. M could do anything and, knowing me as well as he did, it could be something far worse than a naughty spanking.

I walked by the swimming pool, but the skies were hazy and it was too early for the party to resume. The tiki bar was closed up and the maintenance crew was busy cleaning the hot tub. I turned up the path and made for the clubhouse.

Inside, breakfast was over and the dining room was empty. The crew tore down the buffet and cleared the tables. I took a seat at the counter and ordered a cup of coffee. I checked the weather on my phone, took another sip of my coffee and turned my diner stool around, scanning the room. Over in the back corner, across from the manager's office, huddled behind a laptop computer, was the dreadlocked Caribbean musician who had been at one end of the bar the night before, serenading the partiers. *I wonder if he watched Tony's peek-a-boo panty display?* I thought.

I took my coffee and walked over to his table. "I enjoyed your music at the tiki bar last night," I said. At first he looked up at me with a blank expression, but then I could see the spark of recognition. A smile spread over his face and he closed the top on his computer.

"It's you, isn't it, beautiful lady? I know you from the tiki bar last night. You had my friend Tony's fingers dancing up your skirt, didn't you? He is a very lucky man, that Tony, to have a beautiful lady like you to love."

Isaiah had deep brown eyes and a hint of grey in his dreads. He was from the French side of St. Martin, and he worked the resort every year for a month, during the summer. We chatted for a while and he told me about his family back in the islands. He showed me pictures of his fifteen-year-old daughter and her mother, explaining how he missed them both, but being a traveling musician, it wasn't always easy to keep a relationship together. He had just finished messaging his daughter's mother when I walked up.

"I try my best to be faithful to her while I am away, but it is not always so easy," he said, looking sad. "These cabin girls love a Caribbean French man."

He looked at me funny and said, "Can I ask you a question? Do you think I am being unfaithful to my wife if I broute-minou the cabin girls, but I don't dugu dugu them?"

"I'm sorry, Isaiah, what?" I asked bewildered. We both laughed and he explained.

"I love oral sex, pretty lady. I love to eat pussy, as you Americans would say. A lot of Caribbean men refuse to do it, but I guess I'm more French than anything, and I pride myself at giving a woman great pleasure."

I blushed a bit at this, more out of excitement than modesty.

"I'm sorry, have I embarrassed you?"

"No, Isaiah, not at all," I replied. "I appreciate your openness and directness. I'm not sure how to answer your question. I think it's different in every relationship, don't you?"

Isaiah dropped his gaze, nodding his head in agreement, then looked back up at me, from under his heavy eyelids.

"I have a confession to make to you, beautiful lady," he said. "This is a very lonely time for me. I won't be home again for another month. I watched you in the hot tub last night. You are so very sexy. It would give me great pleasure to satisfy you the way you satisfied Tony and that young man. You and I are much alike in that way. We are very generous to our lovers."

He smiled at me, took my hand and said, "Please, would you allow me to lick you until you are satisfied? It would truly be my pleasure."

At this, I did blush, I turned red as a rose. I covered his hand in my other hand and said, "That would be just divine, Isaiah."

We walked together down a wooded path, lush with vines and wild flowers, to a small cabin backed up to the water. A rowboat sat to one side of the cabin. On the other side, two large trees stood with a hammock strung between them. The setting was idyllic and, if I hadn't known we were on a small island in the Great Lakes, I could imagine we were in a tropical paradise.

Isaiah led me over to the hammock, turned me to face him and kissed me sweetly on the mouth. It was so calming being with him. He had such a serene way about him. Any apprehension I felt melted away with his tender touch. He undid my pants and slid them down my thighs, and did the same with my panties. He held the hammock steady for me as I seated myself, then turned and stretched out my half naked body. He joined me, laying down fully clothed beside me. His beaded dreads were tied back with a single lock. Strands of silver hair weaved through them and sparkled, catching the scattered sunlight through the trees. He began kissing my knees and caressing my legs. His long, slender, guitar player fingers slid between my thighs, parting them slightly, and trailed sparks of his touch up to the delicate skin around my pussy.

He positioned himself just so, spread my thighs open, and lowered his mouth on to me. It was pure heaven. I closed my eyes and felt something hot and agile slither circles around my sex. Over and over again, he circled, never touching it, until my vulva were swollen with desire. I had never felt anything like it before. I opened my eyes and looked down at him to make sure, and it was indeed his tongue making love to me.

When he, at last, slipped it into my slit and licked the dripping leaves of my pussy, up and down, I closed my eyes, succumbing to the rush of my cum. My uncontainable desire swept me away as I shivered, my thighs shaking. The orgasm spread outward from my cunt, filling my whole body and spilling out of my mouth with animal-like sex sounds.

He let me lay there for a moment, untouched; he began again. This time, his tongue probed deeper and my hips leapt up to meet it. He sucked my pussy up into his mouth, releasing it; he slurped deep into my gash, giving me a total tongue bath. I alternated between squirming and thrusting, tightened and stiffened as my whole body erupted with another mind numbing spasm of orgasms. It was so powerful I had to force myself to breathe again, inhaling harshly, sucking down air.

Again, he left me to lie there, resting and untouched. My head lay on his lower thigh and I could see his pants bulging with his hard-on. Hungry for cock, I began to stroke him, but he reached down and stopped my hand.

"Pretty lady, please understand," he said to me. "I am a wonderful lover with my mouth, and pleasing a woman with my tongue is my greatest satisfaction. But I'm afraid in other ways I fall short as a lover."

I looked up at Isaiah, not sure what he meant, and he held up his index finger and thumb, spread them an inch apart. "I'm sorry to say, pretty lady, but my little man, is a very little."

"However big he is, Isaiah," I smiled back at him, "I'm sure he could use a good sucking." I pushed his hands away and began untying his sweat-pants. He pulled them off, tossed them to the ground and rolled over so his hard little cock was right by my mouth. It looked like a featherless bird in a nest surrounded by two big brown eggs. I wrapped my lips around his hot mouthful and ran my tongue around its cherry tomato head. He again slipped his tongue into my slutty gash, holding the lips open wide with his long sensual fingers. I ground my pussy into his face as he stiffened his hips to gain deeper penetration into my mouth. His ball sack smashed up against my face and the scent of his sex filled my senses. His hips thrust repeatedly into my mouth. He moved his attentions to my clit, unsheathing it with his fingertips, and applying his hot, wet tongue to my engorged clit.

My thighs began quaking, again. The head of his cock pounded mercilessly against the roof of my mouth. His balls pulled up tight and he began to shoot. His warm jizm filled my mouth with its salty cum butter. I clamped my thighs tight around his head and let go one last massive orgasm.

Isaiah lay still for a few minutes, smiling. "Thank you," he said, "you have no idea how wonderful that was."

He opened his eyes, looked towards me and laughed, "What are you doing, pretty lady?" I had my cell phone in hand, extended at arms-length and pointing back at my face. "Are you taking a selfie with your mouth open and my cum in it?" he asked.

THIRTY THREE

....

FERRY RIDE

After leaving Isaiah, I spent four hours crisscrossing the resort in the rain. By the pool, no one, the Tiki Bar had a female bartender. Although there were a few men in the restaurant eating lunch, they were either hung over or with women. I went into the kitchen to check and see if I could find any willing volunteers, all I found were more women. I considered approaching one of them, but M had been most specific about sucking five cocks to improve my technique. Somehow I didn't think a clit would count.

Dejected, I returned to the room. I was hoping M wouldn't cancel our evening plans. I had been dying to see Frankie Mars for as long as I could remember. After making sure I had collected everything and had the bags ready for our departure, I curled up on the bed and sulked. I had been certain I'd be able to make the deadline, but with the earlier departure and the rain, I had been hip checked. I'm not sure I had ever failed one of M's games and my perfectionist self was going nuts.

When M walked in, he took one look at me and said, "I guess you didn't finish your training. Don't be so glum, GG. There's still the ferry ride. You should be able to find your final assignment on board."

At that pleasant thought, I perked up. I was certain there would be a willing man on the ferry, either a passenger or one of the ferrymen. Things were looking up, at least until we got to the car. Our bags were loaded into the trunk in a torrential downpour. I felt as if nature was conspiring against me. When we arrived at the ferry, there was no one else in line for the ferry: ours was the only car. As M parked, the attendant walked up to the car. M rolled the window down so he could hear the man. "Don't worry folks, it's safe passage to the mainland. It's raining hard but there's no wind so the waves are pretty flat. The passenger lounge is upstairs and it's enclosed so the rain won't get you. I'll be in the wheel house if you need anything."

M rolled up the window and kissed me, "I know you can do this, GG." I smiled, took a deep breath and ventured out into the rain. I headed straight for the passenger cabin, no one there. I wandered along the passageways and finally found the crew, all in the wheelhouse with the door closed. I couldn't believe it, not one horny man aboard. I returned to the car and admitted defeat. "M, there just aren't any men. The way they are hiding from the rain, you'd think they would melt if they got wet."

We sat in silence for a few moments. "I know of one horny man, GG. I'm no stranger but if you can convince me you've learned your lessons well, I'll let you count me as one of your five."

"Oh, M, thank you!" I reached to open his pants but he waved me away. "Not here, in the passenger cabin, just like you would with a stranger. Give me five minutes to get settled, then come up."

As M headed off, I tried to get my head back in the game. I didn't feel at all sexy or flirty. How on earth was I going to give good head? Don't get me wrong, I love to suck M's large, beautiful cock. In fact, it's one of my favorite things to do. Hmm. I get to suck M's cock in public. I took a deep breath and planned my approach.

"Is anyone sitting here?" I asked him as I walked up next to him in the passenger cabin.

"No, would you like to join me?" he asked. I slid onto the seat and began making small talk like I would with any stranger. After a few minutes, I batted my lashes. "All this rain sure makes me horny. I don't suppose you would allow me to give you a blow job?" M grinned and answered, "Why of course you can. Every man dreams of having a beautiful stranger suck his cock."

I was into the role now. I knelt in front of him and unzipped his pants. As I took his cock out, I marveled again at his size. I held the head of his cock in my hand while I licked his balls, sucking first one and then the other into my mouth. As I continued licking and sucking his balls, my hand pulled his cock up, my thumb rubbing across the tip.

I flattened my tongue, running it over the base, traveling up the underside to its head. As I sucked the head into my mouth, M let out a groan. When I met his eyes, he smiled at me. I held eye contact and took him down my throat. I tried in vain to swallow the whole thing; I felt my pussy get hot with the effort. I gagged and squirted as he pushed against the back of my throat. "Someday, I'm going to get this cock down my throat," I mused.

I began moving my mouth up and down his shaft, in time with his thrusts. I cupped his balls in my hand and massaged them. His hand found the back of my head and held me still as he pushed his cock into the back of my throat. I tried to swallow him but his cock was just too big. When I gagged, M moved his hand. I stayed down on him as long as I could and, as I pulled up, I turned my head back and forth, "polishing" the head of his cock with the back of my throat. I was rewarded with a long groan from M. For a time, I continued the up down motion with my new technique. When M grabbed my head with both his hands and began fucking my mouth, I knew I had done a good job. As he pounded me, I felt the heat grow from my pussy, my entire body flushed as I had an orgasm while M fucked my mouth. When he stopped, I rested my head on his leg, too overcome by my cum to move. M stroked my hair and leaned over to kiss my forehead. "GG, you have improved in your cock sucking abilities." "So," I whispered, "I can count this as number five?"

M laughed. "Yes, my love, this one counts."

THIRTY FOUR

....

FRANKIE MARS CONCERT

I ended up driving us to the concert. M was busy on the phone and then later, on my clit, his fingers dancing over and around it, making me cum while I drove. At one point, I drove off the road. "GG, look out!" M shouted as I swerved off the berm and righted the car. "Should I stop playing with you?"

"No, I'm alright," I said. "I've got this. I can handle it." I refocused on driving and M resumed his strumming. Let me tell you the man is dexterous. I must remember to volunteer to drive more often.

We arrived at the Westland Casino in plenty of time for dinner. They seated us and we ate while we waited for the show to begin. The venue was cabaret style. Our seats were unreal.

What a concert, absolutely incredible. Frankie Mars was in top form. He stood upfront striking his classic poses, working the crowd like the mega star he was. Then, he sat behind the piano and played Her Majesty's big hits from there. He still had it, hitting the high notes like only he could. But I missed seeing him with Her Majesty. They were such a great band. We stayed through the encores then headed out to our room.

"What a day," I said to M as I leaned into his side.

"Indeed," M replied, "What a day. I don't know about you, GG, but I'm about ready to fall over."

M let us in the room and I made right for the bathroom. When I came out, he was in bed, ready to sleep. I felt a little disappointed although I tried not to show it. I crawled in next to him, gave him a kiss and snuggled down next to him.

He played at the sleep game for a minute, then turned and pounced. His hands roved over my body, his mouth demanded kisses from mine, kisses which were more like intercourse than kissing; tongues dancing together, twining and untwining. I know I'm depraved but I wanted his cock in my ass with something approaching desperation. As soon as I could sneak in a word I begged, "Please, sir. Please, fuck my ass."

He ignored my pleas, pleasuring my nipples, then my clit, with his fingers. He spread my legs, knelt between them, and placed the head of his beautiful cock against my puckered hole. I smiled as he applied steady pressure, opening my ass to his cock. As the head filled me, my body erupted in a special pain/pleasure orgasm that only happens when a cock enters your ass the first time during a fuck. I treasure this orgasm, short, sweet, limited to the immediate area. As filled with anticipation as it is fulfillment. I could experience it every day and never get tired of it.

As he slid in and out, my need took over. I had been sitting next to him all evening, listening to his voice, seeing his smile, needing his touch.

"I don't need gentle, M, I need a long, hard fucking," I begged. M knows me so well. He pulled out, turned me over onto my knees and reentered me so I could move back toward him as he slid into me. Our pace accelerated, my muscles tensed for an orgasm, it exploded across my body. But this wasn't the orgasm I sought, merely the precursor. Faster and faster, his balls were slamming against my pussy, his thighs against my ass. He held me by the waist and drove into me. Again and again, until my muscles began their orgasmic contraction, my ass gripping his cock as he drove ever deeper into me. This was what I sought. This, the radical orgasm, which stops the mind and suspends me in the bliss.

As the waves of the orgasm receded, M pushed me down onto my stomach and covered my back with his body, lips on my neck, hands holding my hands. Cocooned by his body and his love, he continued to move, slow and gentle, fucking my ass deep and full, as only he can, in the way I've come to crave. My orgasms became smooth and cascading, less cataclysmic, more a state of being.

I never knew I could feel like this.

He owned me.

THIRTY FIVE

....

FROM M TO THEO

We boarded the 9:00 am flight back to California and sat, side-by-side, in first class. The stewardess walked down the aisle and M greeted her in his engaging way.

"I'm well this morning, sir. Thank you" she smiled, replying to his warm greeting. "Can I get you and your wife a cocktail before we depart?"

M smiled at her and replied, "A sparkling water, please for my lovely lady and me," and leaned over and kissed me on the cheek.

Being mistaken for M's wife warmed me all over, bringing the color up in my cheeks. I felt like I was, or rather, like I could be. We fit together, comfortable in our seats and in our coupleness, completely at ease, sharing the joy of another day together. So we were a couple, at least, for as long as it took to fly to California.

The flight was uneventful. M caught up on work on his laptop and I finished a book on my Kindle. I curled up using my jacket for a pillow and gazed out the window until I drifted off to sleep.

Our lustful weekend activities had left me more exhausted than I realized. I awoke some time later to the sound of the stewardess' voice instructing us to prepare for landing. M had draped his jacket over my shoulders and waved down the stewardess to bring me a cup of coffee.

"Good afternoon, lover," M said. "I didn't want to wake you, but your phone has been buzzing with text messages for the past half an hour." Earlier, I had connected to the planes Wi-Fi and placed my phone back in my purse. I pulled it out and checked my messages.

"It was Theo messaging me," I said. "He says he is picking me up from the airport. That's strange, he usually can't be bothered to come and fetch me. He just sends a limo or tells me to grab a cab."

The expression on M's face hardened. He brushed my hair away from my forehead, kissed it, and sat back in his seat.

"Then it would be time for us to behave like strangers," he said. "We wouldn't want to jeopardize our little secret, would we?"

His demeanor changed, becoming proper and impersonal, not the M who owned my cum. "When we land, I'll stay behind. You can exit the plane first and make your way down to baggage claim. I'll lag behind and grab a cup of coffee. I'll wait for you to text me when you and Theo have left the airport before I retrieve my bag."

"Yes, sir," I said, half joking. But M was having none of it. He was dead serious. He distanced himself from me even further. I didn't like it at all, I felt cast away. Now it would be clear to anyone looking on, that we were nothing more than two strangers in the same aisle on the same airplane.

We landed and taxied to the gate. The seat belt sign turned off. I unbuckled, gathered my things, stood and retrieved my bag from the overhead compartment.

"Have a pleasant stay in Los Angeles," I said.

M looked up distracted, and nodded saying, "Thank you. It was nice meeting you." He went back to messaging on his cell phone, and I was dismissed.

I exited the plane and walked down to baggage claim in a state of shock. The whole thing felt surreal. One minute, I had been wrapped in the glow of our connection and the next, nothing.

Thankfully, the bags came quickly. I rolled them out to the curb where Theo had the car waiting with the trunk open. I loaded my bags into the trunk and let myself into car.

"Welcome home, GG," he said. He leaned towards me, gave me a kiss on the cheek, and drove off.

I texted M "we are gone." He answered back "ok" and nothing more.

THIRTY SIX

....

WE FOLLOW OUR HEARTS

We must follow our hearts, or our hearts go cold. There is a moment when you know for sure the person you have committed your life to should be committed, as in institutionalized.

As women, we give up everything to make the marriage work, only to find out our spouses are unwilling to give up the very things keeping them unavailable to us. Whether it is the television, the sports, the pornography, the gambling, the drama, the drugs, the alcohol, the food. The list goes on and on.

So, if hubby was forever distracted by his first love, his addiction, then why was I denying myself my great passion, sex?

It was time for me to live. To indulge in the things which made me feel alive. Be assured, it wasn't hubby's passion, pepperoni pizza (so nasty), a new car (nice, but not sufficient), season tickets to the Clippers (yum, all those hot, sweaty men) or a trip to San Francisco (a four star hotel room with two queen size beds, one for him and one for me - oh joy.).

Enough! Whose life was this I was wasting? It was my life, that's whose. If you are unwilling to live your own life, someone else will be more than happy to take you hostage and live yours for you. Or, as M was fond of saying, "When you die, God doesn't give out a gold star for throwing your life away to please someone else. You get no special commendation for being a doormat."

I could not go on this way for long before I dried up inside. Would I die for my man? Yes. But I would not kill myself for anyone. And that's what it came down to. I was going to have to change everything if I was going to survive. I couldn't take back the lost years, they were gone forever. But I was bound and determined the next ten years were going to make up for the last 10 in unbridled love, passion, and living.

We had made a good start, M and I, but it was only a start. Now was my time to live up to my nickname, the OC butt slut.

THIRTY SEVEN

....

PLAY TIME

This time, M and I were apart for two weeks. I spent the time working at the office and playing the role of perfect OC wife - lunch with the ladies, shop for clothes, dinner at the club with hubby.

How pointless it all seemed.

My mind and clit were in suspended animation, just waiting for M to return.

Our only contact was through text messages. But what text messages! M gave new meaning to the word, 'sexting'. He began sending animations of huge cocks in pussies and asses. I had to check around me for innocent bystanders before looking at my phone. Imagine Theo looking over my shoulder just in time to see a young woman with her mouth, her pussy, and her ass full of cock. During dinner at the club, one of M's texts got me so wound up I had to excuse myself and go into the ladies room to rub one out. Ok, so it was more than one. When I returned to the table ten minutes later, Theo asked me what took me so long. I told him I got my period. Just goes to show how well he pays attention, I haven't had one since my ablation surgery two years ago.

On day seven without M, I went completely mad, surfing the Internet for porn. Wow, did I find some! I know some people think it's shameful, but it does turn me on. Especially the extreme stuff, BDSM, gang bangs, and even ass fisting. I'm not quite sure about doing it, but I felt drawn to watching it. I was rubbing and sliding my fingers into my pussy, but it wasn't enough. I needed big. I needed to be filled. I put four fingers in – still not enough. Then, I decided to see if I could get my fist up there. I twisted and contorted and, oh sweet relief, filled my pussy with my fist. As aroused as I was, I gave myself a good pounding until I'd had a few orgasms. When I could stand it no more, my dirty mind decided to call M and see if by chance he picked up. To my surprise he answered the phone.

"Nikolai Mionchinskaia speaking," he answered.

"Hi M, it's GG. Guess where my hand is?"

"Holding the phone?" he said.

"No, lover, in my pussy. I'm fisting myself."

"Can I call you right back. The valet is pulling up with my car," he said and disconnected. Minutes later the phone rang. It was M. He had called back on Face Time, video phoning me.

"Hello, lover," he said. "It's wonderful to hear your voice, baby. Now, did I hear correctly that my OC butt slut has her fist in her pussy? What inspired this?"

I moved my iPad into position and connected with him. I wanted to make sure he enjoyed the show I was about to put on for him. He was driving from his meeting back to his hotel - probably not the best time, but my libido wouldn't wait. My fingers idly stroked my clit as I finished getting everything into place. "Are you ready, M?" I asked. He shook his head and our eyes met. I smiled and leaned back, giving him an eyeful of pussy.

I stroked my clit, up and down, then slid my fingers in and out of my gash as my thumb continued rubbing my clit. Performing for M was making my slutty self horny as hell. I needed a filled twat, so I dispensed with the warm up and made a fist. I worked it into my pussy, then fucked myself hard with my fist, shoving it into my pussy just as far as I could get it, moved it around, in and out, side-to-side, every way I could. Although I orgasmed, I wasn't getting enough of what I needed. I pushed harder, moved faster. I felt a big cum getting ready to break over me and I focused on keeping my arm moving so when I came, the feelings kept going and going.

Ahh, sweet relief, but I still wanted more.

M had been silent to this point but now became my coach.

"GG, fuck yourself with your fist. That's right. Pull it almost all out then, push it back in. Oh yeah, that's it. Fuck it good, my OC butt slut." I loved hearing his voice and dirty talk. I always made me so hot. I gave myself a couple more orgasms. I was feeling like the ultimate slut, ready for anything.

"Hey, M, do you think I can get my fist in my ass?"

"GG, that just isn't fair," M replied, but I barely heard him. I lubed up my other hand and contorted so I could reach. It wouldn't be easy but I was determined to get my hand up my ass. I didn't think I could do it, but as M cheered me on, I got first two fingers, then three. I was lost in the slutty heat of it. It felt so good having my ass stretched open.

But I was missing the loving attention I always received from M. "The ass of destiny" he would he called it. What I needed was his cock up there, but all I had was my hand, so I tried four fingers. Oh yeah, better. But I wanted my hand up there, like in the porno movies. So I pulled my fingers out and bunched them together. All five together were about as big around as M's fully erect cock. I shoved them up as quickly as I could. I came so hard, my entire body shook with the effort. I had another big orgasm when I fucked my ass with my hand and again, as I pulled it out. As I settled back down I saw M's profile on the screen. He was still driving.

"M, I'm still horny. Do you think I can get this water bottle up my cooch? It looks like a dildo." He looked over and grinned, "Yes, GG, I'm certain you can."

So I grabbed the water bottle, lubed it up and began fucking it like it was a big cock. I rubbed my clit with my other hand. That was more like what I needed. I needed to be completely filled, and my hands just weren't quite big enough. I humped that bottle until I couldn't hump it any longer. My thighs just gave out and I collapsed onto the floor. Winded and panting, I looked at M's handsome face on the screen. He looked like the horny one now.

"When are you coming home?" I whispered.

"Not soon enough, GG. Not soon enough."

THIRTY EIGHT

....

PULLED OVER

Glorious, just glorious. Some days it's just so good to be alive. M was home and I was escaping to meet him in Las Vegas. No amount of Theo's whining could get me down. I listened to his complaining and his objections to my weekend get-away to Vegas, kissed him on the cheek, grabbed my bag and was out the door.

There I was, red Mercedes, windows down, sunglasses on and hair blowing in the wind; smoking hot blond flying down the highway on my way to sin city.

I was rendezvousing with the sexiest man on the planet.

Cruising along Interstate 15 at eighty miles an hour in my halter top and tight, white jeans, the truckers serenaded me as I passed them, their horns bleating out their approval. I had the music turned up, and I was singing along with all my might.

I love road trips. They feel so free and so, well, sexual. The steady vibration of the tires against the highway, a powerful machine beneath me, steering wheel in hand, all at my command. The leather seats would get my bottom all warm and sweaty. On more than one occasion, I had turned the cruise control on, pulled up my skirt, pulled my panties to one side and rubbed out a good one. One hand, gripping the wheel for dear life while the other hand fingered my clit.

As the road spread out before me I began to regret choosing my tight white pants over a loose and easy-to-lift skirt. So I exited Minneola Rd between Barstow and Baker, pulling across the road and off the side of the quiet entrance ramp. I stripped off my tight jeans and clingy panties, tossed them in the back seat and drove off down the road, naked from the waist down.

I set the cruise control to eighty-five, moved my hand between my thighs and began having the most vivid fantasy. With my other hand on the wheel and my eyes on the road, my mind's eye watched M step out of the shadows, come up behind me and run his hands down the length of my naked body. He pulled me backwards on to his lap, facing away from him. He was restraining me, hugging me to him, his arms wrapped around me, pinning my arms to my sides. My legs were wrapped on the outsides of his thighs and he spread them wide apart. My sex was exposed, my pussy and ass hanging open. I longed for him to fill my pussy, but to my dirty delight, I felt his fat cock head pushing up into my ass instead. He firmly planted his long, thick man-meat deep in my ass.

The heat and the desert sun were beating down on me, and I was feeling light headed. That fantasy alone was enough to send me into shivering orgasms. But then, like a desert mirage, I had a vision of a well-muscled man walking up to me, dropping to his knees and sucking my clit into his mouth.

I could almost feel his tongue on my slutty nub, slathering it around and flicking it as its shy little head peaked out from under its swollen hood. I was grinding my ass into the car seat, imagining M's man-meat stretching my brown hole wide open, pummeling my behind.

I got so caught up in my cum I didn't notice my foot flooring the gas pedal. When I looked down at the speedometer I was doing 95 mph. I panicked for a moment, pulling my foot off the accelerator, sitting up straight and taking the steering wheel firmly in both hand. *Whoops, that was close*, I thought, easing the speedometer down to seventy miles per hour before glancing in the review mirror.

"Oh shit, don't tell me," I said under my breath. There was a state patrol car keeping pace with me a quarter mile behind. I watched him in my mirror, praying he hadn't been behind me the whole time. I went to exit at the next rest stop and sure enough, he turned on his flashing lights and followed me.

As I pulled in a parking spot I noticed the rest area was abandoned, and the bathrooms were closed up tight. The desert stretched out to the horizon all around me, not a soul in sight. I looked back through the rear view mirror and saw the officer open his door, get out and walk toward my car. I kept both hands on the steering wheel. I didn't want the state trooper to think I was going for a gun or something. When I looked down between slick red thighs for my purse I panicked.

"Oh no, I'm still naked from the waist down." I looked around for my pants, but they were somewhere behind me, on the floor in the back seat. I crossed my legs in a futile attempt to conceal my cooch.

He approached my car, eyeing the back seat and passenger's seat for contraband as he walked by. "Your driver's license and insurance card, ma'am," he said.

"Yes, sir," I replied, reaching for my purse, retrieving it and handing him my license. But where was my insurance card? In the glove compartment. Damn it!

I smiled up at him and leaned over to the glove compartment, trying to keep my thighs together, which did nothing to hide the fact that my bottom was bare ass naked. He got quite an eyeful as I shuffled around for the card. When I leaned back and handed it to him, he pretended not to have noticed.

"Stay here and keep your hands on the steering wheel where I can see them" he said, then took the license and insurance card and walked back to his patrol car.

I nervously watched him in my rear view mirror. He was sure taking his time. Did I dare put my pants back on? No, I'd better keep my hands on the wheel as he instructed me. He was going to issue a ticket for sure. But would he arrest me, impound the car? Would they give one phone call? Oh god, I didn't want to have to call Theo from jail, I'd never hear the end of it. And worse, I'd be a no show for M in Vegas.

Finally, the patrol car door opened and he strode back to my car. As he came up beside my car, I took off my sunglasses and looked up at him. "Is there a problem officer?" I asked, turning on the charm. GG, I thought to myself, of course there's a problem or why would he have pulled you over.

He gave a stern expression and looked down at me. "I clocked you going 95 mph, ma'am. Yes, I would say that's a problem."

When I looked back up at him again, with a pleading look in my eyes, he had his hand on his baton. "Officer," I looked at his nametag and sounded out his name, "Mionchinskaia. Mionchinskaia?" I asked. "That's my boyfriend's last name, too. Are you Russian?"

Don't be stupid, GG, of course he's Russian, I thought.

"Do I sound Russian, Ma'am?" he said with a southern drawl.

He shuffled around his papers and held out my license and insurance card to me. "I'm going to let you off with a warning this time, GG. My cousin, Nikolai, is expecting you, and he doesn't like to be kept waiting," he said, a handsome smile spreading across his rugged face.

He stood up, looked at me and continued, "But as per his instructions, I must ask you to please get out and step around to the back of your car."

"Yes, sir," I replied, swinging the door open. I tried to keep my thighs together as I lifted my legs up to step out, but it was hopeless. My clean-shaven cooch was spread wide and wet for him to eye if he should choose.

"Now, place your hands on the trunk and spread your feet apart," he ordered. "What?" I said, crossing my hands over my cooch. He stepped back and put a hand on his baton.

Oh my, was this M's idea? "Yes, sir," I said. Naked from the waist down, I leaned forward and placed my hands on the trunk. "Yeow, that's hot!" I pulled them back. He reached into the back seat, grabbed my pants and tossed them to me.

"Here," he said, "It's your choice. You can put your pants on, or you can drape them over the hot metal to protect your hands. Either way you are placing your hands on the trunk." I put the pants under my hands and leaned on them. What was the point of trying to hide my nakedness? He already had a full view of my goodies.

He came up behind me, placed his boot beside my foot and slid my leg further over. I tried to look back to see if there were any passerby's, but he pushed my head back down. The rest area was closed and we were well off the road so it wasn't likely. The hot desert air sucked the perspiration off my skin as fast as it appeared. I was shaking, out of fear or excitement, I wasn't sure.

Officer Mionchinskaia stepped in close. I could feel the hot leather and cold metal of his holster and gun on my thighs as he began to frisk me. He moved his hands down the outside of my arms and back up the insides of my arms. He slid them down my sides and up my back, back down again, stopping just short of my bare hips. Then, he slid his hands in front of me, over my belly and up my front, grabbing my braless breasts under my halter top, one in each hand. He pinched my nipples and I gasped, pushing my ass back against his hips.

He slid his hands off my breasts, then around to my back again and down my body. This time his rough hands continued on past my halter top, over my bare hips and down the sides of my legs. He was kneeling now, my naked sex at eye level. I could feel his hot breath on my exposed parts as his hands circled around to the front of my legs and up over my thighs, brushing my Venus mound on their way to my belly.

He stood up behind me again and took each of my hands, one at a time, off the trunk and brought them around behind me, handcuffing them. "As per my Cousin Nicolai's instructions, Ma'am," he said. My ears perked up.

He circled his hands around my hips and grabbed ahold of my ass with both hands, spreading my naked cheeks apart. He let them go and reached around in front and up between my legs. With one hand, he grabbed my cooch and with the other hand, pulled out his baton and dragged the baton across my butt cheeks, then down the moist crease of my ass and up between my pussy lips. He guided it into my hole with his hand holding my pussy and began stroking my clit. He slid his nightstick in and out of me, in slow motion.

I was being taken on the side of the road by a police officer. Who would believe it? M knew me so well; he must have figured I'd be tripping the clit fantastic on my drive through the desert, and so he put his cousin up to this.

Officer Mionchinskaia pummeled my pussy over and over, using his nightstick with admirable skill, while rubbing my clit into a juicy cum frenzy. I howled and bucked back against his stick, and he complied, shoving it deeper into me, completing my orgasm with a shiver. I would have crumbled to the ground but he held me up, removed the handcuffs and put me back in my car. He handed me my pants and sent me on my way with my salacious warning.

"Make sure to send my regards to my cousin, Ms. GG."

THIRTY NINE

....

THE STRIP, BOOTH SEVEN

I rolled into Las Vegas mid-afternoon. As I stood in line at registration and watched affectionate couples and groups of attractive young men mill about, my hunger returned. I had been without M for ten days, and I could not wait for him to join me. I felt so damn horny without my hot lover and being pulled over had not satisfied the ache in my loins. I missed him being around to fill my bottom the way he did. Big kisses, big hands, and big cock; thinking of him made me shiver in anticipation. I got to the room and looked around. The room seemed too empty without M. I had plenty of time before his plane arrived so I stowed my suitcase in the room.

It had been ten years since I was last in Las Vegas. In fact, before M had come along, during the ten-year sex drought brought on by my passionless marriage, I had considered coming to Vegas and reserving a porn star surrogate for a night. I had researched for hours on end, using the internet, for a solution to my empty pussy. I found it was possible to experience a well-endowed man, who knew how to use his big gift, for a price at the legalized brothels. The thought of this still sent a quiver through my quim, and I was pretty sure, as long as I took pictures and videos documenting it, and a clear series of photos of the cum dripping out of my pussy, M would approve.

You are such an Orange County butt slut, GG, I thought to myself and chuckled. I had adopted my saying as my motto "I'll try anything…twice". Words I planned to live by, now that I'd escaped my gilded cage. I changed into a skirt, closed the hotel room door behind me and made my way down through the casino and out onto the street.

I walked a while, catching glimpses of myself in the large, mirror-like windows lining the strip. *Damn, GG, you look so good I'd fuck you*, I thought, inspecting my reflection. I looked like a sophisticated 35 year old, pert nipples pushing up through my blouse, perky ass twitching beneath my short skirt with every step I took. "What I wouldn't give for a big cock to suck on to pass the time until M gets here." I could feel my slick pussy lips rubbing together in time with my strides.

I turned the corner, heading down a side street and ran headlong into the doorman, welcoming guests off the street into a male strip club.

I couldn't believe my eyes! Darnell, my favorite valet from the country club, stood right in front of me, looking hotter than he ever did back in the OC. "Well hello, Mrs. A. What are you doing here?" Darnell was the good-looking Colombian valet with whom I flirted with outside the country club when he brought around my car following tennis and lunch with the ladies. Somehow our playful banter would always take a turn towards the risqué after he handed me my keys. I took pleasure in grabbing a hold of his hand and placing a twenty-dollar tip in his palm. "When are you going to let me return the favor, Mrs. A? You're always so generous, let me return your generosity with a big tip of my own." We would laugh as I got into my little red Mercedes, spreading my thighs wide to give him a good, long look up my tennis skirt.

And there he was, on the streets of Las Vegas, leaning down, planting a kiss on my neck and taking me by the elbow, leading me into the full nude club. He had his cell phone to his ear making arrangements as he ushered me through the door.

"She's on her way now," Darnell said and slid the phone back into his jean pocket beside his delicious bulge. "No charge, Mrs. A. I'm sorry I won't be able to join you, but I've arranged for someone special to take care of you. I know you're going to like him. Feel free to take a look around the club, then take the stairs up to the second floor. You're in Booth 7." He turned to face me, pushing up against me. He took my ass in his hands, giving me a hot, Latin kiss with lots of tongue, squeezing my cheeks and grinding his hard package against my pussy. "Consider it a thank you for all the lovely leg you've always shared," he whispered in my ear, and then he was gone.

The place was hopping inside. I stood still as my eyes adjusted to the dim light and my overheated skin cooled in the air-conditioned comfort. Women in groups, twosomes and singles, were receiving personal attention, stripping, grinding and bumping. There were naked, ripped young men everywhere. Behind the bars, waiters serving drinks, lap dances at the tables, and every color of hunk working the stages. In short, Disneyland for horny women.

I flushed with excitement at the possibilities, my brain in overdrive. A waiter stepped up to me wearing a speedo and a tuxedo tie and offered me a shot. "No, thank you," I said, feeling shy, "I don't partake."

He smiled back at me and said, "I understand, beautiful, the stiff you want isn't a stiff drink. If you'd like to take a seat at the table over there I'll be right back to serve you this." He took my hand and placed it on his package closing my fingers around his thick joint.

"Oh," I gasped, "that won't be necessary. I have a booth reserved. Booth 7?"

He looked at me, his lips parting in a leering grin. "Ahh, baby, now I understand. You have a date with Destiny."

I felt flustered and must have looked confused. The waiter laughed, "It's what we call him around here, Mr. Destiny Johnson. Booth 7 is right up those stairs, fourth curtain on the left."

I started up the stairs, looking over my shoulder just in time to see my waiter's perfect buns disappear into the crowd. *Boy, would I like to squeeze those,* I thought.

At the landing I made my way down to Booth 7 and pulled the curtain aside to enter. In the center of the candle lit booth was a pit couch and on the couch was a long, lanky man wearing only a towel. My wet pussy clenched in anticipation and excitement at the sight of him.

"Please, come join me," he said in a smooth, deep voice. "Darnell tells me you are a special guest, and I'm to give you the deluxe treatment."

I stepped into the pit and sat down beside the man. He had a rugged handsomeness about him and big gentle hands. He reached over and caressed my hair. "What are you in need of, beautiful?" Before I could answer he leaned over and firmly kissed me on the mouth, his closely trimmed beard tickling my cheek. His towel fell to the side and there, laying on the couch, heavy and thick, was the Johnson of Mr. Destiny. He released me from his deep kiss and, looking in me in the eye, took my hand and placed my fingers around his thick shaft. His Johnson sprang to life, doubling in length and girth. "Oh my god," I gasped. I felt my flesh across my neck and chest flush with excitement as I used both hands to hold his cock, my fingers exploring his magnificent organ. *Damn, if this cock is meant for me, then who am I to argue with my destiny?*

M always called me a closet exhibitionist, and not even thinking I pulled my blouse over my head, revealing stiff full nipples. Only after pulling down my skirt did I remember I hadn't worn panties. I felt my cunt clutching and re-clutching again, anticipating his fat joint between my pussy lips. I could feel the quick steady beat of my heart in my clit. *GG, you are a slut-tress for sure,* I thought. *M will be here in a couple hours and here you are, preparing to suck this huge cock.* A lecherous grin spread across my face. I took a deep breath and said, "Ok, Mr. Johnson, I'm going to suck your big cock. Then you're going to fuck my pussy hard and deep and put a big cream pie in me. But most important, I must have photos and videos, and you're going to take them."

Smiling at me, he reached behind a cushion and pulled out a HD video camera. He put in a fresh memory card, set it on a tripod, turned it towards us and turned it on. He sat back down and spread his thighs open wide, offering his beautiful cock to me. I dove down on his massive tool, trying to swallow the fat head and thick shaft. My bottom went wild as I gagged on him. My ass gripped and my pussy squirted as I tried my best to get the massive thing down my throat. I wrapped both of my hands around his thick trunk as he fucked my mouth. I relaxed my throat muscles and he slid further down into the back of my throat, gagging me until my ass clenched and my pussy swelled. With one hand, he pushed my hungry mouth up and down on his thick member and with the other, he had grabbed ahold of my whole bottom, pushing two fingers up my ass and two into my pussy against my G-spot. He placed his thumb against my clit. With a piston-like motion, he cranked my pussy and ass. Again and again, faster and faster, he worked my bottom into a creamy lather, all the while, deep fucking my throat.

I gagged with ecstasy. I came with great convulsing shakes. I kept one hand on his long thick shaft and moved the other to cup his balls. I could feel his balls tightening, getting ready to shoot my mouth full of his cock cum. I lifted my head just long enough to say, "Cum in my pussy. You have to cum in my pussy and take photos of it dripping out."

He continued to work my pussy, bringing on the most intense cum. I was panting and quivering all over. My skin felt as hot as the desert. He stopped just short of cumming. I could feel the huge rimmed head of his cock dripping a slick juice on my tongue when he pulled out and stood up. He lifted me up onto my hands and knees and stood behind me, forcing my thighs far apart. I moaned in anticipation of being split wide by his magnificent cock. He took a step back and grabbed the camera, positioning it just behind us and to the side. He turned back towards me and said, "Darnell paid for the deluxe fuck, and I'm going to give it to you, honey."

I looked over my shoulder in time to see him grab a bottle of lube and grease up his massive manhood. Just as I turned forward, I felt the fat, slippery knob push up against my bunghole. He stayed still for a moment, teasing my twitching, hungry ass. He forced his cock in my ass with a slow, steady push.

I gasped as he split me open, his long shaft just kept going and going. Only after spreading me wide with his thick root did I feel his heavy, cum filled sack slap up against my throbbing pussy. My body erupted in a kaleidoscope ass cum leaving me seeing stars. Then, he began sliding the whole length of it in and out of me at an ever-faster pace, each time his balls smacked into my swollen lips, making my clit throb in time with his thrusts.

Smack, smack, smack, smack, smack. After each smack, I groaned and pushed back to take it even deeper into my ass. With every penetration I felt him growing larger still. He stopped, withdrawing the great length of shaft from my ass and flipped me over on my back. I grunted and watched his cock twitch as he struggled to contain his cum. He lifted my legs up over his shoulders and began thrusting again, this time deep into my aching pussy. We were riding each other to a mind-exploding cum. As my orgasm began to sweep me away, I looked up at his grimacing face and saw him lose his nut. I could feel the powerful streams of man jam shoot out of his rigid joint. He was pumping me full of his semen. His joint was so thick and my pussy was cumming so hard, I was squeezing his warm cum out around the girth of his cock as fast as he was pumping it into me. He gave one more pussy-pounding thrust; he pulled slowly out, his massive cum flooding out of me.

He stepped back to the camera and zoomed in on the thick mess of creamy pussy juice and man cream dripping down my pussy and over my puckered asshole.

I just lay there, holding my legs up, my throbbing ass and pussy open wide so M could enjoy my slut ass on the video. I was breathing hard and moaning. I coughed and a big glob of cum squirted out my wide-open cunt and rolled down my clenching bottom.

Destiny stepped back and turned off the video camera. He removed the memory card and walked over handing it to me. He took ahold of my hand for a moment and smiled saying, "Stop back any time, beautiful. Call ahead and it's on me."

I found my way to the ladies room and found an empty stall. The bathroom was full of horny, drunk women. They were having fun, but no way could any of them be as thoroughly fucked as I. It took a moment for my swollen pussy to pee. I wiped up and squeezed out a few more drops of Destiny cum before giving my pussy one last juicy wipe. I made myself presentable and left to pick up M at the airport.

I had been a naughty girl. Later in the evening, when I viewed the video with M, if he was pleased with me. I was hoping he would punish me: my mouth, my pussy, and my ass. He would give me a hard spanking and fucking. I had earned my punishment and I would enjoy it.

FORTY

....

GG'S LADY SANDWICH

I drove to the airport and picked up M. On our way back to the hotel, we had fun discussing my adventures as I recounted my wild time with the highway patrol. "And when I read his name-tag," I said to M, "I knew you had to be behind the whole, crazy thing."

"My cousin's text message was classic," M laughed. "'Mission accomplished,' he wrote and then, 'That GG is one hot chick. If you ever want to share her, give me a call.'" M put his hand on my bare thigh and I opened my legs. He slid it up under my skirt and rubbed my clit.

"So you drove all the way to Vegas with no pants on?" M laughed, "That's brazen, even for you, GG."

"You know how I am. Something about the open road. All that free time. I just can't resist playing with myself," I spread my legs wider and pushed my pussy into his hand.

"But it was just the start of it," I said and went on, telling him about seeing Darnell and ending up in the strip club. I described in detail my encounter with Mr. Destiny.

"I made sure to take pictures and," I paused for effect, "there's a video, too."

M gave me his sly look and said, "That's my GG, OC butt slut to the core.

THE NEXT MORNING, I WOKE UP, STRETCHED CAT-LIKE AND GOT TURNED ON ALL OVER AGAIN. M and I had finished our evening watching my strip club sex video and rubbing each other out. It was an incredible turn on for both of us. M pulled me backwards on his lap, and I rode him while on the screen my alter ego GG got fucked hard. The four of us, screen GG, Mr. Destiny, M and I all came to an explosive climax together.

We retired, completely spent, and M wrapped me in his tight, lean body until we both fell sleep. Waking up with the memory of our sex play brought a blush to my cheeks. In my former life, I could never have imagined the things I was doing.

I was pulled from my half-sleep as M awoke. He smothered me in hugs and kisses. He rolled over and called room service; I showered quickly and joined him at the table. The coffee smelled heavenly and I quietly enjoyed my java fix. "Do we have anything planned today, M?" I asked.

"Unfortunately, I have a couple of hours of work to attend to so I have taken the liberty of scheduling a massage for you. You could use a little pampering after yesterday's debauchery."

I blushed. "Thank you, hotness. A massage sounds wonderful."

"M, I'M BACK," I CALLED AS I WALKED INTO THE SUITE. I found him sitting at the desk. We kissed and I reached for his cock but he stopped me. "We'll have time later. For right now, I want you to freshen up and put on something sexy. I have something special planned for this evening. I've arranged for you to experience what you have longed for, for all these years. M patted me on my behind, his fingers tracing the contour of my ass.

What does my naughty man have in mind for me now? I wondered.

M moved to the couch and pulled out his MacBook Air, returning emails and checking accounts. I excused myself and retired to the bathroom to freshen up. Our luxurious hotel suite had a beautiful living area with a couch, a love seat, and a reclining chair. There was a kitchen and dinette, and through double doors, a bedroom with mirrors on the walls and a king size bed. The bathroom was as big as a normal hotel room. It had a large Jacuzzi tub to one side and a commode and walk-in shower to the other. I peeled off my clothing and ran the water. The steam rose from the hot shower, fogging over the mirrors. Man-smell was still wafting up from my slick, juicy bottom. The scent triggered a shiver up my spine and a spontaneous cunt clutching, a flash-bang, aftermath orgasm. I held on to the shower door until I stopped cumming, savoring the memories and sensations.

Well, the smell may wash away, but I won't soon forget the memories of such dirty pleasure. I finished my shower, dried off and moisturized my legs, backside and breasts. I wrapped a towel around my head and another around my middle, positioning it just so to tease M, revealing ample cleavage, a glimpse of butt cheeks and a flash of shiny pink pussy flesh. I was ready for some of M's big cock loving, more than ready for him to take me.

As I walked through the bedroom, I was surprised to hear voices coming from the other room. I entered the living room to find M seated in the recliner and two attractive women sitting side by side on the couch.

"GG, do come in and join us," M said, indicating I should take a seat between the women.

They moved aside for me as I made my way to the couch. In a vain attempt at modesty, I tried to keep my towel in place as I sat down and crossed my legs.

"Ladies, this is who I'd like you to meet. This is GG," M said, "and GG, these lovely ladies are Fiona and Delilah."

We said our hellos all around, shaking hands and kissing cheeks. Fiona had shoulder length brown hair and a short skirt with a sequined top. She was petite with pert little breasts, the nipples pushing through her blouse. She had what I would refer to as a stripper's body, sensual and sinewy. Delilah was curvy and busty. A natural red head, she wore her hair up, accenting her long elegant neck and plunging neckline, which fell open exposing her soft, rounded bosoms. Her dress had hiked up when I seated myself between them, and her pale, smooth thigh flesh pressed up against my naked hip.

"GG, it's a pleasure to meet you," Fiona said, turning to stroke my hair and slide her hand down the length of my arm, taking my hand and interlacing her fingers through mine. "M has told us all about you. He is fond of you, you know," she said as she placed my hand on Delilah's warm knee. "You are a very luck girl."

Fiona leaned across me towards Delilah, lifting her leg and straddling me to reach her. As she draped her slender, tanned thigh over my hips, her tiny skirt slid up to her bare pussy. It was an incredible turn-on, to smell her soft scented skin and feel her clean-shaven pussy pressed against me. She reached right into Delilah's bra and began caressing her luscious boobs. The two of them were kissing, their tongues darting in and out in a hot slithering dance. My towel had fallen open and Fiona was grinding her cunt against my nakedness. Fiona took my hand and forced it up Delilah's leg, pushing her legs open as we went. Delilah's thighs spread wide as my hand pushed against her damp crotch. Fiona reached into her panties and pushed her finger into her warm, wet hole. Delilah moaned.

Fiona pulled out her fingers, stood up and took me by the hand, pulling me off the couch and pushing me down between those soft, pink thighs. I watched as she took ahold of Delilah's panties and pulled them down, over her ankles and over her feet. I was eye-level with her big swollen pussy. Fiona spread the thick lips opened and teased the unusually large clitoris, grabbed a hold of my hair and pushed my face into Delilah's hot, juicy sex. I gasped for a moment then began licking and sucking her succulent gash, bringing my own hands up to spread her heavy lips apart. The smell and taste of her succulent hole were enough to give me short, little pussy-gasms.

I was down on the floor between her thighs with my naked ass up in the air, eating pussy. The heady musk of her dripping cunt was intoxicating. I pushed a finger into her and slid it in and out as I worked on her swollen clit.

Fiona stripped out of her blouse and skirt and came up behind me, grabbing my hips and ass, spreading my butt open and pushing her hot little snatch against my open bottom, like she was about to fuck me doggy style with her pussy.

She pushed my face hard into Delilah's snatch saying, "Eat that pussy good, GG." She slapped my ass hard, grabbed my full cunt with both her hands and squeezed it. That was all it took, I was cumming, but she slapped my ass again and said, "You pay attention to that pussy you're eating. Lick it all over and slide your tongue in her hole and suck her good." She slapped my ass twice more, harder this time. I was pushing my ass back into the spanking like the slut I am, savoring the pleasure/pain. She began kneading my ass with her fingers, pressing them into my cheeks and sinking her thumbs in my pussy. She kept pressing, releasing, and rubbing me vigorously.

Fiona put two fingers in me and began churning in and out of my pussy with her tiny hand. She was adding fingers as she went along until she had four fingers inside me, pumping them rapidly. I came again; she pulled out her hand and slapped me hard saying, "That's no way to eat a pussy, GG. I can see you need to be trained in the proper treatment of a horny slut. Let me show you how to do it."

She pulled me backwards, stood me up and turned me towards her. She kissed me deeply and passionately, sucking the pussy juice off my tongue, and took my place down between Delilah's thighs. She had a small bottle of lubricant in her hand and she began applying it liberally up and down into Delilah's pussy and ass.

Delilah pulled her legs up to her chest spreading her knees as wide apart as she could manage, giving Fiona complete entry. "Oh yes, please, Fiona," she pleaded, she had a blissful look on her face, "please, fist me." She was flushed with arousal, her face, neck, and chest burned a rosy red.

"Now watch me, GG," Fiona said. She brought the tips of her four lube-dripping fingers and thumb together, compressing her hand into a compact wedge-like shape. She inserted the tip of it into Delilah. She continued pushing it in, spreading her cunt further and further open, slipping in past her knuckles; her whole hand disappeared into Delilah's gash.

"Once you have your hand in there, GG, it's time to close your fist." Fiona seemed to be clenching her fist inside Delilah's pussy. Delilah squirmed and moaned, cumming all over Fiona's arm.

Fiona continued inserting her arm until it was forearm deep. She was pumping it in and out of Delilah, slow at first, then picking up the pace, pounding like a sensual piston, never too hard, just hard enough.

Delilah had thrown her head back. She had her mouth open wide and she was licking her lips and rolling her eyes, moaning and grunting, grinding down on Fiona's in-thrust. Fiona quickly withdrew her hand, vigorously massaging her clit, and Delilah orgasmed , gasping.

"Now you, GG," Fiona took me by the hand and pulled me down in front of Delilah's swollen pussy lips.

"Oh," I exclaimed, standing on my knees between those smooth, pink thighs. I folded up my fingers into the wedge like shape and placed the tips against her juicy labia. Fiona squeezed the lubricant in her palm and rubbed it all over my fingers. As I began to insert my hand in Delilah's pussy, Fiona kissed my mouth and fondled my breasts. I couldn't help myself, I came right then and there. The hot slippery wetness of her pussy surrounded my fingers. My hand slipped fully into Delilah's fleshy cunt and the muscles of her vagina tightened around me. She moaned and pulled her legs up and to the sides of her full, round bosoms, spreading wide open for me.

"Now make a fist, GG," Fiona said. I curled up my fingers in Delilah's hot, wet pussy. Fiona surprised me, sliding her hand down my back and up between my legs. I jumped as she pushed her fingers up into me. "Ooh, what a tight, wet pussy you have, GG," she said. I couldn't help myself, I immediately assumed the position, tilting my ass up to meet her probing fingers. Somehow, I managed to keep my hand in Delilah's pussy as Fiona finger fucked me intensely.

As I pumped my fist in and out of Delilah's juicy cunt, my own pussy began clenching and unclenching, gripping hard on

Fiona's fingers. "Oh you are loving this, aren't you, GG?" Fiona withdrew her fingers. I felt her squeeze the lubricant on my pussy and rub it around and up into me. "Harder, GG. Fist that pussy like you're a long, thick cock fucking that horny slut."

I began fucking Delilah's pussy with my fist. She squirmed and moaned, her muscles contracting around my arm as she came again. I leaned back, right onto Fiona's hand. She was pushing the whole thing up my dripping cunt.

Oh my god, I thought, *This woman is fisting me.* I gasped and shuddered as she closed her hand into a fist. It was like a thick cock with a big swollen head, only it was twisting and bending in unimaginable ways. I came hard, shaking and crying out with the pleasure/pain.

Fiona pushed me forward, penetrating deep into my pussy and forcing my arm up Delilah's pussy. Fiona grabbed my hair and forced my mouth down onto Delilah's huge swollen clit. I sucked for all I was worth as Fiona sent me into cum orbit.

M was getting quite an eyeful. Delilah on the couch, legs up, grinding and moaning, me on my knees up between her thighs and Fiona up behind me doggy-style. As I licked, sucked, fisted and fucked Delilah, Fiona was fisting me. M snuggled in behind Fiona and when she looked back and nodded, he slammed his rock hard cock into her, adding Fiona's cum sounds to the melody.

What a scene. We were cum-howling like a bitch pack in heat.

FORTY ONE

....

M-ECSTACY

Fiona and Delilah cleaned themselves up. The four of us kissed and hugged all the way around, saying our goodbyes. Then, it was just M and I. Too drained to do function, I thanked M with a big kiss and went straight to bed, satiated.

My heart was filled with a warmth having everything to do with him. *This man. This handsome, hot man. He's for me.* M saw my wild, untamed needs and filled them. Sometimes without me even knowing I had them.

I lay there, cuddled under the covers, breathing in the dark and the quiet, drifting in and out of sleep and floating in the bliss of my afterglow. I felt the welcome shaking of the bed, of M climbing in to join me under the covers. I opened my eyes, seeking his gaze and found instead his beautiful cock, right there, ready to be sucked.

I was exhausted, but knew he must be in great need of release after witnessing the three of us in our depraved sex dance. I shifted closer, closing my lips around the tip, sucking him in deep. He was soft so I was able to get all of him in my mouth. As I sucked and licked, I could feel his cock begin to grow. I let him slide in and out of my mouth as he got larger. I cupped his balls with my hand and continued to suck him. I've made it my goal to deep throat his entire length. On this day, I was so relaxed I was almost able to.

I took his erect cock into my mouth and when the tip touched the back of my throat, I swallowed and swallowed, relaxing and pushing against it. Almost...then I gagged. I tried to ignore the need to pull away as I pushed my mouth further onto his cock, even as I gagged. When I could take no more, I pulled back. I gasped for breath, but my hand took over for my mouth, rubbing his saliva-slickened cock. Now he was the one gasping, responding to the steady jerking motion I was giving him. It felt so good to make my man as hot and needy as he made me.

Twice more, I tried to deep throat his beautiful prick. By now, it was so large I couldn't get it into my throat at all. As my hand took over for the third time, encircling the shaft and teasing the head with the tips of my fingers, M growled and pulled me up into his arms, kissing me with unbridled passion as he lay me back and buried his cock, balls deep, into my pussy. My cunt contracted around his cock as his kiss swallowed my gasp. We moved as one, pounding together, so hard I thought we'd both break. As I looked into his eyes, I could see the effort it took him to keep from cumming. I held on, unwilling to cum again without him. I thought my heart would stop before he finally nodded, ever so slightly, signaling the end was imminent. I went over the edge with him as his cock shot cum into my cunt. He threw his head back and growled with abandon.

After the pounding stopped, we lay together and spooned. We softly talked and laughed about the wonderful evening we had. Lost, I was totally lost in the gritty, sensual afterglow. I could never have imagined a weekend so perfect, so fulfilling.

We both slept hard through the night.

FORTY TWO

....

BILLY RETURNS

I didn't ever want to forget our trip. It was outrageous, unexpected, and so hot. A truly epic Las Vegas adventure. What happened there was not staying there – no way. It was coming back with me to the OC. The morning after, M had sent me off with a hug, a kiss, and a pat on my behind. He climbed into a limo and headed for the airport; I drove down the road, heading back to sunny OC.

I wasn't exactly well rested, but I was well used. I had a smile on my face and a delicious soreness in my bum. Nothing too bad, just enough to keep the weekend foremost in my mind. Somewhere along Cajon Pass my iPhone buzzed. I grabbed it off the passenger seat, "Hello, this is GG."

"Hello, GG," came a voice I couldn't quite place, "Hello, can you hear me?"

"Yes, I can hear you fine," I said, "Who is this?"

"GG, it's Billy," he said, "Billy Rowen."

No way, I thought. Stacy was going to be so jealous. She hadn't heard from Tommy since the night of the Tool Box concert, nine months earlier. Tommy had promised he would get ahold of her, but when the band passed through Kansas City, he hadn't called. Billy and the band had been around the world since I'd last seen him. Those nine months had been the wildest time of my life, all because of my magic man, M.

"Billy," I said, "what a pleasant surprise. To what do I owe this pleasure?"

"GG, my love," he sounded excited to hear my voice. "It's so good to hear you. How have you been? Well, I hope. I've thought of you often GG, about our night together. Listen, the tour is winding down, and I'll be in town next month. I'd love to see you. Tool Box is at the Honda Center. Can I send a car to pick you up?"

"Yes, Billy," I said, surprising myself, "that sounds fun. Can you text me the specifics?"

"That's great," Billy said. "I'll get you the information by this evening. I've missed you, GG. I brought you something special back from China. I think you will really like it. Ciao."

Odd, I felt uncomfortable. Why was I feeling like I was betraying M? Our relationship wasn't exclusive. He knew all about my flirting, and I was sure he must have lovers all over the world. Why did I feel like I was being unfaithful to him?

FORTY THREE

....

COUNTRY CLUB PARTY

My life in OC continued on, same as it ever was. Except Theo was becoming more and more attentive. He was lavishing me with attention, rather than treating me as an afterthought. Our twenty-year anniversary approached, perhaps explaining his actions. But the truth was, his attentiveness was no longer necessary nor wanted. My daily life was still in the marriage, but my heart and body had moved on. Besides, his doting seem gratuitous and insincere, more like his therapist suggesting he might want to acknowledge me if he wanted to save the marriage.

Give the guy a break, you say? Well, try this on and see what you think. After ten years without sex and eight years without being touched, hubby is all of the sudden asking me if I'd like for him to "make my toes curl." Excuse me for saying, but not on your life. The days when his attention would have been welcome are long gone, honey.

He moped around for about a minute after I turned him down. Next thing I knew, he was back on the couch engrossed in season three of The Big Bang Theory. Besides, we had a business event to attend together later in the evening, so why make waves over a little thing like sex?

Like I said, same as it ever was.

THE EVENING AFFAIR PROMISED TO BE DULL: A GATHERING OF THEO'S BUSINESS CONTACTS, VENDORS AND CLIENTS. The cocktail party was the kick-off event of a weekend dedicated to networking, seminars and golf, with a smattering of social events and a whole lot of drinking. Events like this one turned me sober ten years ago after I saw one of my friends overindulge out of boredom and make a complete fool of herself. Following the event, her husband shipped her off to detox and divorced her. I never saw her again, and I never drank again.

I managed to avoid the last event hubby attended, but with his radar working overtime and M being busy anyway, I decided to put on my sexy best and try to convince him nothing had changed. For this evening, I chose strappy *Stuart Weitzman* shoes in metallic sparkle. My cashmere dress fell to mid-thigh showing off my tanned and toned legs. The sleeves were long and billowy with a fitted cuff and they flounced as I walked. My back was bare from the bottom of the collar to the bottom of my tailbone, saving the dress from being too demure. I felt sexy and I wished M were there to see me. And then undress me!

As we got to the club, my favorite valet and secret strip club facilitator, Darnell, opened the door of the car for me with an appreciative and knowing smile. "Good evening, Mrs. A. Good to see you. Will you be dining in the main room?"

"No, Darnell, we're here for the private cocktail party in the Bayside room," I replied.

"Ahh, business then. Well, enjoy yourself, Mrs. A. You look stunning as usual."

Theo shot Darnell a warning look and placed his hand in the small of my back, guiding me into the club. Even this small touch felt wrong to me. I managed to suppress the desire to pull away and distracted myself by asking him what his goals were for the evening. "Well, there's a rather large potential client here I would like to meet and talk with concerning a strategic business partnership. Other than that, just checking in with everyone," he replied. "Do you think you can keep yourself amused, GG? I know how you hate these affairs."

I rolled my eyes at him. "Of course I can keep myself amused, dear. Just send up a flare if you need me." He was much better than I was at mingling and the self-obsessed conversation that passed as intellectual at these events. For twenty years, he would bring me to these affairs, only to disappear after we had made an entrance, leaving me to fend for myself. I had perfected floating around, chatting but never engaging for long with the businessmen who populated those events. I had no desire to get to know them and even less desire in having meaningless conversation of the sort they were capable of after a few drinks.

I had just re-entered the Bayside room when the special energetic tingle I felt when M was around me tickled my skin. Startled, I stopped and looked at the crowd, trying to identify the reason for the tingle. Of course, it was my wishful thinking that it could be M. I walked over to the windows and looked out. I felt so lonely in the middle of a crowd of people, many of who were known to me. I just didn't feel right without M.

"Looking for someone?" M breathed into my ear. My heart leapt into my throat.

"You're here! But how?" I whispered as I turned to him.

"No, GG, don't turn around. Go over to your husband and tell him you've got a migraine and you are going to lie down. Then, find Darnell. He has my instructions."

"Yes, sir," I replied. But he had already moved on. My heart beat double-time. I was excited and nervous at the same time - my beloved M and my husband in the same room, at the same time. In my wildest fantasies I never would have imagined this scenario. I turned from the window and went looking for hubby.

When I found him, he was regaling his vendors and customers with a story I had heard at least a hundred times. I tapped my toe as I waited at his side, smiling and laughing at the appropriate times, until he finished. As I was leaning in to inform Theo I had a migraine and was leaving, M approached the group. Theo leaned in and whispered to me "I've been waiting for months to meet this man, do not embarrass me." I stood by as the two men were introduced and once they began talking, I made my escape.

I walked to the valet stand and found Darnell. "Mrs. A, I have special instructions for you. Please, follow me." Bemused, I followed him past the valet stand and into an entrance used by the employees. He led me down a long, dark hall, past the kitchen and up the back stairs. He let me into one of the private rooms through a hidden entrance next to the bookcase. "Ok, Mrs. A, my next instructions are a bit strange. You are to go to the window and bend over." "It's ok, Darnell. I'm used to these games," I assured him as I crossed the room to the window and bent over the back of a chair.

I wasn't expecting what happened next. Darnell had followed me across the room, running his hands up my legs and under my skirt to my bottom. He pulled aside the string on my panties and cupped my pussy in his hand. "Ahh, Mrs. A, just as hot and juicy as I imagined." His fingers ran up and down my gash, brushing my clit with each stroke. Then, he plunged two fingers into my wet cunt and finger fucked me. My back arched and I pushed back onto his fingers as his thumb rubbed my clit, bringing me to a delicious orgasm. I felt the tip of his cock at my wet opening, but he made no move to enter me. I tried to push back onto him, but he kept the same relative position. "Mrs. A, I can't do this without asking, are you ok with this?" "Oh Darnell," I breathed, "I've wanted this for oh so long. Please fuck my pussy." My words were all he needed. He slid his cock into me like a man lost in the desert who found water. His hands gripped my hips, and he drove into me hard and fast, pounding me for all those times we had flirted but never touched. I came hard, my pussy contracting around Darnell's cock. His rhythm increased and he shot his load into my cunt.

He leaned over and kissed my back. "Don't move, Mrs. A. I need to take a picture of our cream pie." He pulled out and stood back to take a picture - or three - of my dripping pussy before handing me a towel. "I've sent the pictures to your phone. I'm to go and leave you here, alone. Wait here until 10pm for the gentleman to join you." I stood up and kissed him. "Thank you, Darnell, for a lovely cum."

I had fallen asleep curled up on the couch in front of the fireplace. Sometime later, maybe minutes, maybe hours, M placed a gentle kiss on my neck, his lips hovering while I woke up. "Did you like your surprise?" he whispered in my ear. "My love, which one? The surprise where you were here at this conference?"

"No, GG. The one where you and Darnell consummated your flirtation at long last."

"Both, my darling, both. Thank you, that was so sweet. What are you doing here?"

"Your husband's company has been chasing business with one of my subsidiaries for quite some time. Since I would be able to surprise you and meet him, I decided it was time to listen to what he had to say."

"Ahh, so what do you think?"

"I think," purred M, "that my director of purchasing is quite capable of distracting your husband for the next hour or two while I enjoy his beautiful wife."

A shiver started in my pussy and spread throughout my body. I stretched my still-sleepy body and curled around my lover. Such a delightful surprise. My hand found his hard cock and grasped it through his pants. We kissed, one of those sweet kisses full of soft lips and dancing tongues. As the heat spread throughout my body, I tried to push to a sitting position, but M pushed me back to the couch. "Relax, GG. Tonight I want to pleasure you."

His hands lifted the hem of my skirt and pulled my underwear to the side. Fingers roamed over my still-swollen clit and plunged into my cunt: first two, then three. I arched into his hands, wanting more but unable to ask. I shouldn't have been shy about asking, but I still was. Asking to have my pussy filled up with his fingers just seemed so slutty and dirty. But how I wanted it. M's thumb strummed my clit as his fingers thrust into my cooch. My orgasm built, heat racing along my skin. I stood at the edge of the cliff for what seemed like eternity when M pulled his hand out and moved his fingers from side-to-side over my enlarged clit, eliciting a long, hot cum. When his fingers released me, I fell into the valley of after-gasm, panting and shuddering.

I pulled my lips to his and kissed my gratitude into his mouth. His fingers began again and I ground my cunt into them with unruly abandon. "My, my, GG, I do believe you need this," M commented, driving his four fingers into me. He pressed me back into the couch, placing his palm on my breastbone. "Don't move. I've got something you need." His fingers danced in and out of my wet hole, first in me, then on my clit, bringing me close to cumming but never letting me over the line. I was trying with all my might to stay still when he shoved his entire hand into my cunt. "Ahh," I moaned.

"Shhh, GG, be quiet." M continued the mind-boggling pressure, his entire fist pushing into my cunt, then pulling almost out and back in. There is nothing quite like it and I came like a freight train, straining to stay still and stay silent. Oh. My. "Fuck me, M, fuck me hard," I whispered around the edges of my pleasure explosion.

I don't know how long he pleasured me. Time had no meaning for me when he fist-fucked me. He pulled his fist out one last time, bent over and kissed me. "Go to sleep, GG." His hand stroked my hair and out I went, dreaming of hot, hot fucking with my hot, hot man.

FORTY FOUR

....

SUSHI AND ME

M was scheduled to be in Los Angeles for the rest of the week, so we had plenty of opportunities to be together. Stacy was hinting around about coming out to visit. I had agreed, thinking we three might be able to recapture the spirit of the sweet and sultry first night we spent together.

I was sitting across the table from M and Stacy. We had just picked her up at the airport and now we were enjoying sushi at the top of the Ritz. The views of the city and sunset were spectacular, and the food was just as good. I enjoyed watching the interplay between my love and my best friend. To a casual observer, it would have seemed they were the couple.

Which is what M had planned. We had enjoyed Stacy's company in our bed before. It had been great fun, but she hadn't been ready to take the step, which would allow us to be the threesome he and I wanted. He was hoping a little extra attention would perhaps open doors to unexplored territory.

All of this gave me time to sit back and watch. I dropped my napkin and went to pick it up, and sure enough, under the table his hand was on her pussy, her hand was on his cock. They were trying to be surreptitious but it would be hard to miss. A whisper here and a nuzzle there, arms moving under the table.

I wasn't the only one who had noticed. Our waitress, a tall, leggy brunette, was aware of the play happening at her table. She seemed to be enjoying it, leaning over to show cleavage to M when she brought each new hand roll, fingers lingering a bit too long on his arm.

I was getting quite heated, sitting across from my lovebirds. After a bit, I thought, why not take care of this? I excused myself and went to the restroom. I sat on the toilet and rubbed my clit. Oh, it felt so good. I had worn a skirt with no panties as I often did when I was with M. My first cum was fast and not enough, so I visualized M licking Stacy's pussy and rubbed out cum number two. Just as I finished, I heard someone walk into the restroom. A little gratuitous listening couldn't deter me, so I went for it on the third cum, pumping my fingers in and out of my pussy and pinching my nipple and moaning a little as I came.

When I stepped out of the stall, our waitress was standing there. She reached out and took my hand, brought it up to her face and smelled my fingers. She took her time licking my fingers while her eyes stayed focused on mine. Seeing acceptance, she put my fingers in her mouth and sucked on them. I had a mini-cum then, my eyes half closing and my knees going weak, shaking from the hot seduction in her eyes. Then, she kissed me. I saw the desire in her eyes and felt the passion in her kiss.

As she pulled away, I dug in my purse for the room key. I held it out to her, "Please, when you're off work, come visit us." She took it, smiled and headed back to the floor.

I slid back into the booth, thinking M is never going to believe this! He noticed the satisfied grin on my face and knew

I'd been in the restroom taking care of myself, but he was going to be so surprised when I told him what had happened. Just then, the waitress stopped by the table and leaned over me, whispering in my ear "I'm off at 11."

AFTER A WALK AROUND LA LIVE, STACY, M, AND I RETURNED TO THE ROOM. We were sitting on the couch in an unconscious reflection of our first encounter. M kissed Stacy, then me, as he slid his hand around her and teased her nipple with his fingers. Everything seemed to be headed in the right direction, and by right, I mean all of us naked and in the same bed, when Stacy had a change of heart. With a dramatic flourish she grabbed her purse and left the room. M gave me his 'what the hell just happened' look.

"I told you she wants you. The only reason she agrees to come join us is to get your attention, hoping she will have you to herself."

"Ahh, one can always hope," M whispered in my ear as he was nuzzling my neck. "I know you love to eat pussy with me, GG."

I snuggled in close to him and whispered in his ear. "I might have a surprise for you, lover. Remember our hot waitress from tonight, the one with the great legs? Well, she walked in on me in the restroom when I was rubbing one out."

"Do tell," I had M's full attention.

"Well, she licked my fingers and then kissed me. I gave her our room key. I hope that was ok?" I said.

"Is that what the whispering was about?" He smiled and teased my ear with his tongue. "I don't see any problem with it, do you?"

"No, sir. She gets off at 11 p.m."

We had plenty of time before eleven and we weren't sure she would show, so we had a party of our own. Since M had returned to town from his extended trip, we had wild sex almost every day. I decided to break things up by treating him to a massage.

I worked on his feet first, since he felt travel most keenly there. I had him moaning into the pillow as I moved up to his calves. Wow, were they tight. As I worked the knots out of his muscles, my eyes drank in his hot body with the long defined muscles. I grinned to myself and leaned over to kiss his butt cheek as my hand slid between his legs to find his balls.

"Now, GG, that's not regulation massage," he said with mock sternness. He rolled me over and gave me a mischievous grin. "Now it's your turn, lie on your stomach."

We switched places and he massaged my shoulders and neck, working on my tension spots. I was blissed out when I heard a quiet knock as the door opened. "Hello, it's Deanna. May I come in?"

"Yes, please!" I said. "We have been massaging each other. Care to join us?"

Deanna sauntered into the room, dropped her purse and gave us the once over. "Wow, you two are a hot couple," she said. She smiled and shrugged out of her clothes, baring her long limbs and sensuous curves. She walked over to the bed, leaned in to plant a wet kiss on M, then a long, wet one on me.

I've been kissed by girls before, but she was an expert. Her tongue circled my lips, then danced tip-to-tip with my tongue before plunging deep into my mouth. Only our mouths touched and yet I almost came. As she pulled back, I opened my eyes and looked into hers, knowing this night was going to be special.

"Deanna, I'm GG and this is M," I said. M rose to his knees and leaned in to return our new friend's kiss with one of his own. I could see the sparks flying as their lips and tongues danced. "So lovely to meet you," M said. "You've had a long day I'm certain, perhaps you would enjoy a massage?"

"A massage sounds amazing. I've been working since 10 a.m." Deanna lay her long curvy body down between us. M and I locked eyes over her body, unspoken but understood, let's show her a good time. We massaged her feet first, M on her left side, me on her right. She moaned her approval and gratitude, "Oh, this is so wonderful, thank you."

After a thorough foot massage, we moved in unison up her legs, by unspoken agreement avoided her beautiful ass for now and worked on her back. M had always told me I had a natural talent for eating pussy, I just needed some more practice. I was beyond excited this was happening. I'd always found women as attractive as I did men, but, aside from our night back east with Erica and the salacious evening in Vegas, I was a novice.

The more I massaged her, the more turned on I became. I wanted to lick her pussy, suck her nipples, investigate every part of her with my fingers and tongue. Beginning at the nape of her neck was an intricate, brightly colored tattoo, which ran across her shoulder blade and around her side, disappearing under her ribcage. My fascination with it grew in direct proportion to my desire to see and touch her nipples.

M leaned forward and kissed Deanna's neck as his hand slid between her legs, brushing her pussy. She turned on her back, opening her legs and hooking her arm behind my neck, pulling me down into another spine-tingling kiss. As M fingered her pussy, her hand reached for mine. She began running her fingers up and down my gash, coaxing my clit to come out of hiding. Her exploration became more insistent and my pussy rewarded her with my cum; a blinding explosion of heat and light, as she rolled my clit between two of her fingers and plundered my mouth with her tongue.

She released my mouth and met my eyes, grinning. "I do love a woman who knows how to cum," Deanna said. I blushed an even brighter shade of red. M saved me from having to reply. "Do you mind if we eat your pussy together? I promised GG I would give her some pointers."

"Only if I get to eat her pussy at the same time," Deanna replied.

What girl could say no to that offer? Not a butt slut like myself! I found my face between Deanna's legs, M's body curved against my back, his head resting on my shoulder. Deanna had already commenced the most delicious lapping of my labia, staying away from my clit but still sending little electric jolts from the tip of her tongue throughout my body.

M coached me, "Now lick all over her pussy. Yes, perfect." He nibbled on my earlobe as his breath warmed my ear. "Then spread her pussy lips open with your fingers, good. Now slide your tongue up and down the creamy slit from stiff nub to juicy hole."

I was trying as hard as I could to stay focused but Deanna had other ideas. Her tongue circled my clit, once, twice, three times; then she began sucking on it as her fingers slid into my gash, fingering me as only another woman could. M pinched my nipples and pushed his hard cock against my ass. The combination of being nestled between them and tasting pussy was so hot that I had an explosive orgasm, pushing my pussy into her face. Deanna never let up for even an instant, not allowing my orgasm to end.

When I returned from the free fall of my cum, I found myself still licking Deanna's tasty slit. I stuck my tongue into her gash, invading it like she had invaded my mouth. I felt M's hands on my breasts holding my nipples as the head of his cock rested against my hinter-hole.

"Nice," M whispered into my ear, "now insert two fingers in her gash and push in and out while you flick her clit with the tip of your tongue. Use your middle two fingers, leaving your first finger free and outside her pussy. Each time you pull your fingers out and slide them back in, your first finger will slide against the hot wet folds between her hole and her clit while you lick the tip of it."

I was getting into eating pussy despite the extreme distraction of Deanna munching on mine and M pushing against my ass and pulling on my nipples. I wanted to make her cum. It seemed only fair. I tried to think of what to do next. My coach must have sensed my hesitation. "You're doing great, GG, now place your tongue firmly on her clit and rapidly push/pull the two middle fingers in and out of her pussy, apply firm pressure against her G-spot every time. Yes, just like that. Find her rhythm, you'll feel her tense, yes, you're doing great." Deanna let out a groan and ground her pussy into my face.

"Good work, GG," M whispered as he slid his cock up into me, balls deep. I could feel the vibrations from Deanna's moan throughout my gash. I sucked her clit like I would suck a cock, keeping her in ecstasy as M pounded my ass. *This must be heaven*, I thought, before all thoughts left my head.

In the middle of my cum, the hotel room burst open and Stacy came rushing in.

"What's going on here?" she said. "Oh my god, I guess I'll need my own room." Her angry voice penetrated my cum-addled brain.

"Stacy, relax, come join us," M said in his most seductive voice.

"You KNOW I don't do girls, M!" Stacy stomped towards her suitcase, grabbing it and making to leave. "I don't know what I was thinking. I should have never come to California to visit you two."

M whispered to us, "I'll go take care of Stacy, if that's ok with you ladies." I grunted affirmatively as Deanna chuckled. "I'd rather have GG to myself, anyway. Guys are ok, but not really my thing."

M pulled out of me and walked over to Stacy grabbing her bags from her. He ran his hands across her breasts, pinched her nipples, lifted her skirt and smacked her ass.

"Stacy, you are too much in your head. Bend over and let me help you relax." She put up a halfhearted fight, then relented, spreading her legs and putting her hands on her knees. M slid his cock into her pussy and commenced banging her silly.

Although I could hear them, I couldn't see them. Deanna had pulled me up so that I was lying face-to-face with her. "Why do you hang out with them?" she asked me.

"M is my lover and Stacy is my best friend. She introduced us. I think she expected to be M's girl but it didn't work out the way she had planned."

"Well, it doesn't matter. We're here and that's all I care about." Deanna wrapped her hot body around mine and kissed me. When her fingers found my cooch, all thoughts of M and Stacy left my mind. She brought me to an orgasm in under a minute; she slid her whole hand into my pussy. With her palm up and her fingers pressed on my G-spot, she began jiggling my insides. I lost my head in my most extreme orgasm ever, over and over again.

I HAD NO RECOLLECTION OF FALLING ASLEEP. The last thing I remembered was beautiful Deanna owning my cum like a goddess. I looked around the room and saw Stacy and M tangled together in the next bed, but Deanna was nowhere to be found.

I pushed back the covers to get up and go to the bathroom. I looked down at my body and laughed. Deanna had written her cell phone number on my belly right above my pussy. And next to the number she had written, "For a good time, call."

FORTY FIVE

....

DESERT RENDEVOUS

M had been summoned out of the country on business. Things had heated up on his big project in Dubai and he was in back-to-back meetings. Our communication had been sporadic. The week dragged on with precious little contact. His schedule and the time difference made it impossible to connect. At the two-week mark I'd begun moping around like a lovesick teenager. Theo asked me at least a dozen times if I was sick. It was as good an excuse as any I so I said told him yes.

Lying in my bed half asleep, I felt my phone vibrate. I'd begun sleeping with it, just in case. I squinted at the screen. The text from M sat me straight up in bed, "GG, get your bikini ready, I'll meet you in the desert at our favorite spa in two days' time." My brain exploded with excitement. I texted back, "I'll be there, love. Can't wait to see you, miss you so." I found it impossible to sleep knowing he would be back soon, so I sat up and began making plans. I would need new sexy nightwear and perhaps a new bikini. Certainly a new vibrator and some lube. I had used all of mine rubbing my clit over the last two weeks.

In spite of my excitement, I fell back asleep and slept until noon. When I got up, I found coffee and a note from Theo waiting for me. "GG, I think you should go see the doctor today. You've had this virus for a while and don't seem to be getting better. I'll be at therapy and then at the office, call me when you get a chance." I made an appointment and went off to see the doctor. Her recommendation was rest. Perfect, I thought. I asked if resting at the spa would count. She laughed and gave her blessing. I dashed around buying necessities and rushed home so I could be on the couch before Theo returned.

When he walked in I stretched and yawned. "How was your day, Theo?"

"Good, GG. We signed..." I stopped listening. I knew his daily rundown by heart, it never changed. Nothing ever changed around here. As he reached the end of his monologue, he looked at me. "Did you go to the doctor like I've been asking you to do?"

"Yes, she was able to fit me into her schedule today," I replied. "She thinks I'm over the worst of it and should rest." I shifted around on the couch, looking to see what Theo was up to. He was absorbed in the mail, perfect timing. "Mimi asked me to go to the desert," I interjected, "and Doc thinks the rest would do me good."

"Fine, fine, go to the desert. Just don't make me sick, I'm too busy," he harrumphed, without looking up.

"We'll be leaving tomorrow morning and I'm driving."

"Ok," he said over his shoulder as he walked off toward the bedrooms, "I'm going to grab dinner at the club. Don't wait up, I'll be late."

"OK, Theo." Yes! I was free for the rest of the night. When he left, I got up, packed my things and headed to the hot tub for a little pre-desert warm-up. I liked to place my clit in front of the jets, experiencing a lovely cum, or more. It's the way I managed to survive my non-physical marriage. Before M and I began our affair, the hot tub had provided my only effortless orgasms. M's entrance into my life changed everything, even my hot tub orgasms. Sometimes, he would call or text me while I was soaking, spinning erotic tales for my enjoyment. My orgasms were so much stronger during his stories. After a cum-filled night of M spinning a hot story in my ear while he watched me cum via Skype, he christened my hot tub orgasms, "bubble-gasms." Every time I got in to soak, his nickname flitted through my consciousness, warming me.

Tonight, the sky above was filled with stars, the misty atmosphere turned dry and crisp. As the moon came up over the mountains, I sighed in pleasure. Soon, M would hold me in his arms, kiss me like I needed to be kissed and fill my pussy with his magnificent cock. My *bubble-gasms* came fast and hard as I previewed our reunion in my mind. Panting and satiated, I pulled my clit away from the jets and slid into the recliner seat. I looked out over the bay, enjoying the serenity of the evening.

THE NEXT DAY ARRIVED DRY AND HOT AS THE SANTA ANA WINDS BLEW IN FROM THE DESERT. I'm one of the few people who love the hot, windy weather. I phoned Theo to let him know I was leaving, tossed my bag in the back of my red Mercedes and headed for my liaison with M. As usual, a trickle of fear entered my thoughts. I was certain something would go wrong, my life had never been this enjoyable for this long. Then, I heard the voice of my therapist asking if I thought it was healthy to let one person be responsible for my happiness. I always replied, "He isn't responsible" but I think we both knew I was kidding myself. As usual, I stuffed these thoughts into the vault in the lower level of my brain and locked the door. No way was I going to let psychobabble drag me down.

I arrived at the resort mid-afternoon and checked into our favorite accommodation, the Al Capone suite. More than a room, it was a small apartment close to the hot spring pools. Built in the roaring Twenties of river cobbles and Spanish tile, the small apartment had a romantic charm all its own. The kitchen and living room formed an early version of a great room, with a beautiful cobblestone fireplace for the cold desert nights. The bedroom seemed smallish with the king size bed in it. The low ceiling made it feel as if you were tucked into a nest. The stained glass cast multicolored sunbeams across the rooms.

First order of business, a long soak in the mineral waters. Floating in the warm water with the sun on my face healed the misery I had been feeling since M left on this trip. I thought being apart would get easier as we spent more time together but instead it had become more difficult. M had wormed his way deep into my heart. Only in this safe place outside my "real" life, where I was reminded of our time together, was I able to admit just how much he mattered to me.

After my soak, I went to the spa to meet my masseuse, Matthew, for my ninety-minute Watsu massage. Although I had heard of this type of water massage years ago, I couldn't find a practitioner until our first trip to the desert spa. For me, Watsu felt like a meditation in the form of a water ballet danced by the massage therapist, using my body as a prop. Not everyone enjoys the total surrender required for relaxation to take effect, but I was born to Watsu. I let go all of my cares and worries as Matthew twirled me through the water. When he was finished, I wandered back to the room and took a long, dreamless nap.

Upon awakening, I stretched and, remembering where I was, smiled. Only a few more hours until M returned. I padded out to the living room, where a cheery fire and a delicious salmon salad greeted me. I curled up with my favorite steamy erotic novel and ate between the sex scenes. I finished my salad, and for dessert, I pulled the new vibrator from my suitcase and gave it a test run. With the vibrator in one hand and the novel in another, I went on a multiple orgasm adventure without leaving the room. As midnight approached with no word from M, I turned off the lights and slept.

I WAS HAVING THE MOST LUXURIOUS DREAM WHEN M KISSED MY NECK, SLID HIS HAND DOWN MY NAKED BACK, CUPPED MY ASS AND GAVE IT A GENTLE SQUEEZE. "The Ass of Destiny," he whispered, right before his large, hard cock slid into my pussy. He settled his weight down onto me, pinning me to the bed.

"M, you're back," I whispered as I tried to push back against his cock.

In response, he kissed my shoulder, my neck, my ear, whispering into it, "Be quiet, GG, it's time to get fucked." He pulled out of me, moved to the side and rolled me over on my back. His hands claimed my breasts, fingers rolling my nipples to peaks. M climbed between my legs and rubbed his swollen cock-head up and down my pussy. He pushed his hot staff into me, taking me in smooth, fluid motions. I melted into his body, the first cum of our coupling roaring through my body, drenching my skin in heat. M's pace increased until he was pounding into me. My muscles clenched hard around his cock as another cum had me scratching at the bed in ecstasy. I felt him grow as he neared completion, then felt the explosion of man juice flood my pussy. He continued thrusting until he had filled my pussy to overflowing with hard cock and hot cum.

"I've missed you, GG," M nuzzled my face, his lips seeking mine. I half turned and he kissed me, soft lips massaging mine, opening them, his tongue sliding across my top lip before engaging my tongue in a slow, delicate dance. Never before had I felt this cherished and loved. A single tear rolled down my face as I realized just how in love with M I had become.

"I've missed you, M," I replied, licking his bottom lip between words. "Two weeks seemed an eternity." As we continued kissing, I felt his cock harden against my leg. M rolled me onto my back and slid his cock between my legs, against my clit. I ground my pussy into his cock, hoping he'd slide in, but instead he tapped my pussy with his rock hard cock at the same time he kissed me. The fire ignited in my gut, and I writhed under him, begging for his cock to plunder me.

After what seemed an eternity, M lifted my ass with one hand and plunged his cock balls deep. We kissed as if we had been parted for decades. Before I realized, I was moaning my orgasm into his mouth as my pussy contracted around his cock. M continued his thrusts until I had finished, then he stopped thrusting, cock still in place.

"Tell me, GG, what adventures have you had since I last saw you?"

"I haven't done a thing," I confessed, "except lie around the house and mope. I've been utterly miserable to be around."

M laughed, "I find that hard to believe, my oversexed Goddess."

He kissed my neck then rolled us over so he could flip on the bedside lamp. His eyes roved all over my face and down to where my breasts rested on his chest. "This won't do, I want to see you."

I sat up, enjoying the look on his handsome face. He told me, without words, how desirable he found me. His hands reached up and cradled my breasts, his thumbs grazing my erect nipples. His gaze and his hands moved lower until his hands rested on my thighs. "As much as I'd love to leave my cock where it is, I need to see your ass. I've been dreaming of it since Tokyo. Hands and knees, GG."

I wiggled on his cock as I lifted off him, taking my time as his gaze roved over me. I lifted my leg over him and turned around, kneeling and looking over my shoulder at him. Our eyes caught and held as I went down onto hands and knees. He sat up, running his hands all over my ass and planting a kiss on my left butt cheek. Then, without warning, *smack*! My entire body shook with desire, the pain of the spank turned to white-hot need. My eyes told him what he wanted to hear - more please. He held my gaze for as long as I could focus but when the smacks had heated up my ass and every additional swat made my pussy ooze, my eyes closed and my head turned forward, my back arched and my ass shoved back to M. Once my cheeks flamed red he began rubbing my clit between his fingers until I came hard. Then, *smack*! A hard whack at the moment I came, making my pleasure so intense I howled loud and long, pulling a chuckle from M.

"You like that, GG?" he asked.

"Yes, yes, yes!" I was panting so hard I had trouble getting the words out. I felt his hand in the middle of my back, pushing my head and chest down to the bed. His talented fingers sent me on another cum vacation while I felt his cock penetrate my pussy, just the head, until he felt me ready to cum again. Then he slid it home, balls deep and pounding hard. He fucked me like I needed fucking and my mind left for outer space as my body entered the land of continuous cumming.

"GG, breathe," I heard M say. I took a breath and my mind drifted around the room, refusing to obey any direction I gave it. M was whispering in my ear, "Breathe, beautiful girl or I'll give you mouth to mouth, which means we'll have to stop fucking."

That got through my space trip - *stop fucking?* No way. I focused enough to breathe again, then tried to push back on M's glorious cock, causing him to chuckle. I was stretched out on the bed, M's weight pinning me to the mattress.

"My insatiable, GG, do you ever get enough?" M began moving his cock in and out, then he pulled out of my pussy and slid into my ass, without missing a beat.

Ass cums are so different from pussy cums and M owned my ass. He had me cum-howling at the moon within seconds, my muscles clenching hard on M's cock. M placed his thumb in my mouth as his teeth sank into my shoulder. He drove his rock hard cock into my ass. I could feel his cock expanding and lengthening, a sure sign his cum was not far off. I sucked harder on his thumb, concentrating on holding off my cum until M's had begun. When I felt his hot juice in my ass, I bit his thumb and let myself fall off the cliff and fly the thermals of the cum winds with my love.

FORTY SIX

....

JOSHUA TREE

The desert sunrise glowed golden on the walls of the bedroom. It was the first thing I noticed when I opened my eyes. The second thing I noticed was M's body curved around mine. His deep, even breathing meant he was still asleep. I lay there savoring this rare moment of togetherness. My entire life I had craved this togetherness, and I had found it in an illicit affair set up by my friend, Stacy. How strange life can be. I found my most secret desire in the arms of a forbidden lover.

I snuggled back against him, prepared to wait until he woke up, treasuring this closeness. I felt the moment he awoke. M always said our time in the desert was a bubble existing outside the stream of life, a respite from responsibility and the expectations of others. But I digress. M's hand grasped my breast, his fingers rolling my nipple to a hard peak before he pinched it. My ass pushed back into his morning wood and sexual desire ignited in my core.

"Good morning, lover. So wonderful to wake up in your arms." I ground my ass into his cock just in case he had any doubts about my preferred activity.

"Yes, GG, wonderful and sexy," M replied. The tip of his cock edged into my wet gash as his hand continued to caress my breast. Oh how I wanted his cock inside me. "Please, M, fuck me."

"My impatient love, you always want to rush right to the main course," M scolded. "Right now, feel your body, enjoy the anticipation, let me rub your clit, wake the sleeping panther." His other hand had captured my clit and he proceeded to roll clit and nipple in time, then pinched, pulled and released them in a most wondrous way. The flush spread from my clit and nipple as I felt the need to cum but was held back by M's steady pull, release, pull, release. My back arched, my head tucked under his chin, my bottom trembled and the moisture dripped from my cunt, coating the head of his cock with moisture. I ached for a cum. "M, please, please," I begged, "Let me come."

"GG, you need to wait a little longer," M whispered as he began kissing my neck. "I'm not ready for you to cum." His fingers pulled my nipple away from my chest, pinching hard, his other hand making my clit hum when his cock rammed into my empty pussy, filling it and bringing me to a fiery orgasm, multicolored ribbons danced across my vision and fireworks covered my skin in color sensations. M's cock changed angle and found my spot, bringing me to another orgasm, distinct and different from the first orgasm. I found myself laughing as my brain launched to outer space, my body bucking on M's hard cock.

"I AM SO HUNGRY, I THINK I COULD EAT TWO BREAKFASTS. MAYBE I'LL TRY THE MACADAMIA COCONUT FRENCH TOAST WITH OUR USUAL EGGS AND BACON." M chuckled, "Sex does that to you. How about we share the French toast? Then, we can grab an early lunch after we float."

I stretched and smiled at him. "Perfect solution as usual. I'm so happy we're here. I've missed you so much."

"Ah, GG, I know. I've missed you, too," M caressed my cheek with his hand. "After lunch let's hike Joshua Tree, get some exercise."

"I knew you were going to suggest that! Can't we just lay around and soak up some rays?"

"I must get some exercise. It's a long flight from Dubai and I'll be back in the air far too soon. You are welcome to stay here if you'd rather sunbathe."

I leaned in close. "Don't be silly, lover, I'm not letting you out of my sight." Just then, our breakfast arrived and we both dug in, all conversation lost as we focused on eating.

"I WATCHED A HONEY BEE DRINK A DROP OF WATER FROM THE STEPS AND A HUMMINGBIRD VISIT EVERY FLOWER IN THE TREE HANGING OVER THE HOT POOL," I WHISPERED INTO M'S EAR. "How's your meditation going?"

M's reply was a kiss and a smile. "It sounds like your float went better than my meditation. My mind is just too active and my body wants to move," M replied. "I'm ready for lunch and a hike."

We wolfed down lunch, then changed, hopped into my car and cruised out toward Joshua Tree. We stopped for daypacks and water in Desert Hot Springs. The weather could not have been better, low 80's with a light breeze. The drive was spectacular. Before long, we were parked next to the Lost Hills Mine trail.

I worked out every day. As an OC wife, being fit was not optional, it was part of the job description. Since M wanted to hike a strenuous trail, I was happy my conditioning was being put to something other than ornamental use.

"Look, the wild flowers are blooming. Spring time in the desert is my favorite," M stated. "I've always wanted to see the stamp mill up here at the mine site. The mine operator found it abandoned at a mine in Nevada and moved it over here. It amazes me how settlers were able to survive and thrive in such a forbidding environment."

"Why, M, I didn't realize you were interested in the Wild West," I looked at the ground ahead of us, scanning the area for rattlesnakes as we walked. The trail was empty, we were alone. M wrapped his arm around my shoulders. "I'm interested in many things, GG. You've barely scratched the surface, my dear." He smiled and gave me one of those mind blowing kisses, curling my toes and flushing my cheeks.

"If you keep kissing me, I'm going to undress and beg for more," I said. M chuckled and kept walking, holding my hand as we hiked up the canyon. Forty minutes later we made the top of the trail and looked out into Pleasant Valley. We sat on a rock and shared a snack. The desert was beautiful, calm and yet, it could be such a dangerous place. Hmm, kind of like my dalliance with M. Beautiful, calm, yet so dangerous. I was still wondering what on earth I was going to do with him and Theo. It didn't seem like I could continue to pull off my double life and yet, I couldn't see any way out of my current situation. Oh well, something else to think about later.

"Thanks for joining me, GG, I needed to get out and move, enjoy some nature. I've been cooped up in too many boardrooms and planes these last few weeks."

"I'm glad I came. It's beautiful out here. I've lived in California all my life and never visited this park. It's hard to believe," I responded as I leaned into him. As much as I loved sex with M, these moments of closeness fed my soul. They were cherished memories when I was trapped at meaningless dinners back in the OC.

We gathered our things up and started on the trail back towards the car. "We've had our hike and we still have plenty of time to get back to the spa for a couples water massage," M said, smiling and pulling me to him and kissing me on the forehead.

FORTY SEVEN

....

THE ENVELOPE

We made it back to the resort, changed into our swimsuits and walked down to the large Watsu pool for our couples massage. The warm buoyant waters and the therapeutic embrace of our massage therapists, Matthew and Stephanie, made for a blissful 90 minutes. After they returned us to reality and delivered us into each other's arms, M and I hugged for several minutes. Hand-in-hand, we stepped from the pool and helped each other into our robes. Together, we walked back to our room.

The sun was about to dip behind the mountains. A late afternoon breeze was cooling the desert. Along the path, a roadrunner eyed us before dashing off into the dry bush. We rounded the corner to our suite and walked through the gate.

"Monsieur and Mademoiselle," a stately gentlemen in a white tuxedo jacket and white Bermuda shorts greeted us, "your dinner is served." I looked at M and he gave me his heart-melting smile. "After you, my love," he said.

We finished our dessert, eating by candlelight. Then we sat and sipped sparkling water and gazed up at the Milky Way's dazzling display splashed across the crystal clear desert skies. Our conversation flowed and we joked in a lighthearted way that only the truly intimate can. When we fell silent, I was awed by the perfection of the moment. I was at peace for the first time in years.

In the silence, I looked over to M and he smiled serenely back at me. He sat forward and placed a small gift wrapped box and a card on the table before me. I tilted my head to one side, posing an unasked question, retrieved the box and card and unwrapped them. On the cover of the card was a single rose, and inside the words: "May our love always be a source of magic and abundant gifts without end."

I unwrapped the gift box and opened it. Within it was a gold antique necklace of a dragonfly with a dazzling mother of pearl inlay and precious gems scattered across its wings.

"Oh, M," I said, touched almost to tears, "thank you."

M stepped around the table and up behind me, taking the necklace, placing it around my neck and fastening it. He leaned down and kissed me on the cheek. He placed yet another, longer envelope on the table in front of me and walked back to his side of the table, seating himself.

"What's this?" I asked as I opened it. Inside was an airplane ticket.

"My darling, GG, the day after tomorrow I leave for Dubai for eighteen months. I will be taking up residence there until the construction on the new building is complete. They've asked me to personally oversee the project and there's no way I can turn them down."

It felt like my heart was being torn out of my chest. *Was this his way of breaking it off with me?* If this was good-bye, I didn't think I could stand it.

He must have seen how crest fallen my face was. "No lover, you misunderstand me," he said, "I would like you to accompany me. I'd like you to join me in Dubai."

Shaken, I stared blankly down at my hands, speechless. "I don't know what to say, M," I managed to get out. This was the moment I had most hoped for and most dreaded.

"Just say you will accompany me," he smiled.

"It's not that simple, M," I replied.

We sat in silence for the better part of a minute. He reached towards me. "Come," he said, lifting my chin to look at him, "we will talk about it later."

He offered his hand to me and I took it.

FORTY EIGHT

....

NO REPLY

The rest of our evening was idyllic. A leisurely midnight walk to the hot spring pools. A luxurious soak in the starlit waters. A moonlit stroll back to our suite, wrapped in each other's warm arms, our progress punctuated by sweet, tender kisses.

Back in the room, we dropped our robes, climbed into bed and fell into each other's skin-to-skin embrace. Our lovemaking was the kind where our bodies knew no boundaries, where I ended and M began blurred. Our coupling was a force of nature, an act of God. Our orgasms overcame us with the intensity of a storm surge crashing on the rocky shore. Everything in its path swept away, nothing left behind.

I DIDN'T REMEMBER FALLING ASLEEP. When I woke, I lifted my head and squinted at the clock on the nightstand. It was 5 am. I turned to M's side of the bed to look for him, but he was gone. "Maybe he got up and went down to the hot pools," I thought, pulling the covers over my head. But something didn't feel right. I threw the covers off and jumped out of bed, looking around the room. M's bag was gone. On the dresser was the airline ticket envelope.

I opened the envelope and found a note from M.

Dearest GG,

Please accept my apologies for springing my big changes on you last night. It was unfair of me to put you on the spot.

I've made some assumptions about our relationship that I had no right to make. I can understand now, why you didn't respond to my offer. I can't realistically expect you to drop everything in your life and run off with me to Dubai.

While in so many ways you've reclaimed yourself in this last year, there are still so many things you have to resolve before you can move on.

You have a life in Orange County. You have a home. You have friends. And most of all, you have a husband.

With much love,

M

I put the letter down and picked up the envelope and looked inside it. The ticket was still there. It had my name on it.

Now what was I going to do?

FORTY NINE

....

HELLO DUBAI?

I cried for a while. I packed my things, loaded the crimson roadster and drove back to OC. Billy would be in town tomorrow night. If anything could take my mind off my troubles, a good rock show and spending the evening with my old friend certainly could do it.

I arrived back in OC late morning. I pulled into my side of the garage, grabbed my things and went on in. As soon as I walked through the door, Theo grilled me. "Where have you been, GG? You haven't answered my texts since yesterday afternoon. What's gotten into you?" he said.

Of course, I thought to myself, perfect timing. "Not now, Theo," I said in a measured tone.

"You know, GG, you've completely changed in the last nine months," he was working himself up to something. "You don't spend time with me anymore. You're always distracted texting someone or talking on the phone or meeting the Ladies Who Lunch. You're always running off somewhere 'with the girls' for the weekend." He was on a roll.

"I'm starting to think it isn't your girlfriends you're running off to," he sighed deeply and continued. "Listen, if you don't want to be in this marriage any longer, just tell me. I can be out of it in six weeks. Just say the word."

I gave him 'the look'. "Not now, Theo," I shot back. "Or you might just get what you're asking for." I walked into the spare bedroom and slammed the door.

A lot of good that did. I could hear him pacing back and forth outside the door. He knocked softly and said, "You know I don't mean it, GG. I'm just concerned about you." I started crying again. "Please, Theo," I said through the door, "just leave me alone."

I threw myself on the bed with a flourish and for ten minutes balled my eyes out.

I sat up and thought, "What's gotten into you, GG?" I stared at my forlorn face in my vanity mirror. "Well, will you look who's getting all dramatic now," I said to myself. "Who, you ask?" I said, "Why, you are." What's this all about, anyway? I sighed deeply, wiped my eyes, blew my nose and pulled myself together.

It should be simple, shouldn't it? You just listen to your heart, follow your bliss, do the right thing and it will all work out, like in a fairy tale. The prince rescues the damsel in distress and they ride off together on his white stallion.

Only, life is never that simple.

Nothing was clear to me anymore. As much as I adored and desired M, when push came to shove I just wasn't ready to ride off into the sunset with him.

I know. What am I, crazy? Women wait their whole lives for someone like M and still it never happens for them. And there I was, about to let him fly out of my life, walking away from the opportunity to be at his side.

On the other hand, some people would call my life in Orange County perfect. It was certainly secure. I had a beautiful house, didn't I? Plenty of money, a beautiful car, lots of friends and there were an abundance of attractive and wealthy men surrounding me. Although my marriage to Theo wasn't passionate, I had discovered I was pretty much free to do as I pleased. So what if Theo was as predictable as the Fourth of July, minus the fireworks. That could be a good thing, right?

On the other hand, M was a wondrous lover, maybe the perfect lover. He understood I was just beginning my self-re-discovery, just beginning to acknowledge my true desires. And he took such joy in sharing those discoveries with me.

The minutes and hours were ticking by. The magic of the last 12 months was drifting away. Why wasn't I more upset? Why was I just accepting this was how it was going to end? I imagined him getting ready for his trip, packing his bags, taking the limo to the airport, checking in, all without me. My heart ached, but I quickly pushed the sadness away. I would not succumb to childish sentimentality. I had the heart of a free woman at last. I was empowered. I wasn't going to let any man take my freedom away from me, ever again. Besides, M had probably been my rebound romance. It had just been a matter of time until we went our separate ways.

The time had come and it was over. "It just ended much sooner than I had imagined," I thought, feeling forlorn again.

"Now stop that, GG. It was nothing more than a fling for you anyway. Girl, you are just beginning your transformation. You need time and room to grow, to be free, to express yourself." Then, the voice in my head said, *for all you know, the women in Dubai have to wear the burka*. I giggled at that thought, imagining me in a burka with a thigh highs and crotchless panties underneath.

Soon, M would be off on a new adventure without me and I would be free to continue my self-discovery on my own. There was a world full of fascinating men and women out there and I wanted to experience them.

My iPhone vibrated in my blue jeans' back pocket. Distracted, I pulled it out. It was M.

GG,

I'm on the plane and they are about to close the doors. The seat beside me is empty. You're not here and I understand why. Maybe someday, further down the line. We will see, won't we, GG?

Good-bye.

I love you.

M

I sat there, numb. I couldn't respond. I just stared at the screen.

"He said 'I love you,'" I said to myself. "He said 'I love you.'"

"GG," I said, sitting bolt upright, "snap out of it. He's leaving. He loves you."

Oh, my god. I began texting frantically.

"I love you, M. I love you." And hit send.

But it was too late. My text just hung there and the message appeared 'unable to complete.' The airplane doors had closed and my fate was sealed.

I love you, M, I said to myself. And I want to be with you.

But he was gone.

H.C. MANN

AUTHOR NOTES

We hope you enjoyed our first erotic novel. If so, please consider leaving a review on Amazon. We are a husband and wife team who discovered that writing an erotic novel together is an advanced form of foreplay. Maybe GG's escapades will serve a similar purpose for you and your partner.

Some acknowledgements are in order...

The valuable input of our editor, Buffie Peterson, made for a better book. Our indispensable beta readers include many friends, some we cannot name and two we would like to thank personally, Lindsey Peterson and Tracy Cole.

The next book chronicling GG's adventures should be out in 2016. Please read on for an excerpt from "Pulled Over and Spanked." Please visit our website, http://www.hcmann.com, to sign up for updates.

Hannah and Charles Mann
Newport Beach CA

H.C. MANN

PULLED OVER AND SPANKED

....

M smiled, slid his fingers into my wet gash and hooked his thumb into my ass. His mouth hovered over my pussy: his breath warm on my skin. His tongue flicked my clit, once, twice and then a flurry of clit tingling contact. His tender teasing was more than I could handle. I tried to arch into him, but he had his arm draped across my abdomen, holding me down. My need burned white hot but M held me on the razor's edge of unfulfilled climax. I was certain I could take no more when he raised his eyes to mine, enjoying my arousal. He lowered his mouth onto me, sucked my mound into his mouth and lapped my clit. "Yes, yes, please more," I gasped, straining for the orgasm just beyond my reach. It was so close. "Please M, please," I begged. His teeth grazed my clit and a kaleidoscope of shapes and colors painted my skin. Heat rose from my clit and raced across my skin as my cum struggled to break free from M's control.

The pounding on the door jerked me awake and out of my dream lover's arms.

"GG, what's going on in there?" Theo yelled. "Open this door right now or I'll break it down."

I slid out of bed and opened the door. "What do you want, Theo? It's 6 AM for heaven's sake and I was finally asleep." *And just about to cum, dammit.*

"I thought I heard you talking to someone. Are you talking in your sleep again? You only do that when you get anxious."

"The way you've been stalking me the last few weeks makes me anxious. Now please, I need to get some sleep."

Theo huffed at me as I closed the door on him and went back to bed.

Then it hit me; M was gone. I curled into a fetal position, rocking as I tried to contain my sobs. What had I done? My thoughts ran the hamster wheel in my brain, around and around, never getting anywhere. A life without M seemed like a life without color or joy. Had my hasty decision put me back into my gilded prison?

Snap out of it, GG, there's more to life than M, I thought but without conviction. It was too early to call my therapist, so I grabbed the phone and speed dialed Stacy. When she picked, up I cried even harder.

"What's wrong, honey?"

"Stacy, M's gone," I started sobbing and shaking uncontrollably. "He's gone. What am I going to do?"

Stacy was silent for a moment. "Did you say M's gone? What do you mean? Oh my God, he's dead? How? GG, you're blubbering. I can't understand you. Honey, take a deep breath and tell me what happened."

I tried to compose myself. "No, No, not dead," I choked out. "Gone, as in left; moved to Dubai. He asked me to go with him, and I chickened out. I couldn't do it. Now he's gone, and I can't stand it. Stacy, I love him, and I let him go. Walk out of my life."

"Oh honey, I'm sorry. Why Dubai? Isn't that in Iowa?" Stacy hesitated. "Never mind, do you need me to come out? I can get on a plane tomorrow."

"Please Stacy, would you? Theo is driving me crazy. And now I can't stop crying. He already thinks I've lost it." I looked up into the mirror across from the bed. My eyes opened wide, "Oh no, I have. I've lost M."

"GG, it's going to be ok. I've got to go so I can make reservations. I'll call when I know what time I'll be there."

We hung up and I took some deep breaths to calm myself. I had to pull it together and get on with my life. My phone vibrated, incoming message. I grabbed it, hoping beyond hope that it would be M. Instead, it was a text from Billy.

"Hi GG. The car will be there at 6 to pick you up. Can't wait to see you." In all of the trauma, I forgot about the concert tonight. I debated canceling, but decided to go anyway. I confirmed with Billy, and dragged myself to the shower. Time to rejoin the human race.

AFTER A LONG DAY OF GETTING THEO ON A PLANE TO SAN FRANCISCO AND CATCHING UP ON WORK, I WAS MORE THAN READY TO GET OUT OF THE HOUSE. I dressed in my concert sexy and ran out to meet the limo. I slid into the lush interior, feeling calmer than I had all day. A large bouquet of roses filled the limo. The card read "To a beautiful evening with a beautiful lady, thanks for joining me." I poured myself a glass of Perrier and sat back to enjoy the ride to the Honda Center. A night with my favorite 80's band, Tool Box, and Billy was just what I needed, and Stacy would arrive tomorrow.

I will get over him, I will, I thought. If only I could believe it.

The limousine pulled up to the stage door entrance and a security guard opened my door. "Good evening, ma'am," a young man in a t-shirt with 'security' printed across the front and tattoos from his elbows to his wrists greeted me. "Please follow me. I'm to take you directly to Mr. Rowan." He handed me a backstage laminate, and I clipped it to a belt loop.

I followed him backstage through the tangle of lighting trusses, PA equipment and stagehands. The familiar pre-concert anticipation filled my stomach with sequenced butterflies. I do love a good rock concert, and Tool Box could still put on a high-energy show, for a band that had been around since the eighties. Billy was standing on the side of the stage, giving orders to one of the crew, as the security guard deposited me and moved off. I watched him in his element, clearly comfortable and in charge. My eyes strayed to his package wrapped in its loose pants and I blushed, red hot, all over. My time with M had pushed my one hot night with Billy right out of my mind.

"Ahh, GG, you made it." Billy gave me a chaste kiss and a hug. In my ear he whispered, "You're as sexy as ever, beautiful." Then he pulled back and took me by the hand, leading me around the stage, calling out instructions as we went. It was surreal being on the performers' side of a concert. Looking out into the hall, I was seeing what the band would see. The place was abuzz with excitement and anticipation. The doors had just opened and the arena had begun filling with fans.

Billy took my hand and led me away. "I'm done here for now, let's head back to the dressing rooms."

We turned the corner and walked hand in hand down the stairs. "I'm so glad this is the last night of this tour. Seems like I've been on the road with these guys forever."

I smiled back at him, "I heard Tool Box is recording a new record after this. Will you be staying in LA with them?"

"Yes, I'm going to be their high priced babysitter. I'll be happy to stay in one place. Maybe I'll get to see more of you."

"I think that could be arranged, Mr. Rowan." I giggled. "I almost didn't know who the security guard was talking about."

"Not everyone knows me as Billy," he replied as he led me into the meet and greet area. We made small talk, never mentioning our hot night together. I asked him questions about his daughter and the tour, still feeling too tender to chance talking about myself. I was half afraid my pain would pour out, and I'd break down again.

Tommy Tool separated himself from a clutch of female admirers and drifted over to us. "Hey, aren't you the girl who was with that hot red head, Stacy wasn't it?" he asked. "Is she here tonight?"

"Hi Tommy. No, she couldn't make it tonight, but she's coming in for a visit tomorrow," I replied.

"That's great. Maybe Billy can set something up so we can get together. She's a great girl. Did you know she likes jeeps?"

"She does? No, I didn't know that," I said, feeling amused. "I'm sure, we can she'd love to see you again. Maybe we could come up to L.A. and visit you in the studio?"

"Perfect," Tommy smiled and turned toward Billy, "Hey man, we got a problem in the dressing room, could you come give me a hand? They served us Miller Light and our rider clearly specifies Bud Light."

"I'll see to it, Tommy," Billy turned to me and kissed me on the cheek. "I might be awhile, GG. You can hang out here or grab a security guard and have him take you to our seats."

"Sure, Billy. I'll be fine here."

I found a comfortable chair off to the side and did some people watching. Talk about an interesting crowd, the partiers ran from groupies to starlets; from gophers to promoters. And there I was, alone with my feelings again. As I waited for Billy's return, I pondered my sudden lack of emotion. I guess I could chalk it up to shock. One minute M and I were enjoying each other at our favorite resort, the next minute he was on his way to Dubai, gone from my life forever. I knew I had done the right thing, I couldn't just run off at the drop of a hat. I owed Theo and my friends something more than a disappearing act. I was already feeling much better. Getting out was a really good idea.

So much better I think I'm already over him That thought lasted about a second before the dark clouds rolled back in. I ached deep in my bones. It felt like nothing would ever be right again."

Just as my wallowing was leading to fresh tears, my phone vibrated. A text from Stacy: "My plane lands 11:30 am." I texted her back, "I will pick you up at the airport. Theo went to San Francisco but will be back tomorrow evening. He is thrilled you're coming to visit." *Hmm, maybe I should get those two together. They seem to get along great. That would sure solve some of my problems.*

Stacy replied, "Hope you're ok, Honey. I'll be there soon so hang in there."

Stacy was a godsend. Only two people knew about M: Stacy and Jee Sun. Oh, and my therapist, Nicki. I was desperate to talk about what had happened, and Stacy was my forever confidant.

The meet and greet area had emptied out by the time Bill returned. He led me to a small balcony on the side of the stage that looked down on the band.

"What do you think?" Billy asked

"Wonderful. This is beautiful, Billy. Nice to be out of the crowd. And it's great for watching the stage."

"I agree. Over the years I've found a different perspective now and then gives me ideas to keep the acts fresh and interesting. Although tonight I must admit to different motives, having you to myself for a bit." He leaned over to me and kissed the top of my head.

"So, world traveler, how was the tour?" I asked.

"It turned out to be one of the easier tours I've managed. Now that the band is older, they value their sleep far more than getting into trouble. Aside from a tight spot in Brazil when customs found a joint in Tommy's bag, we had no problems. The entire crew is ready to be off the road, though. It's been a long year."

"I would love to be able to travel to all those places. Maybe someday I'll have the time and money. You mentioned you'd be staying in L.A. now? For how long?"

"Yes, the crew is doing the load in and setup at the recording studio early tomorrow. We expect to take the next six months off from the road and focus on writing some new material and mixing a live album we recorded of the world tour. Who knows, if all goes well we might even get a start a on an album of the new material. Strike while the irons hot. At our age, it's anyone's guess if they will get the chance again."

Just then the lights went down. We turned to watch the band make its entrance and were met by an explosion of pyrotechnics. The arena roared to life with thunderous power chords and the sound of Tommy's wailing voice. The crowd sprang to their feet, fists pounding into the air and throngs of middle-aged women waving frantically at the stage. The deep sounds of the bass guitar made the whole place rumble. I was definitely getting turned on. I felt like the arena was one big vibrator, and I was sitting on it.

It has always been that way for me. Concerts are my ultimate aphrodisiac. I was half hoping Billy would make a move but I could see he was still "at work". I was starting to think the night we shared was forgotten. Billy had always been a gentleman, maybe too much so.

It was a fantastic concert, Tool Box really delivered, and Tommy was still the star of the show. If only Stacy could have been there. As the band began its big finale, Billy turned and gave me a hug. "I'm afraid it's time for me to get back to work. I was hoping to ask you to join me for a late dinner, GG, but I'm having issues with the promoter and the hall I need to iron out." He looked annoyed and disappointed, so I put on my best, 'I understand' face. "Could we get together later this week? Maybe you and Stacy can come up and watch a session?"

"We would love that. Thanks for asking. I'm beat anyway and Stacy's plane lands early tomorrow."

"Good, then it's a date. I'll text you tomorrow with the details."

The security guard escorted me back to the limo. As I headed for home, my thoughts returned M. Thank goodness Stacy would be here tomorrow. I needed distraction and advice.

www.ingramcontent.com/pod-product-compliance
Lightning Source LLC
Chambersburg PA
CBHW070901180626
46817CB00003B/861